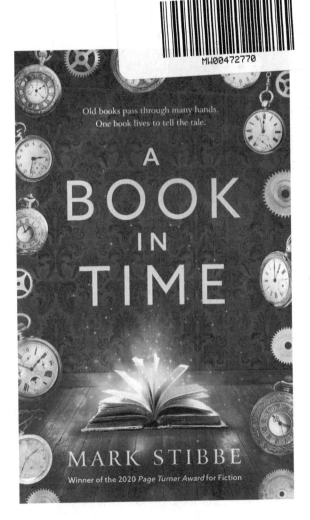

Old books pass through many hands.
One book lives to tell the tale.

A
BOOK
IN
TIME

MARK STIBBE

Winner of the 2020 *Page Turner Award* for Fiction

BOOKLAB

First published 2023 by Bella Books UK,
a Pawprint/Imprint of BookLab
www.thebooklab.co.uk

British Library Cataloguing in Publication Data
A catalogue record for this book is available from the British
Library.

ISBN 978-1-3999-4335-2

Cover design by Esther Kotecha

Printed in the UK

Dedication

I dedicate this book to my darling, beloved wife Cherith,
who has believed in it, and me, as no other ever has
or could, and whose constant encouragements have
fuelled my perseverance and brought hope whenever
despair has come knocking at my doors.
I am eternally grateful and forever blessed.

When I was little, my ambition was to grow up to be a book. Not a writer. People can be killed like ants. Writers are not hard to kill either. But not books: however systematically you try to destroy them, there is always a chance that a copy will survive and continue to enjoy a shelf-life in some corner on an out-of-the-way library somewhere in Reykjavik, Valladolid or Vancouver.

Amos Oz

Contents

Part 1

1805-1806

Calm let me slumber in that dark repose,
Till the last morn its orient beams disclose:
Then, when the great Archangel's potent sound
Shall echo thro' Creation's ample round,
Wak'd from the sleep of death with joy survey
The opening splendours of eternal day.

Elizabeth Carter of Deal (1717-1806)

I was conceived in a hot bath in Deal and born, twelve months later, on a mahogany table in Holt. My mother was called Emily Swanson. She was eighty-seven years old when she finally delivered me. She was so overcome that from that day forth she often held me to her chest as she shuffled about the cottage. When she looked at me it was impossible not to notice the adoration in her eyes. Sometimes she would bow, her skin wrinkled like the pages of an antique book. Then she would kiss me.

Once, when a howling wind was buffeting the windows of the cottage, and the flames were trembling in the guttering candles, she held me so close I thought I was going to disappear into her heart. When at last she separated me from her heaving chest she stared and stared at me, her head shaking from side to side and her eyes filled with a melancholy beyond the reach of words. Then a tear formed in her left eye, filling the lens until it spilled from her cheek and fell upon my front.

I thought my spine would break.

My mother lived for just six months after she had brought me into the world. In that time visitors came to pay homage. Young lovers and old lovers and enough blue-stockinged women to fill a library. They journeyed through any weather. When they stood within our panelled parlour room, they strove to outdo one another with their praise.

"You are an emancipator," one said.

"The bravest of women," another added.

"A connoisseur of love," a third exclaimed.

At every knock on the door, my mother would force herself up from her rocking chair and call upon Miss Eliza Reed. Miss Reed and she had been like sisters for four score years. Miss Reed had thinning white hair and smoked a dirty clay pipe once owned by a long dead blacksmith. She had found it while digging up onions in our walled garden and had whooped with joy when she realised it was still in good working order. She often wondered out loud about what scenes the pipe had witnessed in this house and grounds. "How strange a thing it is," she would say, "that the things we cannot live without outlive us."

Reedie, as she was known to my mother, would often smoke this diminutive white pipe in bed until one day she fell asleep, and her sheets caught fire. Billowing with smoke, she descended from the top floor of the cottage to the scullery screeching like a demon. My mother doused the flames with water she always kept in a bucket by the door, "in case poor Reedie ever had a conflagration."

Whenever visitors came to the house, such as those travelling to pay respects at the small shrine of our home, my mother would shout upstairs, "Swiggies, Reedie! Swiggies!"

Swiggies was her word for port wine served in crystal glasses, accompanied by a silver plate of biscuits and pâté. Mother would serve her guests with homely sacraments from these makeshift chalices and patens. Many left our doors with faces glowing.

Some were lost for words.

These were halcyon days.

I thought they would never end.

On Christmas Eve, one of my mother's oldest friends paid us a visit. Elizabeth Carter was her name and she had travelled all the way from Kent – no small feat because she was as advanced in years as my mother. When she stepped into the parlour, she was wearing a white bonnet with pale blue ribbons tied above her cloudy hair. She had a scarf and a thick brown coat, which she now took off with my mother's assistance.

"How are you, my dear?" my mother asked. There was the hint of a sigh in her voice that indicated to me that she knew the answer even before she asked the question.

"The coach to London was overcrowded, and the thick smoke in the city made the air unbreathable. People are milling about at night for unholy entertainment. Some are wearing the ghastliest costumes, influenced by outrageous French fashions."

Elizabeth continued as my mother hung up her coat.

"I was pleased to arrive at Holt. The houses here look even lovelier with a mantle of snow upon them and, of course, it is good to be near the coast. I'm happy to be here and even happier to see you, Emily. Congratulations are in order."

My mother was holding me with one hand while helping her friend with the other. Elizabeth's eyes widened as she stared at me, a broad smile extending from her chaffed lips.

"Better late than never," my mother said, and they both laughed. I felt her body shake with it.

My mother took Elizabeth by the hand and adopted a voice of mock gravity. "Others are not allowed beyond the parlour," she said as she led her to a staircase filled with books. "But you can come beyond the veil into the most holy place."

"Look there!" my mother said as we ascended. She pointed to a book – *Sir Isaac Newton's Philosophy Explained for the Use of Ladies*. It was translated from the Italian by none other than the same Elizabeth Carter. Both women read out the title simultaneously, emphasizing the word "ladies" in a mocking manner. Both laughed heartily.

"I was twenty-one when I wrote that," Elizabeth said. "What would I do for such youthful wit and energy now." She struggled up the last few steps and followed us into the drawing room, just as the grandfather clock chimed six times. This was my favourite room in my mother's house. The place where she wrote.

There was a desk in one corner with papers covered in my mother's scrawl. A smaller table stood against an adjoining wall; it bore an old King James Bible and a Hebrew lexicon. A writer's chair stood in the centre of the room, its armrests long and wide enough for books to be read and written. This was where we often sat, my mother and I, warmed by the red-hot coals in the cast-iron grate. Here we would rest while mother drifted in and out of sleep, sometimes scratching vagrant thoughts upon the pages with her trusty quill before they shuffled off into the night.

"Please sit in my writer's chair," my mother said.

"No, no," Elizabeth protested.

Seeing there was no point in arguing, my mother yielded while Elizabeth settled into an armchair.

"How are things in Deal?" my mother asked.

"We are still watchful in case Bonaparte tries to invade our shores, but in truth, the smuggling is the greatest threat."

"Is it still bad?"

"Worse than ever. There are contraband goods passing hands everywhere. No one is immune. Even our legislators are at it. The revenue cutters are outnumbered and the dragoons on the shores are constantly outwitted. I don't know what's to be done about it."

"I am sorry to hear that. I am relieved to say that it is not such a problem this far up the east coast."

"You are fortunate," Elizabeth said, shifting in her seat.

"It is good to spend this Christmas together," my mother said, sheltering me beneath a tawny throw.

"Ah Emily, I have missed our conversations," our visitor replied, grimacing with pain in her chair. "Do you remember our days conversing with the others at Elizabeth Montagu's house in London?"

"I will never forget them. The finest women I have ever met were at the Montagu's."

"Fanny Burney," Elizabeth said.

My mother added, "Hannah More."

"And you," Elizabeth said.

"No, you!"

They both laughed.

"Her Mayfair house was a Temple for rational conversation, virtue, and female friendship."

"And a tribute to Chinoiserie," my mother added. "Do you remember those Chinese screens?"

"And the oriental desk with the carved elephants," Elizabeth said. "I do miss those days. I rarely go out now. From time to time, people visit me, but their visits are unreasonably long and after just ten minutes I am corky and restless. There are only a few souls whose company and conversations I love. You are preeminent among those, my dear. I feel a very affecting pleasure to be here with you."

"The distance is painful," my mother said. "And we are not getting any younger. How is your health?"

"I have been suffering more and more from beastly headaches. And my physician tells me I have St Anthony's fire."

"I am so sorry."

"I suffer from increasing burning sensations and my aches leave me in a lifeless state."

"We will both be in a lifeless state before too long," my mother said.

I shuddered.

Elizabeth took out a box, applied some snuff and sneezed. "To keep me awake. I fall asleep on a whim these days and I don't want to do that tonight, of all nights."

"Why do you say that?"

"My dear, you of all people must be feeling the same intimations of mortality. This may be the last Christmas together. We may not see each other again, at least this side of death's door."

Another shudder.

"Then it's high time I said thank you," my mother said.

"For what?"

"For many things, but especially that you taught me Hebrew. It was an honour. No other woman surpasses you for knowledge of the ancient ones. Dr Johnson said as much."

"Not everything he said is true," Elizabeth said, and with that their laughter filled the room again.

When the merriment subsided, my mother spoke. "I am so grateful that you taught me to read the Song of Songs in the Hebrew tongue. Without your help, my love – or at least the expression of it – would have remained dormant, and this life . . ." she lifted me to her heart, "would never have poured out of me."

"It was a privilege, Emily."

"Few but you would have thought that way," my mother replied. "I was unworthy of your company, let alone the company of all these other women, so bright and intellectual."

Elizabeth said, "Such walls will not remain. There will come a time when they will be no more, when every soul, both male and female, will be seen for what they are, created in the image of God, one and the same in equality and honour."

"That is truly a time to imagine," my mother said. "And a thought to inspire our dreams as we sleep tonight."

When my mother awakened, it was Christmas Day. She and Elizabeth rose and trudged through the snow to church while Reedie stayed behind to adorn the downstairs rooms and prepare the Christmas lunch. Mother said that it was important to celebrate the Feast of the Nativity, eating sweets by the fire and laughing with friends. It was even more important, she said, to commemorate the birth of the Christ Child.

My mother carried me to the parish church, bundled in a woollen scarf. We sat in a pew adorned by rosemary and bay as the parson, standing in a pulpit covered with wreaths of holly and sprigs of ivy, extolled the virtues of Mary, the mother of the divine child. Throughout the service I stared at a window which portrayed the holy mother in an ultramarine robe cradling the baby, her eyes sweet with adoration. I trembled with wonder at the spectacle of such warm and sacred nurturing.

On the way home, my mother lamented the fact that there were so few people at divine service that day, and those that were present had not put on their Sunday clothes, but their work-a-day garments. "It is like bringing a dirty and worn-out book to a king," she said. "No one would think of doing such a thing. No, such a gift should be bound in luxurious and golden-lettered covers."

Elizabeth replied that it was the same on the shores of Kent, and that Christmas Day was not celebrated as it ought to be. Her father, she said, had always tried to make it a sacred feast when he was the Vicar of St George's Church in Deal. He had sought to make the people glad at the remembrance of the birth of Christ, encouraging one and all joyfully to receive him as their Redeemer. It was a season illuminated by the true light, he used to say, and so it should be celebrated with shiny and not glum faces, and people should give generously to the poor, remembering that God loves a cheerful giver.

On our return to the cottage, we found the parlour filled with candles and the dining room table adorned with nuts and fruits. Reedie had made a visit the previous afternoon to the shops before the light faded. She said that the windows of the poultry shop in Holt had been decorated with holly and bright red berries and that the grocer's shop had been filled with small, swollen baskets full of chestnuts or full-bearded hazelnuts. She told of clusters of grapes hanging from the ceilings and Norfolk biffins arranged in the shape of pyramids on the counter. She brought two of these apples out of a cotton pouch attached to the front of her apron. They seemed to glow with a dark red hue. She told us that she had found some Spanish onions for the stuffing and the gravy.

"The goose will be here in no time," she added.

As Mother and Elizabeth waited, they drank a glass of port-wine by the open fire. They sat on the two rocking chairs next to the hearth, a red and green throw over their knees. When she announced that lunch was ready, Reedie ushered us into the dining room where she served the feast, disappearing as soon as she had left the food, allowing the two friends to talk beyond her hearing.

After dinner, Elizabeth and my mother returned to the sitting room while Reedie cleared the table and cleaned the dining room. When we ascended the stairs to my mother's writing room, we found that Reedie had left bowls of candied fruits, figs, and nuts on the desk. There was also a silver tray with two porcelain cups and saucers on a table by the captain's chair. The room was filled with the scent of cinnamon and freshly brewed coffee. As several dry logs crackled in the grate, the two friends sipped their drinks and munched some sweets.

Elizabeth said, "The parson was right to venerate the Virgin this morning in his homily. I just wish that gentlemen in holy orders could do the same for Eve, the Mother of All living."

My mother roused herself from the edge of a nap. She muttered, "Men have always regarded Eve as inferior to Adam."

The silence that followed was interrupted by the sound of Reedie singing at the sink downstairs.

Then Elizabeth said, "I was studying the Hebrew text of the opening chapters of Genesis again last week."

"And?"

"And I saw something there that may one day change the hard hearts of stubborn men."

I could tell that my mother was intrigued.

"When the Holy Scriptures describe Eve as Adam's helper, this is not a demeaning word, as if to say that Eve is to be his cook, his maid-of-all-works, his slave." Elizabeth paused to drink some more coffee before continuing. "Far from it. The word in Hebrew is used elsewhere of Jehovah himself, where God's help means instructing man in the truth of his inscrutable ways."

"That is interesting," my mother said.

"And you know what it means, of course, Emily? It means that Eve was never meant to be Adam's lowly servant. She was meant to be his equal, his teacher, his source of wisdom."

"How is it that we have not heard this?"

"I can think of two reasons. Firstly, the interpretation and preaching of the Scriptures has been the province of men alone since time immemorial. And secondly, these men decided that 'helper' means what Milton understood it to mean, that it is the task of women to serve men with 'dulcet creams' and the like."

"My dear Elizabeth! What a revelation! If this was to be preached from the pulpits throughout the land, men like Dr Johnson would have to revise their opinions. Wasn't it he who said that a woman preaching is like a dog walking on its hind legs, a thing not done well?"

Elizabeth laughed. "I told you yesterday that Dr Johnson is sometimes wrong."

"Very wrong," my mother agreed.

The conversation turned this way and that. Then, after some games of whist, Elizabeth yielded to her infirmities and rose to her feet. She headed up to her bedroom to read before she slept.

Reedie returned to tidy the room.

My mother helped her and, before turning in herself, said thank you, adding that it was the finest Christmas meal that she had ever made, and that she was the truest of all friends.

The next day, after a late breakfast, my mother and her guest conversed in the drawing room. After an hour, Elizabeth started to ask my mother about the man who had long ago seized her heart with a love so high, so deep, so long, and so wide that it had left her wanting no other.

"I did not know you then, Emily," Elizabeth said. "You were but twenty years of age."

"Twenty-one, to be precise," my mother said.

"Who was he?"

"I cannot name him."

"Was he a phantom, or physical?"

My mother said. "My body was alive with love. Every sense, every sinew, throbbed with the force of it, as if I had been struck by a thousand lightning bolts and transfigured by the light within them."

"When you speak like this, Emily, you sound like our beloved Julian, of nearby Norwich fame."

As she mentioned the mystic's name, my mother seemed to vibrate. She began to speak words not her own. "We need to fall, and we need to be aware of it, for if we did not fall, we should not know how weak and wretched we are of ourselves, nor should we know our Maker's marvellous love so fully."

"So, you fell from grace when you fell in love."

"I did not fall. I ascended."

"My dear Emily, you speak in riddles."

"Perhaps," my mother said.

Elizabeth leaned back in her chair and smiled. "You are not going to give me a lucid answer to my questions, and that is of course proper and no doubt prudent. Forgive me."

"My dear friend, there is nothing to forgive. I am not being evasive. It is just that words fail us so atrociously when it comes to describing the bliss of true and lasting love."

"But it didn't last."

"Its effects did. What is it Sarah Edwards once said? I feel his nearness to me, and my dearness to him."

The clock chimed and my mother stood. "I fear the time has come," she said.

Elizabeth nodded.

When they descended the stairs to the parlour, our visitor's coachman was warming himself by the open fire, drinking a flagon of stout ale poured for him by Reedie.

Elizabeth tied her bonnet, donned her shawl and coat, and made to go. "You know," she said, "the country is divided. Some say that what you've done is miraculous, others blasphemous."

My mother stood and looked into her friend's eyes, holding me even closer. "And what do you say?"

Elizabeth paused and then stepped forward, holding both my mother's hands in hers. "I say that, thanks to you, women have found a voice. And not just women like me . . . *All* women."

I was caught in the heart of their embrace.

"Then we have both fulfilled our destiny on behalf of other women," my mother said, her voice confident.

Tears filled Elizabeth's eyes. "Tish, tish," she said. "I must be on my way. Coachman, it's time to leave."

"Yes, my lady," he said.

"I hope the journey home goes without incident," my mother said. "I have never known it so icy."

"There will be outrageous politicians and talkative lawyers on the coach to Deal, but I shall survive."

My mother smiled. "Thank you for making the effort to see me, especially when the weather is so bad. Please give my love to Kent and to . . . what was it you said in your recent letter?"

"The whistling wind, the beating rain, and the dashing waves," Elizabeth answered.

"Yes, that was it. So beautifully put."

Before she walked out into the cold street, Elizabeth turned. "I took my last long walk at twilight exactly a year ago. I heard the owl sing his farewell note to the departing shadows of night, and I thought of you, and of our friendship. I'm glad I came this Christmastide."

"I am too," my mother said.

"All shall be well," Elizabeth said.

"And all manner of thing shall be well," my mother replied.

The next moment, our visitor was gone.

My mother wept at the turning of the key.

Two evenings later, when the front door had closed for the last time that day and Reedie had retired, my mother sat with me on the uneven slates of the parlour, humming by the fire. After a while, the chair began to slow its metronomic to and fro until its creaky legs fell silent. The coals in the grate throbbed red and gold as the light in the room began to die.

It was a sudden gust of wind blowing down the chimney that startled her. She seemed confused, like a sailor cast adrift, no compass or moon by which to navigate. Then she saw me in her lap and a smile began to make its way across her face and her eyes glimmered in the half light. "My child," she whispered. "My only child."

Gathering her woollen scarf, she stared into the fireplace. "I was dreaming of him again," she whispered.

She looked down upon the slabs before the grate.

"We lay upon a rug and kissed beside a blazing hearth."

The embers blushed.

"We were one, completely one, as you and I are one. And we kissed like there were no tomorrows."

A teardrop formed in her eye then seemed to freeze.

"That is why you were born. So late I know, but not too late."

She lifted me and pressed me to her face.

"I want you to tell the world." She took a deep breath. "I want you to sing our song of love. Sing to those who have not loved and yet who long to love. Sing to those who need awakening from the winter of indifference. Sing it in the morning, sing it in the evening. Sing it to the prince and sing it to the orphan. Let generations hear my song."

And then she giggled. "You truly are my poetry," she said. "We speak in love-inspired pentameters!" With that she laughed and laughed until she coughed so coarsely that I thought I would be unhinged.

My mother began to make her way across the freezing floor to the winding stairs. She gathered me under her left arm while with her right she held a candle. She trod so carefully that the spiral staircase seemed to last forever. No matter, though, for either side the walls were lined with wooden shelves and ancient, well-thumbed books. Every inch of space was occupied by busts and ephemera lying upright and on their sides.

It always was my favourite journey.

Up, up, up the stairs with books for walls.

Up to her bedroom.

That night my mother slept exhausted by my side, a bony finger resting on my golden headband.

A man came knocking at our door, a tricorn hat beneath one arm. The other arm he had lost at Trafalgar, or so he said, when a ball from a Frenchie's canon took it from his shoulder. Only the swift appliance of a tourniquet and a cauterizing torch had saved him. Judging by the constant contortions of his shoulders, he was still sore from the mutilation.

My mother was weak and worn so Reedie took his cape and hat, once he had awkwardly removed them with one hand. Reedie introduced our guest. Tobias Inkley was his name.

"Miss Swanson," he said as he drew a brown parcel one-handed from his raven jacket, "I have come to tell you that you have exceeded all our expectations. Although you have courted much controversy this has served to attract attention and your name is on the lips of everyone in the land. You have provided a welcome distraction from the war."

As Mister Inkley mentioned the war, he bowed his head. Then he clawed like a crow at the bow of the parcel. "One hundred pounds," he said as he placed a text block of white banknotes on his knee.

My mother stared at him from under her fraying shawl. "All monies are to go to Mister Wilberforce's cause." My mother stroked me as we sat beside the fire.

"Are you sure?"

"As sure as my soul is in this book, and this book is in my soul."

"Then I will tell my colleagues."

After finishing his tea, he departed.

At the end of the month, his languid frame appeared once more, and my mother signed the papers.

"I bequeath it all," she said, "to the cause of the abolitionists, so that there will be neither slaves nor masters, but all will be one."

"And what of your pride and joy?" the man asked, pointing at me.

She paused, then said, "I have taken care of it."

"But who will be the guardian?"

"Billy Massingham."

"Who?"

"The young man who cares for our windows," Reedie said as she lit a tallow candle on the mantelpiece above the hearth.

"Why should he be given such a great entrustment?"

"He saved us from paying window tax."

Reedie pointed to a blocked window in the dining room.

"That would have been the eighth window," my mother said.

Our visitor looked as if he understood and nodded.

"We place great confidence in the young man," my mother said, concluding the conversation.

"Then I will make sure that your trust is honoured."

Reedie fetched the man's hat and cape, and he left our cottage, his worn naval boots crunching in the snow.

That same night, Reedie served dinner in the dining room, not in the parlour. She had polished the silver candlesticks and the chamber was now ablaze with light. There was silver everywhere. When Reedie brought the roast chicken, she even carried it on a silver platter.

After Reedie had poured claret with an unsteady hand, my mother spoke. "To what do we owe all this?"

"It is a celebration of our friendship, my dear."

"How lovely," she said. Then she added, "you have been such a dear, dear friend to me. How long is it now?"

"Three score years and ten."

"You have been so faithful to me, Reedie. Especially when he and I . . ."

Reedie interrupted, "Others were blind."

"You were the only one who possessed eyes to see and ears to hear," my mother replied.

"Do you still think of him?" Reedie enquired.

"When I open my eyes at dawn, and when I lay my head upon my pillow at night. Those times especially.

He comes without me even trying to remember him. Throughout the day, little things are prompts and cues that cause me to remember. And then, even when I am asleep, he enters through the door of my dreams. He has the key. He will always have the key, and only he. He never knocks. He does not need to. He is my beloved and my beloved is mine."

"You never thought of any other?"

"Never. I have met handsome men, as have you. And I have admired their outward appearance and their inward personality. But he, he was the only one. No others could compare."

"Is there only ever one soulmate?"

"Only one, my dear. Many become married to one who is not their soulmate and live as strangers in the same home. It is most tragic to see. When you find your soulmate, there is oneness. Complete oneness. Oneness of vision. Oneness of passion. Oneness of language, even."

"Language?"

"Yes, the strings of your hearts are so perfectly tuned to each other that you play the same melodies. Not prepared music, from written scores, but the spontaneous duets of the heart."

"You truly are a poet," Reedie remarked with a smile.

My mother finished a last mouthful of chicken and then sat back in her seat. She looked at her friend, with her fine white hair and her bright blue eyes, her soft round face and her curved nose. She sighed before she spoke. "Your friendship, Reedie, has been lifegiving."

"Emily! Your tone is so . . . so elegiac. You speak as if this is our last supper. My heart will not endure it."

"And what if it is?"

"Well, then, that would be simply dreadful. How shall I go on without you, all alone in this cottage?"

My mother leaned forward. "I have left provision for you. The house and all its contents I leave to you. The only exception is the great gift I give to Billy Massingham."

"But Emily! This cottage is you, and you are this cottage. It will be like a body robbed of its soul."

My mother left the table and walked to her friend, put her arms around her shoulders, and squeezed them.

"Remember," she said. "All will be well."

My mother released her friend.

"Why do you tell me this tonight?" Reedie asked.

"Because the clock of my heart is worn and nearly stopped."

"Emily, I simply cannot bear to hear such things."

"Come now," my mother said, returning to her chair and raising her silver chalice. "A toast."

Reedie was slow and reluctant, but she reciprocated.

"To the end of winter," my mother said.

"When the rains are over and gone," her friend replied, keeping back the tears.

On Easter Day, my mother fell ill. Her face seemed sallower and the light in her eyes dimmer than the embers in her bedroom hearth. I noticed she was trembling when she held me and that her breathing seemed to rise and fall with inconsistent undulations.

It was the arrival of a letter that precipitated my mother's decline. It was from the Vicar of St George's Church in Deal.

Dear Miss Swanson,

I write to inform you of some sad news. Your dear friend Elizabeth Carter passed peacefully on February 19th. She died at home in her room overlooking the sea that she loved so much, in her town house on South Street, Deal. We held the funeral service in St George's Church and buried her body in the graveyard there, in full and certain hope of the resurrection to eternal life, through our Lord Jesus Christ.

I thought you would like to know that in her dying breaths, just after I had administered the blessed sacrament to her for the final time, she mentioned you and besought me to pass onto you a message. She said, "Tell Emily we fought the good fight for women. We have run and we will surely win the prize." And so, I pass this message onto you.

Elizabeth was adamant that I wasn't to tell you about her funeral. She said the journey would be too much for you.

I send my deepest condolences to you. Judging by the number of the great and the good at the service and then at her burial, she was the most extraordinary of women. And judging by what she shared with me, you are too.

May the grace of our Lord Jesus Christ, the love of God, and the fellowship of the Holy Ghost be with Elizabeth, and with you, for evermore.

My mother sobbed.

All that night, Reedie kept watch over her as she slept, perched on an armchair by the grate, her shoulders burdened by the eiderdown and blankets from her bed upstairs.

"Are you all right, my dear?" she asked at dawn, as she stood by the side of the bed.

"I saw him," my mother replied through squinting eyes.

"Him?"

"Yes. He came to me like he did at the beginning . . . over the hills. He knocked on my windowpane. Told me that it was time to get up." My mother was rasping now. "He said the winter was . . . over . . . he said he could hear . . . two turtle doves . . . cooing . . . in the forest."

Reedie bowed, her bedclothes falling like leaves.

My mother stretched out her hand. I could see the bones pressing through her mottled skin as she pointed to me. I was resting on a cushion with a blossoming vine, one my mother once had sewn.

Reedie took me to my mother's side.

"My child," my mother whispered. Her hands were spotted like the foxing on a fading page.

Then she sighed. A long and drawn-out sigh that seemed to come from deep within and head for far away, beyond the stars above. I saw it. It left her like a silken scarf, one that glowed with the strangest deep-green light.

My mother was gone.

Who would hold and kiss me now?

Part 2

1806-1815

My heart is broken by the terrible loss I have sustained in my old friends and companions and my poor soldiers. Believe me, nothing except a battle lost can be half so melancholy as a battle won.

Arthur Wellesley, 1st Duke of Wellington (1769-1852)

After my mother died, I rested on her bedside table, remembering her soothing words, her tender eyes, her trembling touch. I stared and stared at the pillow where she used to lay her head. There I had read her expressions in the night, trying to guess what dreams swirled within her mind, sometimes causing her to smile, other times to wince. The room felt like a bottle whose vintage wine had been decanted. I thought that I would never recover from her absence.

As the months passed by, the mourning took its toll on her companion too, who withered and withered until she could stand no more. When Reedie sensed that she was not long for this life, she summoned Billy Massingham. Before he arrived, she held me for the last time. We both felt the connection with my mother. The unending profusion of her tears dismantled me.

"Dear Emily," she said, opening my covers and looking deep into my soul. "How you burned with love. But the candle of your life is carried up the stairs to the place of rest." Then she put me down upon her knee. "I will not be long after you now, my dear, dear friend."

Reedie fell asleep, her head resting on a cushion.

When the clock struck ten, there was a knock and she stirred. "Come in!" she cried, her voice loud but croaky.

Billy Massingham stood at the threshold, cap in hand. "How are you Miss Reed?"

"It's time," she said. She took me in her hands, shaking and unsteady, and lifted me. "She wanted you to have this."

Billy's eyes glistened.

"Take it with my blessing."

He held me to his chest.

"You know I will treasure this," he said.

"Pass me that pipe," she said.

Her small clay pipe was on the shelf above the fire. Its bowl was stuffed with tobacco.

"Are you sure?"

"Don't fret," she said. "The maid will be here at midday."

Billy handed it to her.

"Light it for me, would you?"

Billy took one of the tapers for the candles, found a piece of burning kindling in the grate and ignited the tobacco. Clouds of smoke began to rise and fill the room, causing our visitor to cough.

"What will you do?" he asked between splutters.

"I have sold this house, and all its books and prints, just as Emily requested. The new owners will move in as soon as I have passed." She lowered the pipe to her lap and stared out onto the small garden. "Thank you for looking after our windows, Billy."

"Thank you for teaching me how to read," he replied.

"What we have imparted to you," she said, "you can pass onto your sweetheart. Are you married yet?"

"A month ago."

"Ah, that's good. I'm happy for you both."

She turned to look at me. "Whenever you read these poems, do it in remembrance of her. A part of her will be present. It will warm your heart because . . ." She took a strong sip from the lip of her pipe and blew the smoke towards the ceiling. "Because the words burn."

When he saw that Reedie had fallen asleep, Billy took the pipe and placed it back on the shelf, waiting until the embers had died and the last wisps of smoke had disappeared. Then he pulled the throw up towards her waist, leaned forward and kissed her on her forehead.

Billy turned towards the fireplace, stoked the coals, and added a log, before walking out of the parlour and onto the street.

After he had strode one hundred feet with me under his arm, he stopped, looked back at the cottage, and breathed a deep sigh. I could tell he was saying goodbye for the last time.

As was I.

Billy's sweetheart took me to her bosom the moment he carried me into their humble little home. Her name was Sally and, in the evenings, when her work was done, Billy taught her how to read, using my mother's poems. It took her no time before she was reading from my pages. On their first wedding anniversary, they read to each other by candlelight.

After they had been married for over a year, it became clear that Sally and Billy could not have a child, so she used to hold me as my mother once had. Often, when her husband was out cleaning windows, she would talk to me, telling me of her love for Billy, using my mother's words. She even tried writing her own poetry, extolling her love for Billy, but soon gave up, cross with herself that she was mimicking my idioms too much, feeling too keenly the distance between my mother's offerings and her own.

The only regular visitor to Billy's house was his best friend Jonny Parkin, a man with a mischievous smile. When war broke out, they volunteered for the Coldstream Guards and went to Spain to fight against Napoleon. When they returned, they entered the house with sunned and hardened faces and many a tale to tell.

"At the Battle of Salamanca," Jonny said, "I took a bullet to the leg and was subjected to the surgeons."

"We were relieved," Billy said, "when we learned that Jonny had escaped the amputator's saw."

"Not as relieved as my leg," Jonny quipped.

And the two men laughed.

Sally did not, and nor did I.

My mother had once read a play called *The Bacchae* during a week of winter nights, translating it into English as she progressed through the book. When she had come to the death of the king, he had been ripped apart, his limbs torn from his body, and my mother had shuddered at what she had called his *sparagmos*.

Rumours of Jonny's dramatic escape from his own *sparagmos* horrified me. I was already frightened of fire. Now I suffered grave anxieties about dismemberment. Mutilation and incineration, these terrors began to occupy my thoughts, and, in the absence of my mother's comfort, I became much obsessed with anticipations of my own annihilation.

This was not helped when Bonaparte, having been vanquished and exiled, escaped from his confinement and returned to France. Raising an army, he proposed to stir up trouble one more time.

"We're off to war again, my love," Billy said one morning.

"Do you have to go?"

Billy nodded.

"Is Jonny going too?"

Billy nodded again.

"Promise me you will look after each other, as you did in Spain."

Billy nodded a third time, then said, "This time, I want to take this with me." He lifted me to his chest. "Miss Swanson's words bring me great consolation. They calm my nerves. And they remind me that it is love, not war, that makes the world a better place."

Sally made to object, but then refrained. "All right, my love. But I want you back here, safe and sound."

Billy kissed her on the lips.

Then he was away to pack.

On the seventeenth day of June 1815, Billy's company retreated to a farm called Hougoumont. During the last half mile, the sky began to threaten heavy rain. Billy and Jonny were singing,

Over the hills and far away,
He swears he will return one day.
Far from the mountains and the seas,
Back in her arms again he'll be.

When we arrived at the farmhouse, we met the gardener. He was called William and lived in part of the farm. He had left his escape too late and was forced to stay behind with his five-year-old daughter, a wistful girl with ponytails called Anne-Marie. She stared at us as the rain began to fall, her eyes filled with curiosity.

That night, the men took refuge in the building. Candles, lamps, and fires were lit in the house and throughout the stables, barns, and sheds. Billy oversaw the creation of loopholes. He then examined every window both for their strength and line of fire.

By 11pm, when the men had finished improving the defences, they were hungry and exhausted. Some had just bemoaned the lack of victuals when the farmer and his daughter reappeared. "For your . . . stomachs," the man stammered, dragging an old barrel behind him.

Billy removed the lid from the cask. It was full of damp rye loaves, one of which he raised as if it was the sacred host. "Form an orderly line," he said after counting the rations.

One by one, the weary, sodden soldiers walked towards him, taking pieces of the wet bread in their hands. Some gorged it straight away while others nibbled at their portion. When all the men had eaten, Billy broke up the cask and used the wood to light a fire.

At midnight, my guardian took me in his arms and looked at me. He held me close and took a deep breath. I read him once again, even as he read me. His chin was dappled with light grey flecks, as were his sideburns and his once brown and deckered hair. His hazel eyes were bloodshot from the many battles he had seen and the comrades he had loved and lost. His face was more beaten than I had ever noticed, like a book whose mildewed covers had been bumped and chipped until they were a shadow of what they once had been.

Billy studied me by the light of a candle, a thousand memories discharging in his mind.

He smiled until his eyelids began to droop.

"Read to us again, Sarge," a private said. "Yes, read to us," other voices echoed in the chamber and the rafters.

Billy pulled himself from the edge of sleep and began to read my mother's mournful songs of love. As he did it seemed the very moon stood still and everyone on earth was listening. He read eleven poems without wavering, showing them the illustrations in my pages when the poems required it. I heard again my lovely mother's voice and felt a warmth within my leaves. Then, his eyes failing, Billy leaned against the cold stone wall and yawned.

"More," a corporal pleaded.

He was on the point of saying no when the gardener's child appeared once more and walked towards him. One of the soldiers threw bits of biscuit to encourage her as she made her way with careful steps across the floor. She picked each morsel and chewed it, suspiciously at first, until she arrived at Billy's boots.

The girl stared into the sergeant's eyes for several seconds, her head tilted like an inquisitive pup, then she sat at his feet, her dolly falling to the floor as she gazed at me with a wondering look.

She pointed at me.

"Very well," my father said.

He started to read again.

The soldiers slipped beneath their drying capes, hiding their moistened eyes from the other men. Then Anne-Marie stood. She looked at Billy and me with shiny eyes.

Underneath her auburn hair, her face seemed to be aglow with a golden light.

"Sank you," she said. With that, she hopped between the soldiers' boots and went downstairs to find her father.

When the sound of snoring began to fill our floor, Jonny turned and fetched a handkerchief from his backpack. It was folded like a present. He put his finger over his lips to signal to Billy that he was not to draw attention to the burden he bore. As he peeled back one corner, Billy gasped. Jonny put his finger to his lips again. Then he revealed two juicy green apples and a cluster of blood-red cherries.

"From the garden," he whispered. "There's an orchard with apple and cherry trees. I also brought these." He reached into his backpack and drew out a clutch of branches. "The trees in the orchard are hardwood," he whispered. "There's gaps between them and no underwood to speak of, but I managed to use my bayonet to sever some of the stubborn branches for our fire."

Billy began to add the fresh kindling to the dying flames next to us while munching on some of the sweet and succulent cherries. He took a bite out of one of the apples too.

"There's more," Jonny whispered.

He thrust his hands deep into the pack and withdrew a large object, pink in hue, with what looked like a hairy snout.

"It's a pig's head," he said, stifling a laugh.

"Where in God's green earth did you find that?" Billy asked.

"Private Southgate. Used to be a butcher. Owed me a favour. I'll cook it slowly and then we can share it around when the men awake. They can have pork and rum for breakfast."

While Corporal Parkin cooked the beast's head, I rested on some dry straw beside my guardian. He was startled only once in the night by a volley from a piquet in the woods outside, chasing off some riders sniffing at our walls. Besides that, he slept and dreamed while I watched him, grateful of the bond of love that tied us to my mother's heart.

What can I tell you of the battle the next day, except that it was as terrible as I had feared, and as awful an affront to my mother's songs of love as anything could ever be? When the ordeal began, Billy raised me to his nose. He sniffed me and then, while none were watching, pursed his cracking lips and kissed me. "God bless you, Granny Swanson," he whispered. Then he tucked me underneath his redcoat, next to his heart.

Billy shouted a command. The gardener's house filled with white smoke as two hundred muskets fired upon the Frenchmen down below. Two hours later, after constant fusillades, Jonny screamed in pain, clutching his leg as blood seeped from a shrapnel wound.

"Take him to the surgeons!" Billy shouted.

A while later, as fire began to fall upon the farm and its grounds, the gardener, William, appeared upstairs. He had his daughter with him. She was clutching her dolly and shivering.

"Sergeant," he said to Billy. "May I parlez . . . with you." The left side of his grubby face was twitching as he spoke, causing the affected eye to close and open like an unattended shutter on a stormy night.

"Of course, monsieur."

When they and I were in a corridor between the kitchen and the scullery, the father spoke. "The French, they will . . . how you say . . ." He gestured with his hands, miming the sound and impact of artillery. "Zis place . . . my home . . . it will be like hell itself." His eyes were full of tears as he gestured to his pony-tailed daughter. "Please . . . save her."

"We will protect her," Billy said.

He stretched out his hand to honour the agreement.

"Sank you," the gardener said. "She will stay here, under the basin, where she will be safe."

After the gardener left, Billy told the girl to stay put while he went in search of Jonny. Outside, there were bodies everywhere, riddled and smashed, like the apple and cherry trees in the orchard beyond, fractured and splintered almost beyond all recognition.

We entered a barn and found a surgeon wiping the reddened blade of a saw. When we saw his patient, Billy gasped.

"Jonny!"

Billy drew some gin from one of his two canteens. He lifted it to his friend's lips and forced it with his fingers into his mouth and down his throat. Jonny coughed and then came around. He looked at Billy and then at the stump where his leg had been, the bandages leaking blood, and he uttered the most terrible groan I had ever heard.

Billy demanded some laudanum from the surgeon. It was then, as the physician fetched a small bottle, that I saw the remains of Jonny's leg lying on the ground. Blood was oozing out of the severed veins and arteries. Everything within me trembled.

"You'll be alright, Jonny," Billy said.

"I'm not sure I'm going to make it."

"Don't talk like that. Just stay awake."

"Don't go, Billy."

"I have to."

"Why?"

"There's just something I have promised to do."

"What?"

"Get the gardener's little girl to safety."

Jonny nodded.

"I'll be back," Billy said, grasping his mucker's hand. "I promised Sally I'd look after you."

"Same," Jonny said.

Then we stepped back outside, into the inferno.

Billy hurried to the kitchen where he found the little girl cowering beneath the basin. "Come with me," he said. She wavered and then hurled herself into his arms. The next moment, we were running through the smoke and fire of Hougoumont, towards the northern gate.

Two soldiers raised the beam and through the welcome aperture we hastened, up past the sunken track and muddy ponds until we reached the higher ground. All the while, the incendiaries fell upon the walled chateau and its grounds behind us, burning barns and trees, scorching men and horses, whose shrill keening pierced the red sky.

It was while Billy was running that I sensed it. His uniform had disguised it well, but I felt it in his chest – the open tear, the seeping of his lifeblood from a sharp and burning shard.

Billy stopped and took me from my hiding place inside his uniform. He slid his hands over me, lifting me up to his mouth and nose, taking in my scent and texture one more time, pursing his quivering lips and kissing me. Then he gestured to Anne-Marie.

"Here," he gasped.

The girl looked confused.

Then she understood.

She took me, holding her dolly and me to her heart.

As she clutched me, Billy saw a dark-skinned soldier in the uniform of the 73rd Foot emerging from the smoke. He was a broad-shouldered Jamaican man with deep eyes. There was blood on his right hand, and he was clutching his shoulder with his left. A letter was poking out of his buttoned tunic.

"Private Rose? Is that you?"

"Sarge!" the man said.

"Where are you heading?" Billy asked.

"I'm carrying a message from my Commanding officer to the Duke of Wellington."

"Can you take this girl with you?" Billy asked.

The soldier nodded.

And that was that.

Billy walked back down the path towards the burning farm. His back was arched, his uniform was rubbed, and he was limping now. I watched until his stumbling shadow slipped into the smoke that hung about the farm. Then, as the rain began to fall again, we turned and made our way towards safety.

Private Rose led Anne-Marie and me to the top of the ridge, where we came upon the Duke of Wellington, sitting upon his horse, looking through a telescope and issuing orders. When he saw the girl, her skin charred and her skirt torn, his eyes were filled with compassion.

"Where have you come from, young lady?"

"Hougoumont," the girl replied.

The Duke reached out towards her with his canteen. She took the silver vessel and stared for a moment at the engravings on its side.

"A gift from my wife," the Duke said.

She opened the top and took huge gulps of the fresh water inside. Then, remembering her manners, she said, "Pardon," and returned it to the Duke, who restored it to its holster.

"What is that you are carrying?" the Duke asked.

The girl signalled with a bellicose pout and a pronounced frown that I was not to be touched. The Duke, seeing her innocent petulance, settled back into his saddle with a smile.

Then, at the sound of a new barrage, he turned to an aide-de-camp next to him. "Take her," he said. "Look after her. Give her some food. Find her some clothes. Do it. Quickly now, I say."

Then he turned to Private Rose. "I remember you. You fought in Flanders, did you not?"

"Yes, sir."

"And you were wounded there."

The soldier nodded.

"And again now, by the looks of it."

The Duke turned to his right.

"Have this man seen to by my physician," he said.

The wounded Private was led away while we were escorted to a cottage half a mile from the field of battle.

Anne-Marie was cleaned up by one of the wives who had been following her husband across Belgium. Several hours later, the girl was reunited with her relieved and grateful father. It was from him that we learned what had happened after Billy left us.

Jonny had lived to fight another day, although there never was another day of battle for him. He returned to England where he set up a shop selling wooden arms and legs for veterans of war.

As for Billy, we both grieved when we learned that he had died of his wounds, his head resting on Jonny's chest.

As Billy died, his friend sang to him.

Over the hills and far away,
He swears he will return one day.
Far from the mountains and the seas,
Back in her arms again he'll be.

Anne-Marie wept inconsolably when she heard that her rescuer had perished, and would not let go of me, not just that night, but every night thereafter, and every day as well.

I, meanwhile, wept for the man who had adopted me, and for his wife who had looked after me with a mother's love. Wept for the loss of the last physical connection with my own mother, and for the fact that I now had no place to call my home.

Part 3

1815-1843

Belgium! name unromantic and unpoetic, yet
name that whenever uttered has in my ear a
sound, in my heart an echo, such as no other
assemblage of syllables, however sweet or classic,
can produce. Belgium! I repeat the word, now as
I sit alone near midnight. It stirs my world of the
past like a summons to resurrection.

Charlotte Bronte (1816-1855)

For nearly three decades, I was as dishevelled as the penniless soldiers living on the streets. My new guardian held me despite these imperfections. But then, one night when the moon was full, she stopped. Maybe a sense of guilt had superseded her gratitude. Or she had begun to realise that I, being passed onto her in such unnatural circumstances, was undeserving of a true mother's love. I had not been born to her, as I had to my beloved mother, nor had I been accepted as an honoured gift, as was the case with Billy Massingham. I had been a refugee of war, thrust into her care, with no human connection other than the brave sergeant who had stood in the gap between her and the enemies raining fire upon her home. No wonder then, that when her father died in the summer of 1843, she decided to sell the farm and give me away, severing the ropes that bound her to her tormenting memories.

"We're going to move to Bruges," she muttered as she picked me up one morning. "My aunt lives zere." She would often talk in broken English, a respectful nod to Sergeant Billy Massingham.

After travelling by carriage, we boarded a barge at Ghent. This strange vessel was designed like a tavern – the most unusual inn in Europe. It consisted of two large rooms; in one, travellers could sit and read, while in the other, they could partake of a fine meal of up to six courses. These chambers were warmed by fires whose smoke poured from two chimneys. The river was calm, so the motion was unnoticeable. The vessel was towed by horses each side of the canal.

When we arrived at Bruges, it was hard not to be impressed. There were bridges everywhere, two hundred in all, befitting a city whose name seems to have derived from an ancient word meaning *bridge*. Inside the four miles of walls, there were many old-fashioned buildings, wide streets, church buildings, marketplaces, and squares. The main marketplace, called the Burg, was overshadowed by a great belfry 553 steps high, the chime of whose many bells was sonorous and distinctive, playing different tunes every quarter of an hour. This steeple, supported by four pillars, was so tall that it acted as a landmark to guide the mariners.

At one side of this great steeple stood the venerable city hall, designed in the Gothic style, whose life-sized statues of the earls of Flanders had been destroyed during the French Revolution. My curiosity was aroused when I heard that tens of thousands of rare books, manuscripts, and old prints had survived in its library.

My mother would have loved to have browsed among its shelves, blowing the dust off the covers, straining her eyes to see the print.

This city, I also quickly learned, was distinguished for its care of orphans, 300 of whom were housed in hospitals and schools. People said that no other city showed such compassion.

As the days wore on, I found comfort in this.

I was about to be the 301st orphan in Bruges.

Once we had settled into a new cottage adjacent to a canal, bought from the proceeds of her father's farm, my guardian decided to visit an English merchant in the hope of obtaining gainful employment. She had become dextrous at knitting woollen garments, thanks to the fleece from her late father's sheep, and was seeking work.

Out of the population, there were a small number of English traders, one of whom was known to her aunt. For generations, this gentleman's family had been sending shiploads of wool across the English Channel to Dunkirk. They were then transported on barges for three hours along the canal from Ostend, finally disembarking at Bruges. Having arrived at his factory, the wool was then woven into cloth and linen, some of the finest in the world, before being shipped to countries far and wide, or sold in his shop in Bruges.

"He is called John Porter," my guardian remarked. "He is English. He may know a bit more about your history, or at least about your mozer. My aunt has established a meeting for us wiz him."

And so, as the bells of the great steeple struck six in the evening, my guardian and I walked through bustling streets illuminated by burning lamps and serenaded by birdsong. We headed to a tavern called *The Paradise* where we waited at a small wooden table near the entrance. There were many people there talking, shouting, eating, and drinking, taking snuff and smoking cheroots. Some of the men were traders, discussing the business of the day.

In no time at all, or so it seemed, a gentleman in an olive-green jacket and light brown breaches entered the room. He paused, looked to his left, strained his eyes, and spotted us. My guardian had sent a message ahead of us. "You will recognise me from the old, damaged book I shall be holding close to my heart." As the man saw me, his fulsome ruby cheeks expanded into a smile. He walked towards us, greeted by several other men on the way, who recognised him and interrupted his progress with questions about the woollen trade.

Removing his bicorn hat, he bowed. "My name is John Porter. You must be Anne-Marie." He stretched out his hand, reaching for my guardian's fingers. Raising them to his lips, he kissed them. "And this must be your travelling companion." He looked at me, his bushy eyebrows rising and falling as he studied my cover. Then he returned his attention to my guardian and said, "I have heard of this book."

"What have you heard, monsieur? I have had zis in my possession since Waterloo. I know so little about it."

"Its author, Emily Swanson," the man began, and as he mentioned my mother's name, I trembled. "She was in her late eighties when she published this, her only work. Some said that her poems were coarse, and guilty of impropriety, not fitting for a woman to pen, or even think. But many more found them enchanting, romantic, passionate. Some even found them spiritual."

"It is a small mouth to make such a big noise," my guardian said.

"That's true," Mister Porter replied. "It is a slim volume, but people often mistake extent for depth. When Miss Swanson decided to use the sacred language of the Song of Songs to immortalise her own love, this was a bold move."

"She sounds like a revolutionary," my guardian said.

"How did you come by it?"

She began to tell the story of Billy Massingham reading my mother's poems to the soldiers the night before Waterloo, then taking me out of the burning farmhouse.

"Astonishing," Mister Porter said. "The book must have been very precious to him, very precious indeed."

"It was. Mademoiselle Swanson gave it to him. It was the very first edition. It was her baby, or so she said. She treasured it more zan anything, even more zan her closest friend."

"May I?" Mister Porter asked. He took me in his hands, opened my covers, and flicked through my opening pages, studying me with his big bloodshot eyes, before handing me back.

"Are you hungry, my dear?" he asked.

The truth was, she was famished. She had not eaten anything since the Tavern on the Water.

The man patted his chubby fingers on a belly threatening to escape from his purple waistcoat. "Time for some dinner."

He shouted out and within a heartbeat a young woman was at our table. "Good evening, Monsieur Porter."

"It is a *very* good evening, Annabelle, especially now I have some company. From Waterloo, don't you know, where we Englishmen gave that upstart Bonaparte a right old kicking."

The woman nodded.

"We want to provide a good welcome to our city, don't we, Annabelle?"

She nodded again.

"You know what to bring us."

Annabelle left for the kitchens.

"What can I do for you, my dear?" Mister Porter asked. "Don't be shy now. Your aunt has told me that you may have skills relevant to my business and that you are looking for work."

"My fazer had many sheep on ze farm at Hougoumount," my guardian said, her face blushing. "I would help him shear zem every year and knit ze wool into garments."

"What did you do with them?" he asked.

"I sold zem in ze market. My stall was always crowded wiz people wanting zem. I would always be sold out ze same day. I dyed ze wool. Zey were many different colours. I had ze good reputation."

Mister Porter looked at the woollen coat my guardian was wearing, eyeing it from top to bottom. It was an unusual style, especially by the standards of what we had seen in the streets of Bruges.

"Did you make this?"

She nodded.

Mister Porter reached out and touched the coat. He then passed his fingers over the material. "You are a seamstress too?"

Once again, she nodded.

Just then, the food arrived in large bowls resting on wide rimmed plates, accompanied by two jars of yellow-coloured beer. There was steam rising from both the stew and the bread around them.

"The beef is exceptional," Mister Porter said. "And the sauce . . ." he put his fat fingers to his lips and made the sound of a loud kiss. "Let me just put it this way. We English invented gravy, and it is as tasteless as the flour with which it is made. In Bruges, the sauces for both broths and stews are works of art."

He unfolded his napkin and buried one corner into the tiny space between his olive-green cravat and his thick neck.

"Tuck in," he said.

The sound of slurping and chewing followed. Even with the hubbub of all the conversations around us, the noise of Mister Porter's jowls seemed as loud as a maid slopping water from a bucket.

When he had finished, my guardian was still only halfway through her meal. He looked at her, studying to see if she would push her bowl away while there were islands of meat still floating in the ocean of remaining sauce. Sure enough, she did, and sure enough he pounced upon the victuals, lifting his spoon, and plunging it into the dark liquid, stoking his large and gaping mouth with his concentrated shovelling.

"Waste not, want not," he said between gulps.

He patted his belly again, which was now extended, arched like the breasts of a freshly plucked chicken.

Mister Porter quaffed his glass of wine, then looked at me. "What do you mean to do with this?"

"I need to pass it on."

Mister Porter's eyes seemed to widen for a second.

"It is very damaged," he said. "What value it once might have possessed is now long gone, I'm sorry to say, at least while it is in this parlous, unrestored state."

He wiped a trickle of saliva from the side of his mouth.

"Although the illustrations . . ." he seemed to lick his lips. "They are, if I'm not mistaken, by the great artist William Blake."

"Zer are ten of zem."

"I noticed."

"Are zey valuable?"

"Depends on their condition. The book has been very damaged. I suspect the pictures won't fetch as much as they could in this, shall we say, battle-scarred condition."

My guardian winced.

"Did I say something wrong?"

"No, monsieur. It's just that the sergeant wanted me to look after it. I know he would never have asked me if he had thought I would give it to someone who was only interested in the pictures."

Mister Porter looked aghast.

"The book and its illustrations must remain together," he cried.

"I agree," she said.

"May I make a suggestion?" Mister Porter asked.

She nodded.

"I could take the book to a friend of mine, the assistant librarian here in Bruges. He comes to my shop, and we often sup here together. He might be interested in taking your book on as a project. You could either pay him to repair it, or . . ." he paused and smiled.

"Or what?"

"Or you could donate it to the library in lieu of paying him. Here in Bruges, there is a fine and extensive collection of old books situated in the Town Hall. It has many rare volumes and would be a fitting place for yours, once its imperfections have been corrected."

"I cannot afford to pay for zis," my guardian said with a sigh. "Maybe it's time to say adieu."

A frisson of worry disturbed my leaves.

"Listen," Mister Porter said. "The library is the best place for your book. Twenty years ago, Napoleon did one thing right. He ordered all the volumes from two monasteries near Bruges should be given a home in the Town Hall. They had been sequestered during the French Revolution. Boney wanted them to be preserved. It's the perfect resting place for Miss Swanson's book."

My guardian looked at me, her eyes brimming. "You're sure zey'll look after it? It is very precious . . ."

"I am confident they will."

"Zen, zey can have it."

"If you're sure, then I'll send a message to my friend at the library, telling him you will see him first thing tomorrow. His name is Monsieur Bleriot. Take the book to him."

Mister Porter stood. "Can you start work for me after that."

"Yes, monsieur."

"Capital."

With that, he walked out, my guardian following not long afterwards, holding me beneath her shawl.

That night, she slept next to me.

Her hand never left my back, not even when the sun broke through the gap between the half-closed shutters.

When she made to turn over, she took me with her, placing her other hand on top of me, as if in an act of benediction.

I welcomed the blessing, not knowing when I would next receive one from a guardian.

The next morning, my guardian took me to the great square just as the bells in the steeple chimed, marking the eighth hour. Traders were setting up stalls of linen, wool, dimities, camlets, baize, and packets of seeds for making oil. All this took place under the arcades of the Town Hall where Monsieur Bleriot conducted his business in the library.

As we approached it through avenues of trees, my trepidation was superseded by my admiration for the perfect symmetry of the building's façade, effected by the two rows of three perfectly aligned windows and the two main doors, positioned left and right below. Then there were the battlements above, and the golden crests on top of the six dormers, all crowned by six great turrets – three on each side. They rose like rockets, frozen in time, into the blue sky and the scudding clouds.

We entered through the left door and, after my guardian had made an enquiry, an attendant pointed to the library. I saw a picture hanging above his bald head where there hung a framed copy of some verses of Robert Southey, dated 1816. I recognised his name. He was one of the many visitors to my mother's house.

The season of her splendour is gone by,
Yet everywhere its monuments remain;
Temples which rear their stately heads on high,
Canals that intersect the fertile plain,
Wide streets and squares, with many a court and hall
Spacious and undefaced, but ancient all.

When we arrived at the entrance to the library, another attendant opened the doors. Nothing could have prepared me for what happened next. Most mortal men and women would have been in awe of what their eyes observed, the stacks and rows of books from far and near. Some gilded, golden, glorious. Others faded, frayed and colourless. Or they might have been struck by the smell, as my guardian was. The odour of covers, binding, parchment, page and even ink, that lifeblood of the book, all scented by the musty fragrance of antiquity.

For me, it was the sound that most impressed me. Thousands upon thousands of voices, from every tribe and nation, in every language and inflection, like a thunderous waterfall descending upon me all at once. Some notes were tragic, others satirical. Some were comical, others whimsical. Many were more tearful lamentation than merry celebration. But all combined, they made a choir whose voices far surpassed the melody and volume of the bells in the belfry outside.

These sounds cascaded out of every volume, every pamphlet, every print in the bookcases and on the walls in the vast chamber, joining with my voice, my mother's voice, as mine began to sound as well.

I was lost in time, or out of time, surrounded by a great, resounding gathering of ancient witnesses, their words alive, their thoughts revived. As they sang, I seemed to catch a glimpse of tonsured monks and long-haired prophets, noble poets and skilful scribes, their writing now vibrating, resonating, trembling with life.

Then, without warning, this chorus stopped as a man with wispy black sideburns approached. He had a black jacket and waistcoat and black breeches. The only other colour, besides his white cravat, was the gold of his tiny, oval spectacles and the chain which he was now grasping. His entrance had caused the music to stop and fade like an orchestra that had been robbed, in a moment, of its conductor.

Looking at his timepiece, he spoke in a tongue not my mother's. Nevertheless, I seemed to understand him. "I am sorry to appear discourteous," he said. "A new shipment of rare books is about to arrive." His eyes shone for a moment as he said these words. "You'll forgive me if we keep this brief."

The man smiled and, as he did, I felt uneasy. His pursed lips were drawn too far, like curtains being held apart. His eyes betrayed him too. There was avarice there.

My guardian handed me over to him. "I am told by Mister Porter you may be able to help with zis," she said.

The man took me in his hands. He opened me, his hands and fingers moving over and inside my covers and my sheets. There was something covetous about his touch. Not safe and soothing, like the hands of my mother. I wanted to cry out, but I had no voice.

"Monsieur Porter informs me that you are prepared. to release this to me, in return for me applying my skills to it."

"Yes," my guardian said.

"Then we have an agreement."

The man turned to leave, as did my guardian.

I was carried to a staircase, then down to vaults below where the librarian grasped some jangling keys from his pocket, unlocked a gate made of iron bars, and approached a safe.

Just as he was about to unlock it, another younger man stepped out of the shadows.

"What have you there, Master?"

"I think you know."

"Not the Swanson book?"

"The same."

"Will you make a sale today?"

"No, Pierre. I have told you before. Patience is required if we are not to be caught. We must wait until its previous owner is no longer alive. That way there will be no one to contradict our story."

"Are you going to restore it?"

"I am not. When the time comes, I will remove Mister Blake's illustrations and throw the rest into the fire."

Every one of my pages trembled.

"The drawings will be worth a great deal by then," he added.

Monsieur Bleriot made to open the safe, but then turned. "Do not think for a moment of trying to steal this. Miss Swanson's book is under my oversight now."

At the mention of my mother's name, I pined for the safety of her arms, for the motion of her rocking chair, the warmth of the embers in her hearth, and the canopy of her tawny throw.

The librarian unlocked the safe with an iron key that hung about his neck and thrust me inside. When the door slammed shut, I discovered one other occupant – a small book half open, with far more leaves than mine, its velum pages decorated by floral borders, revealing an image of the Virgin Mother with a golden crown and an ultramarine cloak. A boy child lay in her lap, a halo around his head. I could tell that the book was damaged, just as I was. Its coloured edges and corners were faded, as if pressed by many thumbs, and there was evidence of charring, as if the book had been exposed to fire.

Never did I ache for my mother's soothing touch more than then, in the darkness that was visible to me.

In my eerie dormitory, I would have had no conception
of the passing of time had it not been for my companion,
whose chanting marked the progression of days. Eight
hours out of twenty-four, for an hour each occasion,
strange music would rise from the ornate book. The
pages would turn as the songs changed and a picture
from the manuscript would glow, filling the chamber
with a sacred, golden presence.

In the first of these hours, an image would appear
showing Mary being visited by an angel who told her
that she had conceived a child by the intervention of God
himself. She held a book in her hands, which I understood
to be a book of prayer. Over time, I would sense that the
book in the picture and the book next to me were one
and the same. When that revelation came, it rushed into
my heart with a light so bright that I thought my own
pages would burn with it.

In the second hour, a single letter would light up and
a song of celebration would start. It told of a meeting

Mary had with her cousin, whose baby leapt within her, because Mary's offspring was divine and her cousin's child a prophet.

In the third hour, a page would fall open with this child now born. A picture would emerge of his mother kneeling before him, worshipping him with eyes that reminded me of my mother's.

At the fourth hour, another page, this time of the child become a man, whipped by three soldiers, the song dolorous. I always shook when I thought of the lashing of his unprotected back.

At the fifth, an even sadder song as the man carried a cross through a mocking crowd. I could see his mother. She was helping her son by bearing the end of the heavy beam.

With the sixth hour, the man on the cross, transfixed by nails, with blood seeping from his wounds. His mother watching, grief-stricken and helpless. The chant now a forlorn lament, a requiem of love.

With the seventh hour, the book displayed the man being carried down from the cross, his mother holding him, weeping over his beaten body. The chant now solemn, funereal, lamentable.

Then, the final hour, and a page revealing the man alive again, having conquered death, and the mother crowned by God for her extreme devotion and sacrificial love. The chant that now poured from the book was like the freshness of a new day. No darkness in the notes. No mournful minor key. But praise, joy, vitality, with a hint of laughter.

And so, it went on, and on.

Time after time.

The mysterious book that kept these hours never wavered, never waned, but kept its vigils faithfully, marking the hours with a voice that never faltered and a light that never failed.

These eight hours kept me grounded in holy time. And they transformed the space in which we lay, turning it from a melancholy tomb into a joyful sanctuary.

Each time these hours came, I would understand more of this ancient drama, and I would feel an otherworldly sense of unity between my pages and the pages of this book.

It was as if the bond between this mother and her child was the original, and all others a copy.

Including my own mother's love for me and mine for her.

These hours of light and colour continued without ceasing, as surely as night follows day, until I had marked 3600 times through the eight sacred hours, nearly ten years. And then, one day, between the fourth and fifth hours, the lock turned, the door opened and there stood Monsieur Bleriot. He appeared older. There were grey speckles in his hair and his skin was more creased than when I had last seen him.

The librarian took me from the safe and placed me on a table. I found myself resting with my pages face down on the wood, my back arched and upright like the roof of a house. As I balanced there, I saw an iron wood burner in the corner of the room. The flame inside, visible through its two charred windows, was dying and the librarian's assistant was trying to encourage it into life with a poker. I watched in horror as he took hold of a large map and tore it into pieces.

The sound of the callous tearing would forever haunt me. I heard the groans of pain as the paper was crunched, hurled into the flames, and poked into even smaller fragments when it ignited. Entire countries and continents disappeared in the conflagration.

"What about the Book of Hours?" the younger man asked.

"It is not for now," the librarian replied, locking the safe. "We have a prospective buyer for the Swanson book."

He lifted me to his chest, prising his arms apart, like a prodigious pair of scissors. I could feel the pressure building in my spine. The brutal buckling was about to begin. But just as he was about to engage in his murderous disruptions, he was himself disrupted.

By a woman.

A tiny lady with bold eyes and a stern voice.

She had descended the stairs and entered the vault.

"Wait!

The librarian looked surprised.

"Wait, I say!"

The woman set her eyes set upon me.

"Is this Miss Swanson's first edition?" she asked.

"It is, madame."

"What on earth do you mean by treating it in such a manner?"

"I was led to believe that you wanted to purchase Mister Blake's illustrations," Monsieur Bleriot said.

"I want the whole book and I want it intact."

The woman reached out her diminutive hands and seized me from my captor's clutches.

"To destroy a book is to murder a soul," she cried.

"That's foolish," the librarian retorted.

"Foolish, you say! You are the one who is foolish, sir. You are in a library, but do you not read? Books are not dead. They are the living voices of their authors. You do well to remember that before treating their pages like mere kindling."

"Books are books," the man said.

"As good almost kill a man as kill a good book," the woman declared. "Who kills a man kills a reasonable creature, God's image. But he who destroys a good book, kills reason itself, kills the image of God, as it were, in the eye."

"Your words are just vapour," he said.

"My words? They are not mine, as you would know if you cared properly for your charges. They are the words of John Milton. You may well have an original copy somewhere in this library. Let me enlighten you. They are from his speech in defence of unlicensed printing, also known by the title *Areopagita*. Although I hesitate to tell you this, lest you find and desecrate that precious volume too."

The librarian frowned. "What do you propose?"

"I propose that you give me the book for the price of a sovereign, and in return I will not report you, even though my conscience tells me that I may live to regret that."

She proffered a silver coin.

The man snatched the money.

As he did, I looked at the safe in the corner. I could not suffer the thought of leaving my friend behind. I pictured the librarian grasping its binding with both hands, wrenching the book first this way, then that, uttering horrid blasphemies as the binder's obduracy delayed his progress. I imagined the book yelping in pain, like a kicked dog, every time it was subjected to this torment. Until, that is, the dismemberment had been completed. Page upon page separated from the covers. The illuminated leaves placed in a box while the pages without any pictures, bearing only text, were cast into the fire.

I was already petrified by fire, but now I felt the added terror of being severed, fractured, amputated, as if my pages were redundant, lifeless limbs, cast aside by a surgeon on a battlefield.

I longed with every fibre of my being to tell my new guardian to rescue it. But she was not to know. She could not see inside the safe nor hear the chants of desperate lamentation leaking from the microscopic fissures of the prison.

For her, it was time to leave.

She turned away, made for the stairs and was about to ascend when the librarian shouted after us.

"What is your name, madame?"

The woman pivoted and looked back.

"Charlotte Bronte," she said.

Part 4

1844-1860

"But I'll not fear, I will not weep
For those whose bodies rest in sleep;
I know there is a blessed shore,
Opening its ports for me, and mine;
And, gazing Time's wide waters o'er,
I weary for that land divine,
Where we were born, where you and I
Shall meet our Dearest, when we die;
From suffering and corruption free,
Restored into the Deity."

Emily Bronte (1818-1848)

Although she stood under five feet tall, my rescuer possessed an abundance of moral courage. The first thing I noticed about her was her determined eyes. When she chastised the assistant librarian, they seem to grow even bigger, boring into his hard heart like unrelenting drills. Her eyes were brown in colour, like her hair, but when she set her towering forehead against my abuser, they seemed to glow with a preternatural fire. And yet, this was not all there was to them. On New Year's Day of 1844, as she looked at me during the slow journeys from Bruges to Ostend, and then on the Ostend packet to London Bridge, and finally from Euston Station to the north of England, these same eyes displayed a warmer hue. They spoke of a woman whose pain had forged a deeper comprehension of the mysteries of this baffling world, and a softer compassion for those enduring the inexplicable tragedies of this short and troublesome life.

It was especially in the thirteen-hour train journey from London to Leeds that she gazed at me, scrutinising every one of my mother's lines. From time to time, I saw her mouth twitch into a faint smile. At others, her eyes filled with tears which she daubed with a silken handkerchief, lest anyone in the carriage saw them. But somebody had. A lady in a red dress sitting opposite had witnessed the outflow of feeling. Her hair was grey, and her forehead spotted and wrinkled. I estimated she was a good twenty years older than Miss Charlotte.

"What are you reading, my dear?" she asked.

My new mistress shuffled in her seat and gazed into her interrogator's eyes before answering.

"Emily Swanson's book. It's the very first edition."

"How priceless, my darling!" she exclaimed. "That book put the cat among the proverbial pigeons."

"Especially the male pigeons," Miss Charlotte added.

The lady laughed, her ample chest bobbing up and down in time with the rhythm of the locomotive's wheels.

"Forgive me," she said, proffering her hand. "My name is Jane Wheeler."

"And mine is Charlotte Bronte."

"Bronte, you say. That's an interesting name."

"My father is Irish, although he has been in England many years now."

"What does he do?"

"He's the Vicar of Howarth, near Keighley."

"And you, my dear? What do you do? You clearly love to read. But how else do you pass your time?"

"In reading, yes, but also writing."

"A woman who writes!" she cried. "How very daring! I'm so glad to hear that you aren't just a submissive wife."

"I am unmarried," my mistress replied.

"Very wise," she said. "Most men are dunces." She repeated the statement more loudly, as several top-hatted gentlemen winced. "Why are you clutching the book so? Are you in love, my dear?"

"I was in love with a man in Brussels," Miss Charlotte said, her lips trembling. "But he would not return my affections."

"Would not, or *could* not?"

Miss Charlotte's eyes filled.

"How did you come about this edition?" the woman asked, squinting at me from beneath her florid bonnet.

"I was working in Brussels as a teacher when I decided to make a sojourn to Bruges. I had finished my employment and I wanted a brief rest before heading home. During my days there, I went to Mister Porter's to buy some winter garments. It was he who told me that this first edition was in the library. When I heard that, wild dogs could not have stopped me from acquiring it."

"But my dear, if it was in the library, how did you acquire it? Are you borrowing it? Or are you . . ." she leaned towards us and whispered, a mischievous grin on her face, "Are you stealing it?"

"Better than that," Miss Charlotte said.

"Oh, how delightful!" the lady said, clasping her gloved hands together.

"It was about to be destroyed."

I shuddered at the memory.

"The wicked librarian was on the point of dismembering and incinerating this priceless book in the vault of the library. I came upon him just in time and snatched it from the precipice of extinction."

Her tiny hands gripped me.

"I paid the barbarian a sovereign for it but, really, he didn't deserve a penny. So, you see, I'm rescuing it."

This news seemed to send our friend into a hot flush. She withdrew a fan emblazoned with Chinese dragons. When her reddened cheeks had grown pale again, she folded it and looked at Miss Charlotte, then at me. "Tell me, why do you love it so?"

"Because it removed the gags from the mouths of women."

"Women like you?"

"And my two sisters."

"Are they writers as well?"

"They are and they will be."

"What of your father, the clergyman? Does he approve of what you and your sisters are doing?"

"He has written books, including poetry and stories, and has always encouraged us in the free use of our imaginations. When my brother was little, Father bought him a set of toy soldiers in Leeds. We invented all manner of fables about them, scribbling our tales in pencil in tiny books. That was the beginning. We owe so much to Father."

The woman smiled. "In that case, I'll let you read and think, muse and write. I'm sure it will be busy and noisy enough when you are at home in the parsonage. It has been a most pleasant diversion conversing with you. I wish you every success in your writing, and I hope that this precious book is an inspiration to you and your sisters."

Miss Charlotte buried herself once again in my leaves. I, meanwhile, enjoyed the iambic rhythm of the locomotive's wheels.

Several hours later, we arrived in Leeds. We headed to Keighley where we spent the night in a damp hotel. There my new guardian cried in her sleep. I looked on with pity during the watches of the night, wishing that I could have held her, even as she had held me.

The next day, the January skies were a dismal grey as we rode on a fly towards Howarth. On the way, we had to cross a great moor where a savage wind assaulted us. We stopped at many turnpikes; Miss Charlotte had to pay six shillings during just eight miles. One mile from the town itself, we embarked on a steep descent. Then, just as abruptly, we headed back up another sharp incline, ascending more arduously towards the desolate and isolated town, perched on the top of the hill, with the parish church towering above it all like a mighty fortress.

We proceeded past the shops and houses until we arrived at a very narrow street, on which stood the parsonage, a sturdy house made of local millstone grit. Having alighted, Miss Charlotte took me down a gravel walk through a small lawn, bordered by flowers, until we arrived at the front door. She opened it and straight away we were in a clean, sandstone hall. On our right, the door was partly closed; my guardian knocked with a light touch three times.

"Is that you Charlotte?"

"Yes, Papa. I'm home."

Miss Charlotte entered, clutching me to her chest. The room was small and snug, the only chamber besides the dining room to have a carpet. The crimson furniture was illuminated by a dim light passing through two windows. These looked out onto the crowded gravestones in the churchyard beyond. The room was kept warm by a fire burning in an old grate. The walls were lined with bookcases bearing many volumes on a great diversity of topics. I rejoiced at the sight of them.

The parson rose. His eyes, staring from beneath a furrowed and high forehead, seemed to look past us. His face was swarthy, as one who had walked in the bracing air of the moors behind the parsonage, and his features looked as rugged as the ancient rocks that we had passed towards the end of our long journey.

Mister Bronte was tall and dignified. He wore the attire of a clergyman – a long black dress coat, with a huge cravat which rose to the level of his ears, almost as white as his hair.

He marched towards us in determined, decisive movements and then reached out his hand to shake my guardian's. His fingers looked long and thin, like the rest of his lean body.

"How was your journey?" he asked, staring through the round lenses of his broad-rimmed spectacles.

"Long, Father. But I am home now. How is your eyesight?"

"Very poor. I fear I shall be completely blind before too long." His eyes were almost closed as he spoke.

"Then we shall have to do something about that, now that I am home, shan't we?"

"Sit with me a while," he said as he returned to the armchair, took a clay pipe, and lit it.

As the smoke from the bowl began to rise, Miss Charlotte told of her adventures in Brussels and her tussle with the librarian in Bruges. She showed me to him. Mister Bronte inspected me.

"Dear Charlotte, what a find, although it looks somewhat the worse for wear, but this may just be my failing eyes."

"It needs the able touch of an expert restorer, but that is not a matter as urgent as the restoration of your sight, Papa."

"My sight may be failing, my dear, but I'm not too blind to write some sharp letters when I want to."

"What has stoked your ire this time?" Miss Charlotte sighed.

Mister Bronte frowned for a moment then stared into the fire.

"Papa?"

"I conducted a funeral last week, for yet another child who was burned alive because of the clothes she was wearing. The poor girl did not stand a chance and her parents were beside themselves with grief. They could do nothing to stop it and now of course blame themselves. The sound of mourning was worse than the wind howling on the moors."

"I'm so sorry, Papa."

"I am planning to write to the Leeds Mercury. I have already prepared some sentences in my heart, stating that garments of linen and cotton are too prone to catch fire, whereas woollen and silk are much less so. This poor girl's funeral was the ninety first I have taken in this church for a child whose clothes have taken fire. In every one of these accidental ignitions, the child was clothed in cotton or linen. This is yet another terrible and preventable consequence of poverty."

"That is a noble cause, Papa. Let me help you."

"When I am ready, and have the full facts," he said. "Then, when the powder is dry and the barrel loaded, I will discharge my responsibility to the poor children of Howarth."

Mister Bronte was gentle, kind, and open-hearted.

I am sure no parson ever contended more for the rights of the poor within his parish.

During the two years that followed, Mister Bronte's eyesight deteriorated. He became surly, sad, and inert, leaving the cure of souls to his curate, staying in his study, as unhappy as he was unsighted.

In February of 1846, Miss Charlotte took me on a visit to her dear friend Ellen. After Ellen had fussed and fluttered about me like a hungry seagull, Miss Charlotte turned to the subject of her father's eyes. "I think you know Mister William Carr, the surgeon," she said.

"I do. He married a cousin of mine."

Within a week, Miss Charlotte had spoken with Mister Carr. "I'm sure that it will be possible to operate," he said. "But you must wait a few months until his cataracts have hardened."

Five months later, Miss Charlotte announced that she was off to have her father's eyes couched by a Mister Wilson. They remained in lodgings there for one month. The operation lasted fifteen minutes. No anaesthetic was used, and the surgeon lauded the patient for his forbearance. It was followed by weeks of recuperation in a darkened room, during which time Mister Bronte had his eyes covered in bandages. He lived on his usual diet of beef, mutton, bread and butter, and cups of tea.

On their return, Flossy, the family dog, wagged her tail. "The people that walked in darkness have seen a great light!" Mister Bronte proclaimed. Flossy barked several times. Mister Bronte chuckled to hear it and rejoiced even more to see it.

After family prayers the next morning, Mister Bronte narrated the entire procedure to his children at the dining room table. Tabitha, who had cooked and was now serving breakfast, kept mopping her brow with her apron as the Master spoke. But nothing was going to stop him. He had always taken a keen interest in medicine. Many of the books in his study betrayed this fascination. One of them, *Modern Domestic Medicine*, written by a Dr Thomas Graham in 1826, lay open beside me that day in the study. From the master's annotations in the margins of a section on cataracts, I guessed what the siblings must have heard, that Belladonna, a virulent poison from the deadly nightshade, had been used to expand his pupil, resulting in acute pain for about five seconds. When the operation took place, there was a burning sensation. Other patients found this intolerable, but Mister Bronte bore it with firmness. In the procedure, the lens was extracted, meaning the cataract could never return. In the month spent on his back in the dark, the master noted, "I was bled with eight leeches on one occasion, six on another, to prevent inflammation."

How the poor, long-suffering Tabatha stayed upright in the dining room I do not know.

In the days that followed, Mister Bronte often held me in his hands and stared at me with his fresh eyes.

"This is a most intriguing book," he said one evening as Miss Charlotte sat with him in the study. "Miss Swanson was a very astute and careful poet. She left it unclear whether the reader is to take this love affair as literal or allegorical. It is a most Romantic and yet also controversial collection of poems, as mystical as some of Emily's, and yet as sensual as some of John Donne's."

"What do you think, Papa?" Miss Charlotte said. "Does Miss Swanson speak of a spiritual or a human union?"

"It is hard to say. I fear that, at present, my insight has not yet caught up with my eyesight." He paused to suck from his clay pipe. "However, it employs some of the imagery of *The Song of Songs* and the same questions could be asked of those poems too."

As clouds billowed from his pipe, he turned from me and looked at Miss Charlotte.

"One thing I know. The amazing Miss Swanson showed that women are as equals to men when it comes to writing. She demonstrated once and for all that sex, like race, is no disqualification when it comes to the matter of artistic genius. You girls must never forget that."

That summer, when the heather was purple in the hills, and the water sparkling in the brooks, the three daughters set to their writing projects with renewed vigour. Their practice was as regular as the hours I had kept in the safe in the Town Hall library in Bruges. After evening prayer in the dining room, Mister Bronte would go to bed having settled Flossy in the parlour. This took place just after nine o'clock. Once Mister Bronte had settled in his bed, the girls would start their rituals. Some of the time they would sit on the hair-seated chairs at the mahogany dining room table and scribble away on paper. Then, at some moment which they all seemed to recognise, at a level of thought deeper even than intuition, they would stand and start to walk around the table declaiming to one another what they had written in the preceding hour or so.

This march, more like a dance than a walk, would begin slowly, and then become faster and faster. It was as if some unquenchable fire was burning in their hearts, fuelling their imaginations, stoking their passions as they murmured with approval at the luminosity of thought, the profundity of feeling, and the solidarity of purpose in each other's scripts. Whenever this otherworldly ceremony took place, it was as if time stood still and the whole earth paused its rotation to watch and wonder at this nocturnal ritual.

One night stands out above all others in my memory. Mister Bronte was a man much concerned with fire and he forbade anyone from wearing inflammable clothes. Only the study and the dining room had carpets, which was perhaps fortuitous, given the wild stomping that the daughters sometimes imprinted upon the flagstone floor when the strange ecstasy overcame them. There were no curtains on any of the windows and the walls were devoid of paper, tinted instead with a dove-like paint. The whole house, in fact, was sparsely furnished and had a bareness about it that created a sense of unity between the moors outside and the unadorned landscape within. All this, it was known, was Mister Bronte's devising. Every detail was a concession to his scheme of rendering the house as invulnerable as possible to fire.

But not even Mister Bronte's careful calculations and stern stipulations could prevent what happened one night. There was a son too in the house. His name was Branwell and he was a tormented soul, prone to fits of unshakeable melancholy. These he sought to alleviate by excessive drinking. The stupor these wild actions produced performed as an anaesthetic, rendering him unconscious to the pain within, but also mindless of the dangers without.

One night, having fallen fully clothed onto his bed with a lighted candle, he forgot himself and his bedclothes caught fire. The entire house would have burned down had it not been for Anne, who just happened to be passing by the door. Seeing that they were on the point of catastrophe, she hurried to Emily. Emily was the tallest and strongest of the sisters. She pulled Branwell out of bed then ran to the kitchen to fill pitchers of water. The sisters succeeded in dousing the flames. From that night on, it was decided that Branwell should sleep in his father's bedroom.

All this not only had a lasting impact on the sleeping arrangements, it also awakened something in the daughters. Not long afterwards, prayers had been said and Mister Bronte had retired to bed. The girls were in the dining room scribbling away, as was their custom. A conversation began in hushed tones around the table.

"What does fire signify?" Mistress Charlotte asked.

"It is a symbol for mystic love," Miss Emily said. She began reciting, "Set me as a seal upon thine heart, as a seal upon thine arm: for love is strong as death; jealousy is cruel as the grave: the coals thereof are coals of fire, which hath a most vehement flame." Then she looked at me and said, "Emily Swanson had it."

She was right.

"What about you?" Mistress Charlotte said, turning to Anne. "What does fire mean to you?"

"A fire can be a homely thing," she answered. "When we are all gathered around this hearth, it speaks to me of contentment. It soothes the soul when everything is as it should be."

"But it is also a terrible thing," Emily said. "A thing of wild and dangerous power, an element of rage and destruction."

"Precisely," Mistress Charlotte said. "Just as we saw in Branwell's bedroom. That night has made an impression on my soul. I have been inspired by it in the writing of my novel."

Emily and Anne knew, as did I, that while Charlotte had been looking after Mister Bronte during his operation, she had begun writing a story about an orphan called Jane Eyre, who falls in love with a Mister Rochester. As she spoke of fire, Mistress Charlotte grasped some papers and sprang to her feet and the two others with her, their silken dresses sending tiny sparks into the chamber. The strange dance began again as they moved around the table.

Mistress Charlotte told her sisters that she had reached a point in her story when Mister Rochester's mad wife Bertha had set fire to his bedroom in Thornfield Hall.

"Read to us!" her sisters cried.

Miss Charlotte complied.

'Tongues of flame darted round the bed: the curtains were on fire. In the midst of blaze and vapour, Mr.

Rochester lay stretched motionless, in deep sleep. "Wake! wake!" I cried. I shook him, but he only murmured and turned: the smoke had stupefied him.'

Mistress Charlotte's hand was shaking as she read, the leaves in her hand trembling too, just as mine were.

'Not a moment could be lost,' she continued. 'The very sheets were kindling, I rushed to his basin and ewer; fortunately, one was wide and the other deep, and both were filled with water. I heaved them up, deluged the bed and its occupant, flew back to my own room, brought my own water-jug, baptised the couch afresh, and, by God's aid, succeeded in extinguishing the flames which were devouring it.'

As she finished, it was as if the walls of the dining room were on fire, the ceiling and roof gone, and a column of billowing smoke pouring out and up towards the grey clouds in the moonlit firmament.

The three women were on fire and the world with them.

"We are the burning ones!" they cried.

In May, as if to confirm the matter, Mister Bronte preached a sermon at Whitsun, about holy fire. When the girls came home from church, they were flushed with excitement as Tabitha served the Sunday roast. I was in the study but could hear every word.

"You were burning this morning, Papa," Mistress Charlotte said.

"Thank you, my dear," he said.

Emily was next to speak. "You said that the fire of Pentecost was for women too, Papa."

"At the risk of preaching the sermon a second time," Mister Bronte said, "It says plainly in the text that the fire of heaven was for daughters not just sons, for maidservants not just menservants. Why should the Daughters of Eve in our day be denied such an honour? What kind of a Father only grants his sons a gift but excludes his daughters from the same kindness and generosity?"

"Are men and women equal in the sight of God?" Emily asked.

"All are one in Christ Jesus, male and female," Mister Bronte replied.

"If men and women are equal," Anne said. "Then why is it that only men can take holy orders if God is the kind Father you describe?"

"The Church of England is like a prodigious snail," Mister Bronte replied. "It moves without any urgency or celerity, but eventually it reaches the right destination, leaving a messy trail in its wake."

Miss Charlotte laughed. "I love the Church of England, although I do not regard her ministers as infallible. Sorry, Papa."

"The Establishment will always resist change," Anne said. "Look at the publishers. We have had to write our novels under men's names. Without these pseudonyms, Papa, your own daughters would never have been able to prophesy."

"Are you claiming to prophesy?" Mister Bronte asked.

"Only as the wild prophets of the Old Covenant," Emily interrupted. "Raging like fire against what's wrong. You use letters, Papa, as with your constant prophesying to the authorities about the foul water in Howarth. We use stories, stories in which we refuse to reduce women to household fairies, or to mere slaves of dull and witless men. The women in our tales are neither angels nor monsters. They are real women. Flesh and blood. Intelligent. Proud. Strong."

"John Stuart Mill said that women should be imitators and men innovators," Anne said when Emily had finished.

"In that, he was entirely and most miserably mistaken. We, your daughters, are innovators, not imitators. We are creating stories in which women are portrayed in a new and respectful way, in a way that has traditionally been reserved for the depiction of men alone."

"Give me examples," Mister Bronte said.

Miss Emily chimed in first. "My story concerns a woman called Cathy, as wild and free as the moors, a soul whom genteel society tries to mould and control, with disastrous consequences."

"Is this a memoir of your own life, dear Emily," Mister Bronte asked. I could tell he was smiling.

There was no answer.

Miss Anne spoke next. "Mine is about Helen Huntingdon, married to a husband who is abusive, adulterous, and dependent upon drink. She is no longer prepared to tolerate her oppressor and becomes determined to show him that her heart will no longer be his slave. In the end, she liberates herself from a poisonous covenant."

Mister Bronte nodded. "Dear Anne, you may receive some censorious criticisms for that, but I for one support you. It is better to escape an abusive marriage than to stay in peril of your own life."

"And the life of your child, or children," Anne added.

"Mine is called Jane Eyre, Papa," Charlotte said, after everyone had taken some more mouthfuls of the roast. "She is a young woman who falls in love with a man twenty years her senior, married to a mad woman called Bertha. He regards her as his equal in all things except age. With him, Jane is a free being with an independent will."

"Restraint is not always a vice, Charlotte," Mister Bronte said. His voice had changed to that of a preacher.

"When it is an act of free will, I agree, Papa. But when that restraint is an unreasonable imposition of someone else's will on mine or yours, then it can never be said to be a virtue, except in circumstances where the life of the person restrained is endangered."

Mister Bronte nodded.

"And I'm imagining another story," Charlotte said, "about a young and determined woman called Shirley."

"Shirley is a man's name!" Mister Bronte exclaimed.

"Precisely, Papa. My Shirley will be an orphaned girl, an heir to a fortune. She will grow up to become a strong young woman who wears the blue stockings too, just like Elizabeth Carter, the champion of women's education, the dear friend of Emily Swanson."

With that, memories rushed in like a flood, of those days and nights in the enchanted cottage where I was born, when Elizabeth came to stay, and when my mother became more enlivened and impassioned that at any other time during my short life with her.

"It sounds to me," Mister Bronte said to his daughters, "that you are using your stories to try to reform society."

"We have no such grand ambitions," Emily said. "We believe that if a story is a good one, then it is so whatever the sex of its author. And as for reforming society, we are but three small candles, burning for a while, dispelling some of the darkness in this unjust world."

The months that followed confirmed Miss Emily's judgement that they were lamps burning for a short time. Branwell died the following September, after being spurned by the woman he loved, and drinking himself to the edge of insanity. When bronchitis and consumption took him, Mister Bronte held his boy in his arms, crying, "My son! My son!"

The Master was inconsolable again when Emily fell ill shortly afterwards. She had a persistent cough, rapid panting and stabbing pains in her chest but refused to see a doctor. By mid-December, it was clear that she was dying. On the day she passed, she rose in the morning determined to do her sewing, but by the early afternoon, even she could not fight her sickness any longer. She contended to the last, protesting and raging against the encroaching darkness. She had been given enough time to write some poems and only one novel, *Wuthering Heights*.

At her funeral, which the curate took, Mister Bronte walked at the head of the procession behind the coffin. Keeper, Emily's faithful dog, walked next to him, into the church before the service, and out afterwards. I could see in the hound's eyes that he was broken-hearted too. The two, who went side by side, were followed by Mistress Charlotte and Miss Anne, to the site of the burial.

Anne was next.

She had been complaining of a pain in her side since early December. When Mister Bronte learned that his daughter was dying of consumption, with an accompanying congestion of the lungs, he allowed her to go with Mistress Charlotte to the seaside, on the doctor's recommendation. Anne wanted to see the ocean and imbibe its power and its peace. I witnessed the farewell at the parsonage door. Poor Mister Bronte, who had witnessed his wife die, then a son and three daughters, had already seen more suffering than most men would in several lifetimes. When he said goodbye, he held his daughter's hand and simply said, "My dear little Anne." And that was that. She left, never to return. At the end of May, she died beside the sea in Scarborough and was buried in the churchyard there, the only one of the three sisters not to be interred in the Bronte vault.

One month later, after Mistress Charlotte had taken some time to recover at Filey and then Bridlington, she returned home to us. I was relieved and pleased to see her, as was Mister Bronte, who greeted her with an unusual display of affection. The dogs, Keeper and Flossy, were in a very strange ecstasy when she returned. They had been so used to my Mistress's sisters following behind her at the door that they were first confounded and then dismayed by the emptiness. They seemed to know what had happened and were, for a while, inconsolable.

On her return, Mistress Charlotte walked into the dining room. She closed the door behind her. I could tell she was haunted by the absence of her sisters. Not even the snuffling and sniffing of the dogs at the door could rally her from her lamentable distress. She sat for a long time with her head in her hands, the tears pouring through her fingers.

After that, I remained at her bedside, next to a Bible given to Mistress Charlotte at her christening. She opened this volume every night before she slept and every morning after the dark sky turned to grey and she awakened. She read passages out loud to herself, in her sweet, strong voice. To me, she was like a song thrush, tiny and delicate with big staring eyes that observed everything and everyone, even while blinking, and a melodious voice that could make the dawn blush. When she read from these pages, I could understand why she had once said to a friend that the Bible was to her a pure fountain of mercy whose water made an end to wandering thoughts and corrupt hearts. Its words seemed to me to be alive, even though its authors were long since dead.

Mistress Charlotte was the last to pass. She was the oldest, at very nearly 39. The people of Howarth were only expected to live to 28, thanks to the polluted water supply. With Mistress Charlotte, the end came after she married Mister Bronte's long-suffering Irish curate, Arthur Nichols. Mister Bronte had been opposed to the union, on the grounds that Charlotte was not strong enough for marriage, by which he meant childbirth. His concerns turned out to be prescient. Mistress Charlotte died before her first child was born. We were all bereft.

Mister Bronte outlived all his children and went on to reach 84 years of age. In his final months, he was bedridden, but still lively of thought. His curate, Arthur Nichols, lived in the parsonage, as he had been doing during his all-too-brief marriage to Mistress Charlotte. He was now a son to the aged Mister Bronte, caring for him as if he were his very own.

One day, Mister Bronte asked Mister Nichols to bring me to his room. It was the first time I had entered the chamber. When I arrived, Mister Bronte was propped up in bed and wearing a white nightgown, freshly washed and whiter than the walls. There was white stubble on his chin which reminded me of the frosting on Martha's Christmas pudding just two months before. His long, bony fingers rested on a clean towel that had been draped on his eiderdown. He was wearing his round spectacles and his eyes looked fatigued.

"Ah," he said, seeing me in Mister Nichols' hands. "I have not set eyes upon this volume for some years now." His face, soft and sweet, seemed to have lit up on observing me.

"It was Charlotte's favourite and most precious book," Mister Nichols said. "She described it as an endless mine whose treasures she only glimpsed in the darkness."

"What shall we do with it, Arthur?"

"I do not want to keep it," the curate replied. "I can't bear to look upon it. It reminds me always of our lost love. My wish is only to keep the books that Charlotte wrote."

"My daughters wrote such clever books, didn't they? Charlotte's writings are well known now among those who hold genius in high esteem. Something of her soul abides there, something eternal, something durable, as strong as the rocks on the moors."

When Mister Patrick finished speaking, Mister Nichols nodded and then laid me on the towel beneath my master's heart. Even with fresh logs and a strong fire in the grate, he was shivering with cold. It had been a very dismal winter, with snowdrifts so high that the roads to Keighley and Skipton had been almost unpassable. There were snowdrifts up to the top of the wall around the parsonage. His whole frame reminded me of a barren, frozen tree I had once seen on a walk with Mistress Charlotte on the moors, all hunched and skeletal.

"It is time for me to put my house in order," Mister Bronte said, his voice gentle and calm. "I will be amazed if I endure to my birthday. Although my mind is strong, my body grows weaker by the minute, and this infernal

Yorkshire weather is not helping, not helping at all. I seem to be perpetually with cold."

As if to prove the point, he withdrew a handkerchief and sneezed into it. He wiped the end of his nose, which had a reddish glow, and then stuffed the dampened cloth up his sleeve.

"This is my wish. This book is of inestimable value, being the very first edition. But it is in a pitiful condition. It is my will that it should be restored to its original glory."

"Who have you in mind to do this?"

"There is a man in Paris whose reputation for repairing antique books is unsurpassed. I would have you post this, with the following instructions, as soon as possible to him."

The master reached to his table and withdrew a letter. Mister Nichols read it and, as he did, his eyes filled with tears.

"Come now, Arthur. Strengthen yourself in the Lord."

"I'm sorry, Father. It is a beautiful letter. I will send it when the snow relents and recedes."

The master looked out towards the window, onto the graveyard beyond. His thoughts seemed far away for a moment, until they returned. "I have been an ordained minister for fifty-five years," he said. "And I have been the incumbent of Howarth for forty-one of them. My final chapter is almost ended."

As he compared himself with a book, a memory was uncorked in the cellar of his mind and a broad grin appeared on his face. "Have I ever told you, Arthur, what my favourite epitaph is?"

"You have not."

"It was penned by Benjamin Franklin for himself when he was a relatively young man. It goes like this."

The master took me and held me to his chest.

> *"The Body of*
> *B. Franklin, Printer;*
> *Like the Cover of an old Book,*
> *Its Contents torn out,*
> *And stript of its Lettering and Gilding,*
> *Lies here, Food for Worms.*
> *But the Work shall not be wholly lost:*
> *For it will, as he believ'd, appear once more,*
> *In a new & more perfect Edition,*
> *Corrected and amended*
> *By the Author."*

He raised me up as if he were lifting the sacrament in the sanctuary. "Just like this book!" he cried. "And he started to laugh, and as he laughed, Mister Nichols laughed too, until both parsons were laughing in a united synod of merriment. They only stopped when the master began a terrible fit of coughing, at which point, he hurriedly handed me back to Mister Nichols and ushered us out of the room.

That evening, the curate placed me in a box which he wrapped in paper and string. I could hear the scratch of nib and ink upon the covering as he wrote the name and address of my restorer.

A month or so later, I heard the curate's voice, then the rumble of carriage wheels until the endless noise came to an end and I could hear seagulls congregating and calling out above me. After that, there was the soothing undulations of a calm sea.

A new adventure was about to begin.

I was on my way to Paris.

Part 5

1860-1880

Eventually, a good chemist will refine my work to such an extent that it will seem naïve in comparison, and thus I will be remembered solely for clearing the path with this book.

Alfred Bonnardot (1808-1884)

I arrived in Paris nervous at the prospect of my operations, longing for the comforting embrace of my long-lost mother. The exact nature of the procedures was a mystery to me. All I knew was that they were to take place in the backroom of a bookshop located in a glass-covered arcade, just off the *Boulevard des Italiens*. This much I had gleaned from Mister Bronte. I would be restored by a man named Alfred Bonnardot.

When I was removed from the box and wrapping in which I had been transported, I found myself in a room with two long wooden tables. Resting on them were glass test tubes and basins, spatulas, and scalpels. Along the walls, sturdy shelves supported glass and ceramic jars, both big and small, containing various powders, liquids and substances, all testimony to the book restorer's love of chemistry.

It was a strange, disorienting world.

Monsieur Alfred appeared. He was 52 years old when I first saw him, a clean-shaven man with a bulbous nose and a forehead which, over time, ascended higher and higher as his dark hair receded. To compensate for the loss, he grew more and more at the back and sides, curling it inwards, holding it in place with a scented lacquer which he also applied to his thick moustache. He wore a pair of rectangular glasses, held to his ears by tiny frames which he tucked under his drooping hair. He was always impeccably dressed, more like a diner at a fashionable Parisian restaurant than a craftsman in a book restorer's workshop.

The gentleman now standing over me was the Parisian most committed to the art of book preservation, and the most skilled too. As I grew to know him, it seemed to me that Monsieur Alfred was more devoted to the past than the future, consecrating his considerable skills, many of them self-taught, to the noble pursuit of conserving the great artefacts of his city. All this was because he loved Paris with a passion. As one English visitor to the shop said to him, "you are a good son who lives only for his mother." By "mother" he meant Paris. Knowing what it was to live for one's mother, the words resonated with me.

This devotion was evident on the walls of the backroom where there were framed pictures of a mossy, ruined monastery in Paris. These depicted the decaying edifice from different angles. Monsieur Alfred had composed these images with wash and ink when he was just 17 years of age. They were not the work of a great talent. But they were heartfelt.

"They portray, for all time, a twelfth century monastery here in Paris," Monsieur Alfred said to the same visitor to the shop, whom he had permitted into his backroom.

"Where can this ruin be found?" the visitor asked.

"It can't. All the remaining masonry has been removed to make room for a new street."

"That's tragic."

Monsieur Alfred nodded. His single aim in life was to slow down, if not entirely prevent, the ruination of the monuments of time. Over many years, he had collected books whose rarity was a matter of popular knowledge. His reputation not only as a collector but as a restorer of these volumes was without dispute. There was no one more skilled in all of France. Even though he was not festooned with the garlands of the academy, he was considered an expert in the field of restoring old books to their pristine glory and had the rare ability of making hard things simple when explaining how he did it.

I soon discovered, however, that Monsieur Alfred was a contradiction. While dedicated to preserving old books, he could be ruthless with his own. For example, he completely eradicated several hundred copies of a novel, written after the style of Victor Hugo, that he himself had authored and published in 1837. The copies that were in his possession he burned to a cinder. All this gave me some cause for concern. Would he restore me to the book my mother had received in her arms over half a century ago? Or would he hurl me with disdain into a furnace?

Most of what I came to learn about Monsieur Alfred came from his conversations with a young and pale-faced fellow called Jean-Pierre, who was being trained to take over the shop when Monsieur Alfred retired. He and his master spent most evenings in the workshop. The young man would take a dilapidated volume from a bookcase beneath the only window, one that looked out onto the street above. The books on the top shelf were the ones nearest to the end of the queue.

On one of these evenings, Jean-Pierre had been cleaning the room and come upon a copy of a book lying underneath a large walnut cupboard. It had somehow been kicked out of sight where it had been collecting dust for twenty years. Jean-Pierre picked it up, put on a pair of white cotton gloves, and started to wipe the particles off the cover in slow, measured movements. It was then that he saw the name of the author.

"This is written by you, master!"

"What is it?" Monsieur Alfred muttered, his attention on another book he was restoring.

"It's called *Perruque et Noblesse*."

Monsieur Alfred stopped what he was doing and ran across the room. He plucked the book from the startled apprentice and threw it straight into the burning hearth.

"What did you do that for, monsieur?"

"It is a work of utter foolishness. The folly of my youth, to be precise. I thought I had removed all evidence of it. But clearly this one copy" – his eyes were squinting at the conflagration in the hearth as he spoke – "escaped my searching. Well, it is surely extinct now."

That was the end of the matter. It was the only book I ever saw him harm. One of his own.

How grateful I was not to have been authored by him, but rather by my loving mother.

I missed her with all my soul.

One evening, I was aroused by my two carers as they walked through the door. Monsieur Alfred was speaking to Jean-Pierre, preparing him for the visit of Alexandre Dumas. "Alexandre Dumas, the *father*," Monsieur Alfred had emphasised, "not the *son*."

It was clear from the breathless reaction of Jean-Pierre that this was no ordinary mortal and that his presence in the bookshop was heralded as if Napoleon himself was about to arrive. Dumas was the most famous writer in France and had written novels of extraordinary popularity, such as *The Three Musketeers*, *The Count of Monte Christo*, and *The Man in the Iron Mask*. Monsieur Alfred possessed first editions of all three of these classics and had it in mind to ask the author to sign them. "It will add enormous value when we come to sell them," he said. Then he had paused and added, "*If* we sell them."

When the celebrated author arrived, he was not what I expected. The descriptions of him had given me the impression of a cheerful swashbuckler, a *bon vivant* as they say in Paris, a fine diner, the ebullient narrator of amusing and sentimental anecdotes, a white-skinned and urbane nobleman. He was indeed of noble descent, as it turned out, but he was not white, nor black, but had a copper-coloured complexion. Beneath his tight black hair, he had big dark eyes, pronounced lips, and a black moustache as regular as his groomed eyebrows. Though tall, he was stocky and thickset, with a wide face and even wider shoulders above his ample frame. And he was not cheerful or ebullient, at least on the day of our visitation. There seemed to be a melancholy about him, as if he had recently been the bearer of a great sadness.

"I need your help, Monsieur Bonnardot," he said, his eyes darting about the room.

"How may we be of assistance?"

The author reached into a leather satchel and fetched out a book larger than me, with covers worn and faded.

"Can you rescue this?"

Monsieur Alfred donned white gloves and took the volume. He turned it several times before looking at its owner.

"This is very special."

"It is the first edition of the most precious of all my novels," Dumas said. "The only copy, with a value hard to estimate."

"What is its title?" asked Jean-Pierre.

"You won't have heard of it," the author said. "It has, rather sadly, remained in the shadows cast by my more popular stories, some of which I am sure you will know by reputation."

The two men nodded.

"It is called *Georges*," he added.

"I have heard of it," Jean-Pierre interrupted.

Monsieur Dumas continued, "About a boy who grows up in the Isle of France, in a climate far more congenial and temperate than what we're used to here in gloomy, muddy Paris. He is a *mulatto*."

"Is he you?" Jean-Pierre asked.

"In some ways, yes. My grandmother was a black slave, my grandfather a Norman aristocrat. I share in the legacy of that mixing of the races, as you can see by the fact that I am a man of colour too. Neither black, nor white, but somewhere between, like Georges. There is much of Georges in me, and much of me in Georges."

As Mister Alfred opened the book and began to study the pages, our distinguished guest continued.

"The novel is not what people expected. It is neither a defence of slavery, nor a protest. It goes deeper than that. It is about the inequalities between negroes, mulattos, and whites – an inequality that lies at the root of the terrible and pernicious evil of slavery."

Monsieur Alfred, recognizing the gravity of the subject matter, rested the book on the table. He took off his glasses and sat on a stool a few feet in front of our guest, listening to him with an attentiveness as profound and penetrating as any he had used on books.

"Contrary to what people believe, or want to believe, I have not had an easy life," he said. "France prides itself on being a nation of equality, fraternity and liberty, but it has its own walls of division, its own peculiar version of the world's ancient, racial hatreds."

The author took a silk handkerchief from his pocket.

"There are native insiders."

He daubed one eye.

"Then there are people like me, regarded with mistrust, described as foreign and made to feel like outsiders."

The author beckoned for his book which my master passed to him. The author held it close to his bosom.

"Few have read this, but it is my most important story."

He dried his eyes.

"Can you restore it, Monsieur? Can you make it new?"

"I can."

"Ah, that is a relief."

He put away his handkerchief.

"However, there is a problem."

"What is that?"

"I have received great wealth from my books, but I confess to having been wasteful. Is there another way I can pay you?"

Monsieur Alfred smiled and told him of his longing for the author's signature on the three volumes which he now produced. Monsieur Dumas wrote in them using a silver fountain pen.

"And I have one more favour," my master said. "Please read to us from your novel. A favourite passage perhaps."

Dumas paused, then said, "Very well, I will read about Georges, not when he is a twelve-year old boy, at the start of the story, but fourteen years later, when he returns from studying in France, having not seen his ailing, ageing father during that time. At first, his father does not know who he is, but then the young man reveals his identity."

As the candles flickered, the author read.

"It is I, father; it is I; you must remember me," cried Georges; "remember that fourteen years have passed since I have seen you; remember that I am now twenty-six, and if you doubt, here, look at this scar on my forehead, the mark of the blow which M. de Malmédie gave me the day when you so gloriously captured an English flag. Oh! Father, open your arms, and, when you have embraced me and pressed me to your heart, you will no longer doubt that I am your son."

And with these words the stranger threw himself on the neck of the old man, who, looking now at the sky, now at his child, could not believe in so much happiness.

When he had recovered, Monsieur Alfred stood, took the volume from our guest, and promised to have it restored in one month's time. "I give my word."

He was true to his promise. And when Dumas returned, his reunion with his restored book pierced the heart as deeply as Georges' return to his elderly father.

"What will you do with it now?" my master asked.

"I will have to sell it."

With that, the author, clutching his book, turned to leave the room, his shoulders hunched, his head bowed.

In the years that followed, I came to learn more and more about Monsieur Alfred's family. One evening, he picked up a volume that was very ancient and muttered something under his breath.

"What did you say, master?" Jean-Pierre enquired as he mixed some chemicals in a glass bottle.

"I said, *how have you survived*?"

"Who?"

"This book."

He took off his spectacles.

"My dear mother, Marie-Pauline, had twelve children. I am the only one who lived. You could therefore say that I have a compassion for anyone, or anything that, endures the hardships and misfortunes of life. Resilience, Jean-Pierre, is a virtue. Never forget that."

Jean-Pierre answered with a nod, almost a bow.

"Is your mother still alive?" he asked.

"She died when I was twenty-one."

"And your father?"

"I never knew him. I was barely a year old when he died. He was a successful lawyer who left more than enough inheritance for my mother and me. This shop, and many of its rare prints and books, was purchased with it. He was a good provider."

The next moment, the master's wife stormed through the door without any warning. Supper had been ready for quite some time, both for her husband and Jean-Pierre, and was now lying cold on the kitchen table in their apartment near the Pont Neuf. She had reprimanded him without restraint. Before she left, she had screamed at him, "These here," she gesticulated wildly, pointing to the books in the shelves all around her, "these are your mistresses."

When she had departed, Monsieur Alfred turned to Jean-Pierre, who looked like an axed tree on the very point of toppling. "She is right, of course. These books are my obsession. If I have any advice for you, Jean-Pierre, it is this. Do not get married if you want to be a successful repairer of old volumes. No woman wants to compete with a collection of books for the attentions and affections of her husband."

As if to prove the point, in 1858, when the second edition of his work on restoring books and prints was published, there was a party in the shop. The guests were invited into the backroom to see the operating theatre where Master Alfred performed his remarkable surgeries. Afterwards, when only his wife was left behind, clearing all the glasses, washing them in a sink in the workroom, she turned on her husband.

"You never hosted a party for our son's christening."

The remark brought a chilly blast into the chamber.

"I will make it up to Hippolyte one day," he said.

"One day! One day! That is what you always say!" she replied, thrusting a wineglass so roughly onto the wet draining board that its stem shattered. "Now look what you've gone and done!"

Monsieur Alfred tried earnestly to console her, but she shrugged his hands off her, leaving him to withdraw like a penitent dog. A penitent Spaniel, to be precise. Monsieur Alfred, it should be said, was fond of Spaniels. On these the master lavished a love that I never saw with respect to his neglected wife and son. With these long-eared pets he had a most unusual understanding. They knew his moods and he knew their needs, at a level of intuition that was quite remarkable.

"When I was growing up," he said one night to Jean-Pierre, as one of his dogs jumped at his leg, the two front paws insisting on a display of affection. "I can never remember a time when there wasn't one of these little dogs in my mother's apartment. They were as much a part of my childhood and youth as she was. We would walk them every evening, crossing the bridge and walking through the parks and avenues of this fine city. They connect me with those years."

So fond was he of these creatures that four years before my arrival – in 1856 to be exact – he wrote and published a book for ladies about how to care for and feed this breed of dog. It was entitled *Des Petits Chiens de Dames, Specialement de l'Epagneul Nain*. He claimed that it was the first pet care book of its kind, one that spawned a myriad of similar manuals. He was proud of it and when he was accused of triviality and frivolity, he became quite insistent that it was an important work.

One time, he pounded the table and declared, "There is no law which compels those who wish to distract themselves with literature to always make their excursions in one direction."

When he had received the first edition, he waved it at one of the dogs. "Look here," he cried as the little dog sat on its haunches looking up at him, its domed head tilting this way and that. This one was called Victor, after Monsieur Hugo. It was black and white and had matted ears and the sweetest black eyes. "Look! It's all about you, my love." The merry dog had jumped onto its hind legs, rested its white front paws on the book, and then sniffed it with its short nose, while his thick and unkempt tail had wagged with an undisguised pleasure.

"See!" Monsieur Alfred exclaimed to the student narrating the story. "He has the white gloves on his hands as he touches the book, just as we do when we set about our work!"

The master was in love with his dogs. These pets, in return, showed affection only for him. When anyone else entered the room, they would stay in their bed. But when he, their Great Master, entered, they would come running, like gazelles bounding over the hills.

Monsieur Alfred loved dogs more than he loved humans, and books even more than he loved dogs.

I was in safe hands.

As I graduated from the bottom to the middle shelf, and then from the middle to the top shelf, the time for my own evaluation arrived. I had ascended while every other damaged volume ahead of me had undergone their treatment. In every case, Monsieur Alfred had restored the book to its former glory. On no occasion had he thrown the volume into the fire beneath the mantlepiece. On no occasion had he despaired. He had continued with a fine-eyed, single-minded concentration with every folio, every quarto, until he was happy that the work was complete. One illuminated Bible took him months. By the time it was my turn, I had every reason to be content that I would follow the same course. I had no reason for any anxiety.

On the first day of my procedure, a chubby-faced stranger in a purple suit and golden cravat arrived in the operating room.

"Jean-Pierre," Monsieur Alfred said. "Let me introduce you to our guest, Monsieur Grondin. He has come to observe our restoration of Madame Swanson's book. He is a prospective buyer."

"A pleasure," Jean-Pierre said.

"Have a seat," the master said to the guest.

Jean-Pierre lit some candles on the worktable as our guest sat in the one comfortable chair in the room, next to the dogs. From there he watched every stage of the process with keen eyes.

"To begin with," Monsieur Alfred said, "we must look at this volume very carefully. Its author, Emily Swanson, was a celebrated writer in England during the first decade of our century. This is the very first edition ever printed, and it was her most prized possession."

At that moment, I missed my mother more than ever.

"It has been through hard times. I gather that it was in the possession of a British soldier at Waterloo and that some of the damage comes from his time with it. Then, we have also learned that it was rescued in Bruges by the notable English novelist, Charlotte Bronte."

Monsieur Alfred stared at me. His eyes, swollen by the lenses of his spectacles, reminded me of something in a new illustrated work about cephalopods. I had noticed the two open pages, one describing the anatomy of a giant octopus, the other a drawing of the sea monster itself with its prodigious arms and tentacles, and two glassy eyes that seemed to stare at me as if I was its next victim.

"See here, Jean-Pierre," Monsieur Alfred said, pointing with his gloved finger at one of my pages. "This is without doubt a bloodstain. Possibly that of the soldier who was fatally wounded at Waterloo. What shall we do with it?"

"It is of historical significance," the protégé replied. "We shall therefore not remove it."

"Precisely," Monsieur Alfred said. "And what of this?" He pointed now to a page with a grimier stain.

"This looks like grease," Jean-Pierre said. "Possibly from a rifle or a musket. Maybe from some other weapon."

Monsieur Alfred chuckled. "Well done! Well done! And what shall we do with that blemish?"

"We will remove it skilfully."

"Why?"

"Because damage caused by time and negligence is to be repaired," Jean-Pierre said, his voice confident.

"And?" Monsieur Alfred asked his disciple.

"And . . ." the apprentice continued, "damage that is of historical importance must be retained and not removed."

Monsieur Alfred joined in with this second statement, revelling with his protégé in a familiar refrain.

"It is like you often say to me, master. 'To the restorer, a blemish is a beauty spot.'"

"Then let us identify the blemishes that are to be kept and those that require our attention."

Over the next hour, both men examined me. Monsieur Alfred took the lead for the first half hour, while Jean-Pierre took notes with an ink pen. Then the two swapped roles until the work was done.

"We have seventeen tears in the pages," Jean-Pierre summarised. "And then the following stains: 24 grease spots, 6 thumb prints, 4 stains caused by tar or pitch, 3 by mud, 2 by blood."

"We will remove all of these blemishes save the blood stains," Monsieur Alfred said.

"And the thumb prints?"

"We cannot be sure that they are Miss Swanson's. We will therefore treat them, and they must go."

"But what about the *Danse Macabre*?" Jean-Pierre asked.

I knew about this volume. It had caused much discussion when Monsieur Alfred had seen a copy of it in quarto. The volume was a kind of *momento mori*, a Medieval book in which skeletons danced among human beings of all social classes, reminding the reader that time will pass and that their death will one day come. It had possessed many thumbmarks on the page corners, evidence of considerable use over many years. Monsieur Alfred had argued that these stains should remain. "They speak of a religious devotion that has almost entirely disappeared in our century when reason has replaced faith, science has replaced piety," he said. "It is therefore a venerable patina, and it should not under any circumstances be removed." However, in Monsieur Alfred's mind the same was not true for the finger and handprints in Miss Swanson's volume.

With that, my covers were closed, and I was lifted to my master's face, as close as possible to his huge and squinting eyes which now inspected my covers and my back, checking to see what damage had been done. The two men now set to work cleaning off my binding with a soft cloth, wiping the dust off my end papers, polishing my gilt top. "We can restore all this to its original lustre," the master said.

Having completed this initial work, they attended to my front cover, made of a luxury leather from the Moroccan Levant. It was a copper-colour, while the tooling and the edges were gold.

Before he did anything, Monsieur Alfred lifted my covers to his nose and sniffed it, just as my mother used to do. Then he told Jean-Pierre to prepare a jelly of white soap. When that was done, he moistened the end of a fine sponge in it and removed the marks on my front made by constant handling. Three marks of grease would not budge, so he instructed Jean-Pierre to bring him some benzine. The apprentice, however, had anticipated this move and passed him a small jug, already filled with the essential oil. With that, the grease in the smears began to dissolve once alcohol had been added.

Next, the master turned me upside down so that my front was facing the floor. The benzine trickled down my cover towards the lowest edge of my binding. I was aware of a tickling sensation as it ran its course. Then, before the oil had time to evaporate, a cotton cloth wiped the substance away before I was turned right side up again.

"There," the master said. "All the particles of grease have gone."

He picked up a magnifying glass and started to examine my front cover. "There are several spots of ink," he said.

Jean-Pierre walked over to the shelves containing substances and liquids and returned with a small bottle of oxalic acid. The master took another old book made of the same leather as mine. On this book – of no antique value – he applied various liquids before using them on me. After checking that it did not alter the colour of the leather, he allowed a drop to fall, one-by-one, on each of my smears.

"Bring some copper with the alkali," he said. When Jean-Pierre returned, the master neutralised the acid and then applied the water colour to one of the spots. "This spot lost some of its hue," he said to Jean-Pierre, pointing to the lowest stain. "Now it's perfect."

The master then turned to the skin troubles caused by my exposure to the roasting sun in Spain and the damp conditions in Belgium. Most of these problems, such as a slight warping, had been resolved over time by the uniform temperature of his workroom.

"It is good that this leather is so receptive," Jean-Pierre remarked, looking in the direction of the visitor. "Otherwise, we would have needed the binder for a completely new cover."

An hour later, as darkness fell and the Pompadour clock struck six, the day's procedure was over.

"Tomorrow, we will attend to the back and the spine," the master said. "But now it's time for some dinner."

"Come to my house, Monsieur Bonnardhot," the stranger said. "I would like to host you this evening."

"I'll close up," Jean-Pierre said.

"Thank you, my boy."

With that, the two men departed.

The next morning, Jean-Pierre arrived first to prepare the room. He was followed a short while afterwards by the master, his dogs pulling him into the chamber at the end of their leads.

"Where is Monsieur Grondin?" Jean-Pierre asked.

"Well, there's a strange tale."

The master sat down in the armchair while his dogs leaped onto his lap. His apprentice stopped dusting and looked at him, waiting for him to stop petting his spaniels and to share his story.

"I went to his house. It was a most peculiar evening. Before dinner was served, he showed me his private collection of books. And what an ensemble of filth it was."

Jean-Pierre and the dogs were all ears.

"He first asked me if I was a man of discretion, one who could be entrusted with secrets. I replied that I was, provided the secret did not involve breaking the law. He said it did not break man's laws, but that I might consider that it broke a higher, divine law. He then led me to a part of his home that he referred to as the Inferno, where he kept a collection of over 130 rare books under a triple lock in a glass cabinet, in a secret room with a special key."

"Why Inferno?"

"All his books are about filthy topics, about cuckolded husbands, some of them in favour of such an adulterous state, others against. All are extremely valuable, have copper plates, and are preserved in a perfect condition by their bindings. Two of the duodecimos, dating from the fifteenth century, are in their original covers. One of them is entitled *La Fleur Des Calamités du Marriage,* the other, *L'Apologie Des Cornards*. Both are illustrated by woodcuts."

The master looked at his dogs who were now snoring on his lap. He shook his head before continuing.

"Beautiful covers often conceal ugly activities," he said.

Jean-Pierre nodded.

"Anyway, Monsieur Grondin remarked that I was very honoured to see his collection. Very few guests have been permitted entrance, or so he said, and he was keen to emphasize that not one lady has ever been allowed anywhere near it, a fact which did not evoke agreement on my part so much as a deep relief, one that I tried my best to conceal."

Jean-Pierre's face looked a mixture of curiosity and confusion. "Is it not strange that a man who confesses to himself being married should want to collect books on such a dismal subject?"

The master shook his head. "It is common for men to take perverse pleasure observing a storm from a safe harbour."

"Maybe there's another reason," Jean-Pierre said. "Perhaps Monsieur Grondin has himself been cuckolded."

"Whatever the reason," the master said, "he revealed himself to me to be a man of a very peculiar and unscrupulous disposition for a bibliophile, an impression that was only strengthened during dinner."

"What happened?"

"Nothing."

"What do you mean nothing?

"He ate his food, which was perfectly palatable, and I ate mine. We talked about books, and we drank wine. All that was pleasant enough. But it was the dining room rather than the meal that disturbed me. On the walls, there were framed prints of old maps. I recognised them straightaway. They were ripped from an invaluable antique book which I had once restored. The owner had come to me in tears when the pages were cut from his priceless volume. But there was nothing I could do. I had no idea who had stolen them, or where they were."

The master paused.

"Until last night."

"You mean Monsieur Grondin ripped them out of the book and had them framed?"

"Either he did it himself, or he had someone do it for him. In any event, he knew the maps were well-known. It was an act of great stupidity to invite me into the room where they were hanging."

"Or bravado," Jean-Pierre interjected.

"How so?"

"Maybe it was part of a plan to draw you into some sort of collaboration."

"Partners in crime?" the master asked.

"Yes, and in that respect, he did show you something in his home that involved breaking the law. Man's law, as well as God's." He paused and then added, "I take it Monsieur Grondin will not be present for the remaining work on Madame Swanson's book?"

The master nodded.

"And that any hope of him buying it has gone?"

The master nodded again.

Monsieur Alfred then sighed and said, "Grangerizing is something I cannot and will not tolerate."

"Grangerizing?"

I was glad the apprentice asked.

"Well, you already know about the predilection for tearing pictures out of books and either placing them in other books or selling them as prints. It is the most despicable of practices."

Jean-Pierre nodded.

"I have no time for these maniacs," his master continued. "Their acts of vandalism are beyond the pale. Dismembering books is an act so commonplace these days that it is rare to find any complete copies of illustrated works. These unscrupulous people have killed as many books as perhaps have revolutions, rats, worms, fires and the injuries of time put together. They are despicable villains."

The dogs on my master's lap could tell that he was upset. They sat up on their haunches and looked up into his eyes, their ears twitching and their heads tilting this way and that.

Jean-Pierre lowered his voice in his attempt to lower the tension. "I heard not long ago about one man who acquired a copy of a Medieval Book of Hours, a volume of great value, and who then tore out all the beautiful miniatures, framed with golden borders, and sold them as prints. He incinerated the mutilated text."

I shuddered.

"An unpardonable crime," the master said. "The practice is quite fatal to books. If it continues, they will one day be extinct on the earth, all for the sake of a few francs for an engraving, a vignette."

"Is this what you mean by Grangerizing?" Jean-Pierre asked.

"It is. A man called John Granger wrote a bibliographical history of England. It was published full of blank pages so that readers could fill them with portraits they acquired from print stalls in London. This led to the widespread practice of removing illustrations from one book and pasting them in another. Those who do this are called Grangerites, and the practice, Grangerizing. It is sacrilegious!"

Jean-Pierre waited until his master had calmed himself, and his dogs, before speaking. "You have often said that there is a great war between iconoclasts and bibliophiles, master."

"There was a battle last night," the master replied. "Before I left Grondin's rooms, I insisted that he told me what his true purpose was in being in my workshop, observing our restoration of this precious book of poems. He simply said, 'it will be mine!' I replied that it would not, and that it was the very lowest form of courtesy to come into my house with such deceitful and malignant intentions. I told him that he is the very worst of humankind. He is an iconomaniac!"

"Bravo, master!"

Monsieur Alfred gazed at me, then said. "There is something about this book that stirs the passions, no?"

Jean-Pierre nodded.

"He will not have it, though," the master continued. "He may be able to say *Veni*, and he may be able to say *Vidi*, but he will never be able to say *Vici*, not while I have breath in my body."

The apprentice was not the only one cheering now.

That morning, I yielded to Monsieur Alfred's scalpels and spatulas with a new sense of trust. My treatment included the complete restoration of my back cover and spine, and a further look at my front to check that the work was consistent. Then the two men polished every inch of my binding with a siccative varnish from an unshaken bottle. Monsieur Alfred used a small brush to apply the varnish everywhere except on my gilding. He then rubbed it in using a cloth dampened with a small quantity of olive oil, waiting until every part of my front, spine and back was completely dry. This massage left me in a state of deep relaxation, and as shiny as I had been on the day of my birth.

For several fleeting seconds, I recalled the moment I first met the mother who gave me life.

I trembled at the thought of her touch.

Monsieur Alfred then prepared for the afternoon's operations by turning me onto my back and thumbing through my pages. He turned me the other way up so that my page ends were facing towards the floor and then, in gentle and rhythmic movements, shook me to check that there were no loose pages. As he did, a small sheet fell to the floor, like the last leaf of autumn. It was smaller than my pages, and I could see handwriting in black ink on it. I recognised the author without a moment's hesitation. It was Mister Bronte.

"Curious!" Monsieur Alfred said. "I must have wedged this in the book when I received it in the post."

Jean-Pierre retrieved the missive from the cold stone floor. "Shall I?" he said, motioning to his master.

Monsieur Alfred nodded and Jean-Pierre began to read.

Dear Monsieur Bonnardot,

My days are nearly done, so I have no more use for this book, or any other, save my Bible and my prayer book. I would be grateful if you would restore it, and I have provided in this letter the money that I was told would be required for such an undertaking. Please ensure that this volume is well looked after in the future.

I know that of the writing of books there appears to be no end, and that there indeed seems no end to the publishing of books, many of which are not worth the price of the paper on which they are printed, but this book is a notable and priceless exception. It is a thing of unparalleled beauty, although a reader must have eyes to see and ears to hear if they are to penetrate its mysteries and exhume its treasures. I know from your reputation that you will cherish it.

I expect nothing for this task. I have no use of money where I am going. All I ask is that any financial gain is not kept but passed on to the poor children in my parish. There is, in my parish of Howarth, a school whose existence and continuance has been a matter of great concern to me. Any money that is raised by the sale of this volume should be dedicated to the setting up of scholarships for the poorest of the children. You will find details below.

Yours faithfully,
P. Bronte.

"What a great soul!" Jean-Pierre cried.

Monsieur Alfred nodded and said, "We must proceed with the pages if his wishes are to be honoured."

The two men began with fissures and tears.

"Do you remember the words of Richard de Bury in the fourteenth century?" the master asked.

"I do. He said when defects are found in books, they should be repaired at once. Nothing develops more rapidly than a tear, and one that is neglected in the moment must later be repaired with usury."

The two restorers leaned forward at the operating table and joined the edges of the twelve tears on my pages with white paste. They placed a clean piece of white paper underneath each tear, then coated the edges of the tear with the paste. Then they pressed down on the paste with another piece of clean white paper, moving both pieces very carefully to prevent them from becoming glued to the tear. When the paste had dried, they removed the sheets and examined their work. In every case, the tears disappeared, even when they were forced to employ thin pieces of tissue to remove the flaw.

Once this task was completed, the contrast between the colour of the paste and the faded colour of the pages was visible to the naked eye so Monsieur Alfred stained the white lines with potassium permanganate, prepared by Jean-Pierre in warm water. This, once it was applied to the white pasted cracks, then wiped and dried, gave the lines the same pale, yellow tint as the surrounding page.

Next, it was time for them to attend to my stains, removing each one with different substances, from absorbent powders to warm turpentine, from cream of tartar to chloride of lime. In every case, they faded away, as if the ravages of time had been but a passing mist.

When my master was content that he had finished the work, he said, "We must hide this book for a season. Its contents have been attracting the wrong kind of attention. When it is safe, we will auction it."

"And fulfil Mister Bronte's wishes," Jean-Pierre added.

I felt happy when I heard this.

And above all, restored.

It was nearly twenty years later, in the autumn of 1880, that the master, whose back was now bent with age, remembered his vow to sell me at the auction house, giving the money from the sale to the poor children of Howarth parish. This happened on a particularly wet Saturday afternoon when the rain was pummelling the roof of the backroom, making any expeditions out of the shop utterly futile. The prospect of any customers visiting the place was also a forlorn one. Being somewhat incarcerated, Monsieur Alfred had taken me out from under lock and key for the first time in many months to clean me. On opening my covers and inspecting my leaves, he had gasped and called for Jean-Pierre, who had now all but taken over the running of the premises.

"See here!" he cried, pointing to one of my pages.

Jean-Pierre bent down. "It's a bookworm," he said.

For some time, I had been aware of a tingling in my leaves, sometimes pleasurable, at other times uncomfortable.

From the conversation that followed, it became clear that the appearance of such a destructive little creature was uncommon in the workshop. In fact, Monsieur Alfred remarked that he could never recall another situation like it, even with the books that had come to his shop from places faraway and long ago. He seemed at a loss to know what to do about it and was concerned that I would be regarded as damaged goods at an auction, until, that is, Jean-Pierre provided a solution.

"There is a lecture next month at the university, by the English printer, Mister William Blades. He is talking about the enemies of books. I am sure I heard mention of bookworms when the address was announced. There may even be talk of it on the advertising poster. We should take the book to the lecture and ask for the printer's opinion."

The following month, we sat among Parisian bibliophiles in a hall. The bald and bespectacled printer, when he appeared, had a large greying beard and a tall forehead. After being introduced, he began to describe in the most eloquent and impassioned manner some of the varied forces that have, over many years, conspired to injure old and precious books. He talked about chance conflagrations and fanatic incendiarism, and the terrible destruction caused by liquid and vapour, citing examples from history, and indeed his own experience. He then reflected on the damage of dust and rats before arriving at the worm of evil repute, whose activity with edible books had caused such harm throughout the ages, from the time of the Pharaohs to the present day. He called this nefarious predator "the mortal enemy of the bibliophile."

When he came to describe this creature, I shuddered. He said that it possessed a large head and a body that tapered towards three tails. It had two horns, long and straight, as well as hairy, scaled legs. It fed upon the covers and pages of books, leaving tiny perforations, finding nourishment in the hemp and flax, digested into its entrails. He told of how the previous Christmas, a printer from Northampton had found such a worm in a new book on which he was working. He posted the creature to Mister Blades in a little box. When Mister Blades received the creature, he claimed that it was still alive when he removed it from its container and that it seemed to have travelled well. When he placed some tiny fragments of a page of Boethius, printed by Caxton, next to it, it devoured a small piece of the leaf. However, it died several days later.

He proceeded to describe the worst of all the enemies of books, human beings. He decried the destructive habits of some who call themselves bibliophiles, but who are really destroyers. He warned against allowing maids into libraries to dust and clean, without proper and due instruction first, and he went on to advise owners never to allow children anywhere near their books, especially boys between the ages of 6 and 12, who had no reverence for age, either in men or in books, and whose fingers, made sticky by candy, caused terrible harm.

He finished with a rousing reminder of the duty that all book collectors and book owners have towards their charges.

"Looked at rightly," he pronounced, "the possession of any old book is a sacred trust, which a conscientious owner or guardian would as soon think of ignoring as a parent would of neglecting his child. The surest way to preserve your books in health is to treat them as you would your own children."

An enthusiastic ovation followed.

After the noise had died down, the members of the audience filed out of the hall while we headed to the platform where Mister Blades had given his informative address.

The speaker had heard of Monsieur Alfred's reputation and was heartened to meet him, and even more so when I was presented to him. He had heard of my existence and was overjoyed to glance at my pages and my prints. When he saw the evidence of the worm's activity, which had mercifully been confined to a single page, he was only too happy to advise my master as to the remedy.

That very night, on returning from the Sorbonne, Monsieur Alfred worked by lamplight to remove the trail of the worm and the microscopic holes left in its wake.

By the time the sun rose the next morning, all traces of the predator's work had vanished.

I was healthy and new again.

My body now expunged of the ravages of the *anobium*, Monsieur Alfred resolved to put me up for auction.

"But master," Jean-Pierre said. "Would it not be more prudent to sell it here, in the shop? We will have more control."

"True, but if I alert my two wealthiest bibliophiles to the sale, they will bid against one another, driving up the price."

Jean-Pierre yielded.

An hour later, we were proceeding along the Rue des Bons-Enfants when the master stopped abruptly outside no 30, a dishevelled house in the middle of a dirty street. We entered under an open coach gateway, passed under an arch, up a narrow flight of stairs, and finally into the corner of a room with little furniture, illuminated by only two windows, without curtains, that looked out onto the street.

"Is this really the auction room?" Jean-Pierre asked.

I could understand the apprentice's surprise. The chamber was empty, save for a large oak table in the centre, surrounded by a few kitchen chairs, and two rows of benches against the two main walls, one bench higher than the other. Along the smallest wall there was a solitary bookcase containing about ten rare and antique books, and it was there that my master placed me.

As a rocaille clock sounded three o'clock, a group of gentlemen entered. Some were booksellers, others were scholars, and still others were collectors. They made their way to the bookcase and expressed surprise and delight at catching sight of me there. None more so, in fact, than the two bibliophiles whom my master had invited to the auction. They arrived late, jostling together at the top of the narrow stairs, hurrying to the display, both seeking to scrutinise my spine before the other.

When the auctioneer called for order, his assistant began to take the volumes one by one from the shelves, placing each on the table, describing the book to the crowded room, and letting the prospective buyers scrutinise it before the bidding began. For two hours this continued until lamps and candles were lit and I was brought to the table.

The auctioneer, a celebrated bookseller by the name of Monsieur Techener, smiled when he saw me. He was, without doubt, the most educated diviner of rare books. His wide face was endowed with a luminous vitality and his brilliant eyes exhibited a most penetrating discernment. He would not allow anyone present to touch me. Instead, he took great care to open me and lay me down upon my back, stroking me with his gloved hands, pointing to the picture on one page, and the text of my mother's poetry on the other.

"We have an addition to tonight's catalogue – a book so rare and priceless that I forbid anyone from handling it."

There was a murmur in the room until the auctioneer spoke again, his voice loud and commanding.

"This is without doubt the bouquet of the evening. The first edition of Miss Emily Swanson's controversial masterpiece, restored lovingly by Monsieur Bonnardot, and containing some of the finest prints that ever graced a book. This was the author's sole copy, and she cherished it as if it was her only child."

The auctioneer stroked one end of his black moustache.

"The ten illustrations are by William Blake, and this is the only volume adorned by them. The pictures were a special gift from the artist to the author. This unique first edition was a gift to the author from the publishers." The man paused to see if his listeners were captivated. They were. He concluded, "I doubt there has ever been an item more desirable at these auctions."

The men poured over me for several minutes, whispering with one another. Then, as Monsieur Techener roused himself, they withdrew to the benches where they waited for the bidding to begin. Only two men stayed behind with me at the table, Master Alfred and his apprentice. They sat on the worn chairs, guarding me like sentries.

"Gentlemen, I have a private bid at ten thousand francs."

There was a gasp. The highest starting bid for the other volumes had been six hundred francs. This was a royal sum indeed, and one intended to knock all other competitors out of the race.

Eight of the men withdrew.

"Who will offer more for this treasure?"

This seemed to have the effect of awakening the two competitive bibliophiles invited by my master.

"Eleven thousand francs," one said.

"Twelve thousand," his rival shouted.

"Thirty thousand francs!" one of the two men cried. I could hear the intake of breath by the spectators.

The other competitor looked stunned. It seemed that the wildfire had been contained and the bidding had ended.

The fat-faced auctioneer took hold of his marble gavel.

"Once! Twice!" he shouted.

"Wait!"

The voice came from a lady in her mid-twenties with a hat sprouting tall black feathers above her wavy brown hair. She had just burst into the room. With her was a gentleman of similar age who, removing his bowler hat, revealed a receding hairline.

The woman was out of breath from running up the stairs and her youthful face was flushed. She gathered herself, walked up to me and scrutinised my opened pages. Her companion stood a few paces behind her. He smiled at her as she studied me with acquisitive eyes.

"What is the bid?" she asked.

"It stands at thirty thousand francs," the auctioneer said. The sweat was glistening on his forehead.

She seemed unimpressed.

"Fifty thousand, then," she said.

There was uproar.

When the hubbub died down, the auctioneer asked, "Do you have the money for such a bid?"

"I am an author and a woman of means."

"Very well," the auctioneer said. "Going once!"

There was silence.

"Going twice!"

People held their breath.

"Gone! Sold to the English lady!"

"Irish," she said, correcting him.

With that, she wrote out a cheque for the auctioneer while her friend scrutinised my pages.

Then she bent down to the table, took me in her arms, and carried me out of the room, casting a disdainful eye and a triumphant smile at the men whom she had defied and defeated.

I had a new guardian, it seemed.

A woman as formidable as my mother.

Part 6

1880-1924

I was persuaded to show it [*The Heavenly Twins*] to Mr Heinemann as a last chance, and consented reluctantly, for he was the youngest of the publishers and I expected him to be cautious for lack of experience ... [but] Mr Heinemann was in touch with the spirit of his day, if ever a man was.

Sarah Grand, née Frances McCall, (1854-1943)

Minutes later, the man with the receding hair was offering up a toast in a café in Montmartre.

"Frances," he said. "That victory alone was worth the trip from Denver. It was so dramatic I may have to report the incident in my paper. Did you see the looks on some of their faces?"

"I owe you a debt of gratitude, Eugene," Frances said. "If it wasn't for our chance meeting, I would never have acquired this book."

"It's my pleasure," Eugene said. "This is the second time I've struck up a chance friendship on a trip to Paris. The last time, seven years ago, I met a judge. He was responsible for my craving."

"Craving?"

"For books."

Eugene took a sip of claret.

"We met in this city and spent months in the Latin Quarter. Then we headed for London, which is where the craving really started. So, I suppose you owe him thanks as well."

My new mistress smiled.

Eugene then looked grave. "But you must beware, Frances. The disease can come upon people in diverse ways, and not just with violence, in a sudden surge of unfamiliar passion. It can be like the measles, slow and obstinate. In such cases, steps need to be made quickly, or else the malady will overtake you."

"And you, Eugene, are you suffering from the measles?"

"Without doubt, Frances, and there are no applications that can remedy it. I am covered in its sores."

They both laughed.

Then he looked at me. "I'm so glad for your new acquisition. If there is one thing I cannot stand, it is an abandoned, antique book. If I could, I would start a hospital for homeless books and name it the Home for Genteel Volumes in Decayed Circumstances."

Miss Frances smiled.

"You are the new keeper of Miss Swanson's book," he said. "See how beautifully it has been restored, how lovely are its illustrations. Monsieur Bonnardhot is a true artist, as clever and as capable as Mister Blake or even the poet herself."

"Why do you collect rare books?" she asked.

Eugene ordered a carafe. He poured them both a glass and then sat back in his chair.

"There are really three classes of book collectors," he replied. "Those who collect because of vanity, those who collect for learning, and those who collect out of a love for books."

"And which one are you?"

Eugene laughed. "My books know me. When I awake, I cast my eyes about my room to see how my beloved treasures fare, and as I cry cheerily to them, 'Good day to you, sweet friends', how lovingly they beam upon me, and how gladly too."

My mother would have agreed, I thought.

"The judge I befriended claims unjustly that women are hostile to books and even more hostile to bibliomania. I'd love him to meet you. You might change his view."

Frances asked, "Why would a woman be hostile?"

"The judge argues that a wife hates her husband's books because she fears that they may replace her in his affections. The judge is a case in point. His wife could not detest his volumes more if they had been blithe and buxom maidens wandering about his study."

He sighed and drank again from his wine glass.

"A man can easily fall in love with his books, or so the judge is wont to say. They are constant. Whatever the season, whether during the asperity of winter or the drought of summer, they are ever radiant and hopeful, fragrant and helpful."

"Do you believe this too?"

Mister Eugene raised his eyebrows and shook his head.

"And do you think this same jealousy might work in the reverse direction?" Frances asked.

The man looked quizzical.

"If I love Miss Swanson's book in the way that you describe, do you think it possible that such a love will ignite the kind of ire your judge friend claims to see, only in my husband back home?"

"That all depends. Do you love this book, Frances?"

"I hope I will come to love it."

"Then, if you develop a fondness for it that many waters cannot quench, the judge may reply in the affirmative."

He finished his wine.

"You have told me little about your husband, Frances. Forgive me for being forward, but are there ...difficulties?"

I could tell she was upset, not so much by the question, as by her memories, most of which I fancy had been forgotten or superseded during her adventure with Mister Eugene in Paris.

"He is a brute."

A look of concern spread across his face. His playfulness was gone. "Is he ... cruel to you?"

She did not answer.

"I'm sorry, Frances."

"He is strong and twice my age," she said.

"But almost certainly half your intelligence," he interjected. "What is his profession, this tyrant?"

"He is the Army Surgeon General in Warrington."

"A medical man?"

"He is in charge of tending to the soldiers in the barracks in our town, but he spends most of his time applying his skills to the impoverished women who fulfil their lusts simply to survive."

"By skills, I assume you mean other than medical."

My new mistress looked away.

Eugene reached out his hand and touched hers.

"I am sorry."

"You are not responsible, Eugene."

"Nonetheless, I am still sorry."

She smiled. "You are kind, Eugene. I shall miss our friendship. We have had many conversations, such interesting and rational conversations, and I have enjoyed every minute of them."

"As have I, Frances."

He paused.

Then he offered her his card.

Eugene Field.

Managing Editor.

Denver Tribune

With an address in the USA.

"Maybe, Frances, when you're a famous writer, we will meet again. Denver is the perfect resting place if you cross from the east to the west coast. I host many writers when they travel our fine country. I would love to have the honour of doing the same for you."

Frances blushed, smiled, and nodded.

"I must head to the railway station," she said. "It is a long way back to England, and then just as long up north to rainy Warrington. I must not be late. I will risk enraging my husband. I do not want the goodness of this trip undone in a single argument."

"One thing before you go, Frances. This book of yours . . ."

"What about it?"

"It is extremely valuable."

"So?"

"So, there are nefarious souls that would steal it, remove its pictures, and sell them."

"Really?"

"Yes, really."

As he put on his coat, he said, "Bibliomania has a dark side to it. There are men, and they are always men, who want to possess the precious books that belong to another. They cannot stand just to look. They must also conquer. And when they have, they lose interest in that volume and pursue the next that catches their covetous eyes."

"They're like that with women too," Frances muttered.

She placed me within her bag, making sure that I was tucked beneath a wadge of paper at the bottom.

"I will take good care of it."

As he hailed a cab for her, he said, "Let he who tries to steal this book be struck with palsy and all his members blasted. Let bookworms gnaw his entrails and let the flames of hell consume him forever."

"Good gracious, Eugene!"

"Not my words," he said. "They were found in a monastery library in Barcelona. But I think they are apt."

"Goodbye, Eugene," she said with a smile.

"Adieu," he replied.

It turned out Frances was a prophet. When we arrived in Warrington, it was indeed raining, and when her husband found out about her purchase, he drained from her all the new-found vitality she had acquired on her holiday. On returning from the hospital for infectious diseases in the town, he discovered her with me in the drawing room. After interrogating her about her time away, he turned to me.

"A new book?"

"Miss Swanson's famous book of poetry. The very first edition."

"How much did that cost, Frances?"

When she told him, his face turned from pale to red.

"That is an obscene amount of money."

"We can afford it."

"We! You mean I!"

"I will pay you back, if it is such a cause of concern."

"How, Frances?"

She shrugged her shoulders.

"You owe me," the man said.

His scowl then turned to a grin. "You can repay me in ways that are more pleasurable than money."

"And what would that make me?" my new mistress asked. The man shrugged his low shoulders. "I'll tell you, husband. It would make me the same as the women who work on the streets, whose bodies you are constantly investigating in ways that are not just scientific and sanitary, but to your mind, pleasurable."

"Only confusion comes from women speaking on such issues," he said, citing one of his maxims.

That night, my mistress placed me by her bed, and it was from this vantage point that I witnessed the full depravity of her husband. Some nights, when the lights were low, his abuses took the form of a subtle undermining of her intellectual pursuits.

"Women should restrict themselves to housekeeping," he said to her one time. "All this talk of women receiving a higher education, it's a waste of time, don't you think?"

"I do think, yes," she replied.

This ambiguity irked him.

Frances continued undeterred. "To say as you do that women are intellectually inferior and undeserving of a higher education is to ignore the fact that even in our own century there have been the most exceptional women, such as Elizabeth Barrett Browning, the Bronte sisters, and before them, Jane Austen."

"But that's where your argument is faulty."

"How so?"

"Because you are building from the exception and that is always a weak foundation for a proposition."

"These exceptions would become the norm if women were granted the opportunity to demonstrate their equality, but men like you hold us back from developing and using our God-given talents."

Interchanges such as these took place with increasing frequency until the day came when the man recognised his notions were falling on deaf ears. From then on, his assaults became more physical. He would return from the mess in the barracks late at night. My mistress, in the early days of this dark season of her life, would be asleep. He, reeking of tobacco and whiskey, would climb upon her, gratifying his own desires, with no care in the world for hers. She, in turn, would wait until he was done, which sometimes took a while – or not, if he fell asleep – before turning her face to the table where I rested. There I would contemplate her eyes. There was no sadness there, no shame. Just resilience.

Matters reached a head when the surgeon returned from a long day in the hospital. There he had been attending to several of the women who had been compelled by poverty to satisfy the lusts of men. They had told him – when he insisted that it was needful for an accurate diagnosis – some lurid tales. He was sober when he returned home some hours later, having had no time to stray to the mess. Climbing into bed, he insisted on sharing some of the stories with my mistress. These were less titillating than tragic to any rational mind, bearing testimony as they did to the desperate measures the women were compelled to take. He, on the other hand, used them as the springboard for manipulation.

"Why don't you tell me a lewd tale?"

"No."

"Do you not want to please me?"

As his childish pleading fell on deaf ears, the rage within began to boil until the bubbling, stinking mess spilled over from his heart into the bed. He raised himself, pinioned my mistress with his arms and legs, then grasped her throat. "You will do as you're bloody well told!"

With that, his face went puce and his eyes wild. He would have strangled her had he not seen, as a physician should, the fading visage before him. Her eyes were going down like the sun and her life was ebbing away. He stopped, gathered his wits, mumbled something to himself, then fell upon his back, turned over towards the door, closed his eyes and, after several petulant sighs, fell asleep.

My mistress lay on her back, her pretty, oval face turned up towards the ceiling. She seemed lost in a faraway trance among the bleached fauna and turtledoves above. Now in shock, the light and delicate colouring in her complexion had disappeared, leaving her skin white. Her soft, brown, curly hair, normally lopped behind her ears into a chignon, was loose and dishevelled, as if she had been caught in a storm.

Then, as suddenly as she had entered this trance, she returned from it. She shifted her head, turned towards the table beside her, and stared at my spine. She picked me up and started to turn my pages. As she read me, I remembered my mother's mandate. "I want you to sing our song of love. Sing to those who have not loved and yet who long to love. Sing to those who need awakening from the winter of indifference. Sing it in the morning, sing it in the evening. Sing it to the prince and sing it to the orphan. Let generations hear my song."

What would my mother have made of such a man?

What hope would she have held out for such a marriage?

As I stared back at my guardian's eyes, I saw death. Not her own death, but the death of whatever it was she had once enjoyed with the man. And then it was as if my mother spoke to me as my guardian's lips began to tremble. Her words were almost silent, but I heard them.

"Desire without my love is brutish lust," my mistress whispered. "Love, without refined desire, is lost."

And then I knew.

As the discolouring began to spread around her neck, I knew that she had decided to leave him.

It was just a matter of time.

My new guardian had one child called Archie. He had been born nine months after my mistress and her husband had wed. The older he had become, the more he had begun to look like his father, and the more that happened, the more my mistress distanced herself from him. Poor Archie felt this disengagement for the rest of his life. "Even when I was an infant," he said to a friend, "I can never remember her holding, cuddling, or whispering to me. She has never praised me. Never."

One day, on one of the rare occasions I was downstairs and lying on the mahogany pull-out desk in the drawing room, my mistress was visited by a friend called Maud – the wife of an army officer and mother of six-year-old twin boys. When the children were playing on the carpet with Napoleonic soldiers, one of them cut his finger and began to cry. Maud swept to his aid and lifted him onto her lap, soothing him and tending to his wound until the tears stopped.

The boy calmed down and returned to the battlefield on the rug. My mistress turned to Maud. "I wish I could be like you. I have never been able to show Archie the kind of love you show for your boys. I just cannot do it. I've never been able to speak to him as you do."

She paused and looked at a framed picture of her own mother standing near me on the desk. "But then again, my mother didn't do any of that for me, either."

"Then you are not to blame, Frances. How can you expect to give away what you've never received?"

"My mother was not cut out for it," my mistress mused. "She probably would have said that she didn't have time. My father died when I was very young. She had to bring us up on our own. But she was cold and stern, a thick-skinned Yorkshire woman who was so strict and discouraging that my early development in literacy was checked. It took me forever to learn and master my ABC. I lay this entirely at my mother's door."

Maud picked up a book next to her. It was entitled *Two Dear Little Feet*. She had written and published it in 1873. Maud said, "Your story makes this book all the more remarkable."

"Yes, I am quite proud of it, although my mother, of course, did not praise me for it, or for anything else I've done. When I was eleven, unknown to my mother, I wrote some songs and posted them secretly to a publisher. They sent them back in an envelope with a rejection letter, the first of many. When my mother intercepted it, she read the contents and chastised me. She told me that a woman should expect only to do charity work, and then only in a voluntary capacity. That left a lasting impression. And not a healthy one."

"I'm so sorry."

"I think that's why I'm so handicapped when it comes to loving others. If my mother had not withheld love from me, perhaps I would have been a better wife and mother. I would have learned from her own example how to love others. But that was not to be, and the damage has been lasting. I don't see how it can ever be cured."

As she spoke, I remembered my own mother's love. How warm, demonstrable, and unconditional was her affection! How adoring was her gaze! How lavish was her love for me! And I felt pity that my mistress should have suffered such deprivation, and that young Archie had become a victim of this generational wounding. If I could shed tears, I would have, there and then.

"I've noticed," Maud said, her voice soft.

"Noticed what?"

"The way you hold yourself back from being affectionate with your friends. With me. With others. I do not hold it against you, not least now that you've told me why you are the way you are."

"I can only apologise," my mistress said.

"Don't. It was what it was, and you are what you are. I accept you completely. You do not need to change. You have been my friend, you are my friend, and you will always be my friend."

"I'm so grateful to you, Maud. Warrington is such a dreary town and the people here do not seem to understand what I'm trying to say about equality between the sexes, let alone the way I dress."

Both women laughed so loudly at this that the boys paused their re-enactment of Waterloo to look up and smile.

"You are the true champion of Rational Dress in Warrington," Maud said, her voice more playful.

"I have taken more than my fair share of criticism for that," my mistress said.

"I can imagine it didn't go down well at home. Your husband is a stickler for obeying the dress code in the army, isn't he? What did he say when he saw your rebellion?"

"It happened almost exactly three years ago now. I had been wearing what he wanted me to wear, a crinoline dress, just like yours, and high-heeled boots with my toes crushed inside them. He wanted me to don these every day and, as time went by and childbirth had rendered my waistline not as thin as it had been, he would pinch my crinoline more and more tightly until the whalebone was suffocating me. Sometimes I thought my lungs would collapse."

"These dresses are dubious inventions," Maud said. "I've got the hoop in this one caught in a carriage door more than once. For all men's insistence on us protecting our modesty, when these garments fail us, what they reveal leaves nothing to the imagination."

"They are also notoriously unsafe," my mistress said. "Do you remember Caroline Ogilvy? She was burned to death when her crinoline caught fire. As for riding bicycles, that is the most ridiculous idea, and yet men keep insisting that we ride in crinoline, while French ladies are seen bicycling around in bloomers and flat-heeled shoes!"

Both women laughed again.

"I remember when the divided skirt was introduced a few years ago," my mistress continued. "I went out straightaway and bought one. When I went for a ride, my husband humiliated me on the street. He bellowed that loose skirts are for women with loose morals. I have never lived that down with our neighbours."

"Do you think things will ever change?" Maud asked.

"Yes, I do. In fact, you must come and listen to me next month, in the town hall. I shall be giving an address about marriage and the rights of women. It's bound to cause a stir."

"But your own marriage, Frances . . ."

"That's the motivation for my address. What if men were to change from being domestic tyrants into being loving equals? Would not that be a good and healthy alternative to them abusing us?"

Maud watched her boys creating a field of carnage on the bloodred Persian carpet at her feet. Their whispered imitations of cannon balls and musket fire awakened her from her trance.

"Are you going to divorce him?"

"I am going to leave him."

"But people will surely say that you're immoral to desert your husband and your son."

"I am not deserting my son. He has already left home to pursue his own way in life. And as for my husband, it would be far more immoral to stay with such a callous brute."

Frances took an envelope from a small drawer. She drew out the letter inside and held it in her fist towards her friend.

"See this?"

Maud nodded.

"It's a letter from his mistress."

Maud gasped.

"Not only is he an abuser. He is an adulterer too. To stay with such a man would compromise my campaign for women's rights. There is far more integrity in leaving. And leave him I will."

And she did.

It took several more months before my mistress fulfilled her promise. During the days before her departure, I found myself downstairs, lying on a table next to a book that became a fine friend. The volume was far bigger than me; it had a cloth cover and contained over one thousand pages in close print. It was called *Mrs Beeton's Book of Household Management* and included, among many pages describing how to clean your house, over 900 cooking recipes, all of which fascinated me. When my mistress left it open next to me, I would gaze at the instructions, and it occurred to me that preparing a meal had much in common with writing a book. The focus in both, I mused, was to gather familiar ingredients and create a new and unfamiliar unity from them.

It was as I was pondering these things that early one evening, when the surgeon general was working late, three women came to the house at my mistress's invitation. They were called Miss Milly, Miss Emma, and

Miss Jane. All were wearing hoods and scarves, not only to protect them from the chilly northern air, but to keep from being recognised by the neighbours. These ladies were her husband's patients and they had come to my mistress to learn how to read and write.

Mrs Beeton and I were together on the table for these women. My mistress would read from my pages to inspire her guests with a higher form of love, and from the leaves of Mrs Beeton's book to help them with their domestic tasks. All this was born from her compassion for women who were oppressed by men, just as she was.

That evening, my mistress introduced the class by narrating the story of Mrs Beeton's marriage.

"She wed a publisher called Samuel Beeton," she said. "He had already contracted syphilis through his infidelities and was kind enough to share the disease with his young wife."

The women looked uncomfortable.

"I do not share this to judge you, but to indicate how remarkable it was that Mrs Beeton managed to write and publish this huge tome in the twenty-eight years she lived on this earth."

"I thought she lived much longer than that." It was Miss Molly who spoke. "My mum had a lot of her books."

"They were not penned by Mrs Beeton herself," my mistress said. "When she died, not only was the true cause of her death concealed, the fact of her death was as well."

"You're not serious," Miss Emma interjected.

"I do not jest. Her husband and the new publisher mummified her memory for monetary profit."

Miss Jane looked as if she had been turned to stone. At first, I thought she was staring at the flames in the grate, too shocked by these revelations to engage in the conversation. Then I realised she was gazing at the portrait above the mantle shelf, an oil painting of the surgeon general in his uniform, a look of indifference in his dark and arrogant eyes. As she stared at it, an expression of disgust and horror spread across the rouged cheeks of her pretty white face.

"Are you all right, Jane?"

"Who's that?" she asked.

"That," my mistress said, "is my husband."

The three girls shuffled in their seats, casting sideways glances at each other, concern on their faces.

"Why are you looking like that?"

"It's nothing ma'am," Miss Molly said.

My mistress, whose posture had been perfect, began to let her shoulders droop for a moment.

"Has he examined you girls?"

"I wouldn't say *examined*," Miss Molly said.

"What then?"

Suddenly, my mistress understood.

"Oh," she said.

Miss Molly nodded.

"You mean . . ."

My mistress did not finish her sentence. She raised her eyebrows and then simply asked, "All three of you?"

"Sorry," Miss Molly said.

Followed by Miss Emma.

Miss Jane burst into tears.

My mistress looked at them and then began to laugh. To begin with, it was a chuckle. Then it developed, growing from strength to strength until she was almost hysterical.

The girls looked at each other.

"You all right, ma'am?" Miss Molly asked.

My mistress, realizing that her merriment could so readily be regarded as vulgarity, or, worse still, insanity, calmed herself. "I am," she said. "In fact, I am more than all right. You have given me a gift far greater than the one I'm giving you with these classes."

"What's that?" Miss Molly asked, her expression shifting between uncertainty and suspicion.

"You have given me ammunition. I knew he had a mistress. What I did not know was the full extent of his other wanderings. Now I have not just a moral reason for separating myself from him. I can threaten him with the ruin of his reputation."

Maud accompanied my mistress to the Bank Hall, just as she had promised. When they arrived, they found the main chamber packed with an audience mainly composed of women. Some were accompanied by husbands with disapproving faces. At the back, Misses Molly, Emma, and Jane were whispering to each other as they spotted clients among the censorious men. My mistress had invited these women and given them free tickets, telling them in advance what she intended to say.

Unknown to her husband, my mistress had been spending many months reading scientific and medical treatises on infectious diseases, focusing on those transmitted through sexual acts. She had studied them, taking copious notes in a moleskin book. One morning, she left a copy of a medical volume open beside me. When I saw what injury and degradation men cause such women, not to mention their own wives as well, I was shocked and angered. These men were no better in my estimation than those who abused books.

When my mistress entered from the wings to gather the three of us in her arms, the crowd fell quiet and some of the women took a sharp intake of breath. My mistress was dressed in a black charmeuse with black lace, a pearl necklace, and a prodigious hat, adorned with ostrich feathers. She looked beautiful and she looked feminine. Many men harboured the common prejudice that the champions of women's rights were no more than what my mistress called "ugly and aggressive harridans with hairy chins and hatchet jaws." She subverted this notion before she had even opened her mouth. But when she did start to speak, her charm and wit unnerved her critics even more. "I shall represent the opposite of the caricatures provided by our newspapers", she had said to Maud. "I will show them what the New Woman looks and sounds like."

And she could now afford to; after many rejection slips, she had at last succeeded with a novel about an oppressed young woman called Ideala. She finished it one year after arriving in Warrington, but she had put it aside for six years. Then, by chance, she found a solution in E.A. Allen, an obscure publisher based in Ave Maria Lane in London. Writing anonymously, the book had sold well and then been picked up by a larger publisher, Richard Bentley, who reprinted it a further three times the year before my mistress's lecture. She refused to reveal her identity, commenting that her husband had a profound dislike for any association with her unwelcome and unnatural ideas. Nevertheless, the book's success gave her an independent income, one about which her husband had no inkling. It had sold out in Warrington, although no one knew that the author was one who lived among them, nor that she was on the point of delivering this speech – an address on which she had expended as much effort and ingenuity as her dress.

After several anecdotes, which even had the men laughing, she launched into her lecture. "Women of today are in an unsettled state. It may be a state of transition, especially since principles accepted since the beginning of time have been called into question."

No one in the audience seemed to notice that my mistress was giving people a hint about the identity of the author of *Ideala*. The words she had just uttered were taken straight from her book.

She continued. "The future of humanity is inseparable from the issue of morality and the issue of health. For humans to survive, women will have to play a critical role. We will need to rise from our current subservience and show men what it looks like to be people with grander minds and grander bodies. We will no longer tolerate what is unfair, any more than we will tolerate our bodies becoming the objects of men's iniquities. These iniquities not only eat away at the marrow of the soul. They infect the body with terrible diseases such as syphilis."

The gasps were audible now.

"Many men behave as simpletons. Governed by lust rather than reason or abstinence, they harm our bodies as well as our minds. Then, when they infect us, they betray the vilest double standards, castigating and chastising us, while excusing themselves."

Several men started to rise, dragging their unwilling wives to their feet. My mistress was undeterred.

"How is it fair that women can be examined for infectious diseases at a whim, while the law protects men from being inspected for the same purpose, saying that it is beneath their dignity to be treated in this way? Why is it degrading for a man to be scrutinised by a physician in this manner but not a woman?"

With that remark, Misses Molly, Emma, and Jane uttered a cheer and more men started to leave.

"If our nation is to be saved," my mistress said, her voice more voluminous, commanding, resolute, "then the answer lies with us women. We must be free to educate and enlighten our minds, and we must be free to keep our bodies in good health."

She paused and lifted one of her husband's medical volumes on syphilis. She began to read a vivid description by the author of the medical consequences of venereal disease. As more people headed out of the auditorium, she spoke with even greater boldness.

"My message is one of purity as well as politics. If women are to play a full part in society, as they must, then they need to be protected against men's lust. That means that men must learn to control their desires and prevent themselves from behaving like beasts. The threat of infection is a threat to our wombs, to our womanhood, to civilisation itself."

At this, there was an outbreak of further cheering from the women at the back, and a ripple of applause, muted by cotton gloves, from the remaining, unchaperoned women.

"And this brings me to marriage," my mistress said. "I am not like some of my contemporaries, trying to destroy marriage, but to save and enrich it. I hold it true, and have always done so despite many personal challenges, that marriage is the most sacred institution in the world, and it is best not to interfere with it."

At this, the last remaining men left – all bar one, a local reporter from the newspaper, who was taking notes furiously.

"But for marriage to be most effective, men should cease from treating us as victims, and regard us as equal partners."

With that, she reached down, picked me up, and opened my pages. "This book is the first edition of Emily Swanson's love poems, illustrated by William Blake."

There were murmurs.

"Miss Swanson understood the sanctity of marriage. In her poems she celebrated the beauty of this holy estate when a man and a woman love and honour one another equally, cherishing each other as recipients of virtue, not the victims of vice. In it, she says these words."

My mistress found the page and took a deep breath.

Let passion and fidelity unite
And be, like twins from heaven, my delight.

She put me down on the lectern, then placed her soft hand on my cover. "Marriage is the expression of mutual passion in a context of uncompromising fidelity. Passion and fidelity together. Twins from heaven, indeed."

As she mentioned twins, my mistress paused and looked down from the stage at her friend Maud, who was seated on the front row. She smiled at her, and Maud smiled back.

My mistress concluded her speech.

"The answer for advanced women is not to despise marriage, as some are wont to do, but to be the best wives they can be, taking care of their appearance and excelling in charm, while at the same time throwing off all the traditional silliness and feebleness of our sex. This is the New Woman. We are the New Women. If married, the best companion for a man. And if not, the best suited and equipped to make a strong and equal contribution in this world."

The women in the audience stood and clapped.

My mistress took me in her arms, along with her two other books and sat on her chair while the remnant applauded. As I looked up into her face, I could see something. It was like the wave of a hand and the raising of a handkerchief. My mistress was saying farewell.

Later that evening she confronted her husband. "You have been shaming the poor women you've been examining. They have told me. You can either let me leave, or I will go to the newspapers."

At first, he had looked enraged, but then he assumed the appearance of a pitiless and penitent boy.

"I'm sorry," he said.

"Sorry that you've been caught, or sorry that you've hurt me."

He did not answer.

"I will not embarrass you by using your surname when I publish my new book," she said. "I have come up with a new pen name, one that will not connect us in any way."

He was still silent.

"And I do not intend to go through a divorce. It is enough for me that I will be separated from you."

With that, she walked out of the house.

It was a bright, summer day in 1890 when my mistress arrived in London to move into an apartment she had purchased in Kensington. She now called herself Sarah Grand, the name under which she bought the flat and published all her subsequent works. She felt the goodness of the bluer skies and the more stimulating people she met in the city, especially the leaders of the movement for the emancipation of women. As I lay beside her bed, next to her lamp, I watched as she hugged herself on her first night. Here was a sheltered port after a long season of tempest on the open sea. As she lay there, I heard her whisper, "I am no longer afraid. I am free!" Later, she was to tell a visitor that she was so relieved, now that she was no longer at someone's beck and call, free from the exercise of asphyxiating control. Her twenty years of captivity had at last come to an end and she was free, free as a bird to sing her own new songs.

When she opened the curtains that first morning, the light poured into every room. Her heart was so full of my mother's poetry that she recited lines about the long hard winter being over and the rains, the unrelenting showers, being over and gone at long last. It was the closest I ever saw her to shedding a tear. Her joy was infectious. I felt the corners of my pages shudder.

From that day on, her bicycle, which she now used all the time, leaned against the wall outside the foyer to the apartment building. Whenever she set out for a ride, she refused to wear crinoline. Instead, she headed to a tailor in the city and bade him design for her a long tunic over trousers, practical for a female cyclist, and not unfashionable. This attracted unwanted attention to begin with, so she restricted herself to wearing it in the countryside. In the city, she donned a cycling skirt, until one day it was snagged in the spokes. Back she went to her tailored garments, stating that she no longer cared what any man thought of her. "The New Woman has too much healthy enjoyment of life to worry about whether her ankles are visible or not," she would say. "Besides, she has such good ones – and, naturally, she knows it."

After several months, my mistress had met new and notorious female friends in London and together they set about destroying the dead stone wall, as they called it, between themselves and the privileges enjoyed by men. There was much need of that, with the newspapers refusing to report their meetings, the right of free speech denied to them, and the bar from women voting. Professions were divided into masculine and feminine. When a woman endeavoured to perform a function traditionally associated with men, she was decried as "unsexed."

In this battle, my mistress determined that the pen was her only weapon and that she would not engage in activities that were criminal, such as throwing bricks through windows and setting fire to buildings. As an advanced woman, she set about using her writing skills to make the argument for change and worked day after day on *The Heavenly Twins*, a long novel in which her ideas of purity and politics were explored, and in which the injustices suffered by women were exposed, especially those connected with male lust and venereal disease. When she had finished her manuscript, she set about having it published, no small quest when one considers that it dealt so clinically and scientifically about syphilis, a subject deemed to be wholly improper for a woman to discuss.

After thirty refusals, the breakthrough came one afternoon in the summer of 1892 when a gentleman visited the flat. His name was William Heinemann. Two years before, he had set up a new publishing company in Covent Garden dedicated to the translation and publication of foreign books and progressive English-language novels. My mistress ushered him into her drawing room and bade him sit and enjoy her "most prized possession." Taking me in her hands, she passed me to him, while she withdrew to the kitchen to make a pot of tea.

Mister Heinemann, a balding man with a high forehead, admired my trim, spine, and covers, before turning every page with a gentleness and care that seemed to me not only unusual but unique. His dark eyes held a microscopic and incisive gaze, but there was also a kindness, a humanity, in them. At points, as he read my mother's words and scrutinised my illustrations, they seemed to shine beneath his black eyebrows, and a smile would appear, causing his coiffured moustache to twitch and tremble at the turned-up ends.

When my mistress returned with the tea, Mister Heinemann put me to one side, away from the hot liquid.

"I notice it's the very first edition."

"It is priceless, not only in monetary value, but in terms of its literary worth. It is a treasure, and in many ways, far ahead of its times. Miss Swanson had no time for men who said it was not a woman's place to write and speak about issues that were, in their eyes, indecorous."

Mister Heinemann smiled.

"And that brings me to your novel," he said, withdrawing a large bundle of pages from his brown leather briefcase. "In this too, I am happy to see you are ripping up the fences put in place by men and taking new ground for women."

"I am, indeed," my mistress said. "My novel does something that no other has done before."

"And what's that?"

"It exposes and criticizes men's attitudes to sex, and their sexual conduct, both within and outside marriage."

"It is a most daring and original work," Mister Heinemann agreed. "It is most important. The most lucid and vivid description of what you call the New Woman. I should like to publish it."

"Really?"

"Really!" Mister Heinemann said with a smile. "You are a pioneer, a scout who is way ahead of a literary movement that I suspect will become an enormous force for emancipation in this country. With this book, the dead stone wall, as you call it, is well and truly breached."

Mister Heinemann reached into his briefcase and withdrew a brand-new volume. He placed it in my mistress's hands.

"Are you familiar with Ibsen's work?"

"No."

"This is William Archer's translation, *The Doll's House*. There are parallels between the two of you."

My mistress thanked him, and he returned to his seat. After a moment, he looked up and said, "we should discuss terms."

"I have thought about this," my mistress said. "This is a very risky venture for you and I'm sure you're wondering if you'll get any kind of return on your investment. So, I propose that I sell you the copyright for £100, that way I get my novel published and you reduce the risks to your young company."

Mister Heinemann agreed. "We will publish next year. A three-volume edition, for sale at a guinea and a half."

One year later, in the summer of '93, Mister Heinemann called again with a broad smile upon his face.

"It has become a literary sensation," he said. "You have been so clever, Miss Grand. The Women's Righters are championing it because of the marriages of your two female protagonists, but the public is reading it too, thanks to the pranks of the same twins. Since February, it has been a bestseller, and there are no signs of the general enthusiasm abating." He drew out a contract from his briefcase. "I have torn up our original agreement and I have here a much fairer proposal which gives you the most favoured author's royalties." He then drew a cheque from his pocket. "This is what I would have paid you had this new and fairer agreement been in place from the start."

"Twelve hundred pounds!" my mistress said with a gasp.

"You'll be able to enhance your rational dress with that!" he said, and my mistress laughed.

"This is most welcome," she said.

"It's already been reprinted three times and it's only been out six months. It's therefore only right and proper. I have already approached Cassell's about an American single-volume edition. They are going to publish it next year. We will do the same in England."

By the end of the decade, the novel had made my mistress £18,000 richer. It was hailed as the greatest women's rights novel of the day and sold so many copies in the United States that it made the overall bestseller's list for the final decade of the century.

This, and the news that her husband had died, put my mistress in very good spirits as the new century began.

My guardian used her royalties to buy a more spacious flat, from which she travelled far and wide, including in the United States. She lectured for most of the first decade of the new century, then became involved in the Women Writers' Suffrage League, the Women's Suffrage Society, the National Council of Women, and the Tonbridge Wells branch of the National Union of Women's Suffrage Societies. In 1913, she formed part of the National Union of Women's Suffrage Society's pilgrimage to London. She took me with her as four hundred women, and some men, walked the Kentish pilgrim's Way to Hyde Park, stopping for lectures and rallies in villages and towns. The entire walk took thirty days, and as we neared the great city of London, the ranks of the marchers swelled until all that you could see were creased banners and rippling flags, and all you could hear were the shouts and songs of the protesters.

One memory, for me, stands out – my mistress speaking in the open air on Ramsgate Sands. She was a tall and impressive woman, but her stature seemed to grow that day. Standing beneath a great hat, with a red rose set in place by stiff pleats, she began, "I have known some agreeable men in my time, and, as fetchers and carriers of heavy objects, I have known one or two who were of some use too." Having gained their attention, she turned to calculated condescension. "Now it is time not only for women to come of age, but men too. It is the woman's place and privilege to teach the child and since men are currently in a moral infancy it will be our role to teach him to be live up to a new ideal of manhood. It is time for the New Woman to help the man-child up to his feet."

And so, she went on, evoking many cheers.

She aroused other emotions too, as when she reminisced about the cruelty she witnessed in China.

"I don't have many things for which I'm grateful to my late husband, but one blessing in the early days of marriage was that his profession allowed me to travel the world. I shall never forget visiting China and seeing how people there bind their daughter's feet so tightly that it stunts their growth. They do it when the girls are only six or seven years old, and it cripples them with small feet for the rest of their days. All this because men in that culture find small feet attractive. I think this was in part the inspiration for my book, *Two Dear Little Feet*."

She went on to describe how for generations men in Britain had been binding the mouths of their daughters, preventing them from being able to seize their rightful inheritance. As she said this, the roars from the crowd drowned out the cries of the seagulls circling above us.

"Our challenge is not only to create the New Woman but the New Man as well," she said. "I am referring to men who refuse to bind the feet of their wives and daughters, their female employees and friends, and whose cry is freedom too!"

The cheers were long and loud.

As the applause faded, she took me in her hands and raised me above her head.

The crowd fell silent.

"This is the very first edition of Miss Emily Swanson's famous and only book, *The Burning Ones*. It is a celebration of true love, the love of two who live to serve one another, where neither part exercises power to oppress the other but gives power away with a regard for their loved one's worth that is infinitely kind."

Every eye stared at me as the brine in the breeze touched my covers above the bloodred rose of my mistress's hat.

She finished by reading one of my mother's poems. As she did, the entire fabric of my being trembled and trembled as a gust of wind carried my mother's words beyond the thickening crowds and out towards the thunderous surf and the restless sea.

The cheers and applause that followed her speech were longer and more heartfelt than for any other speaker along the Pilgrim's Way, or any of the bold protestors who were to address the massed crowds in

Hyde Park at our journey's end in the City of London. I was never prouder of Miss Sarah than I was that day. As we returned home to her beloved Kent, many of her fellow liberators' hands touched my covers in homage. My spine vibrated with the sound of their songs.

None of us knew that the next year, war would break out, putting an end to all the marches. Women were put to men's work, while the men were away fighting at the front. This assumption of men's roles did more for the women's cause than anything orchestrated by the Suffragists or the Suffragettes. From the munition's factories to the railways, women showed that they were equal to men in capability and ingenuity. While men fought for freedom in the trenches in France, using weapons fashioned by the hands of women back home, women fought for their own freedom at home, using tasks and talents assumed to be the province of men alone. These were my mistress's views, in any case.

During the Great War, as it was called, my mistress opened a depot where she and others collected clothes for refugees and turned parts of old army uniforms into pen wipers. In her spare time, I learned that she had lunches in Margate with the novelist Thomas Hardy and the poet Siegfried Sassoon. All the while, I stood on a shelf in her room, alongside her own books, *The Heavenly Twins*, *Babs the Impossible, Adnam's Orchard* and *The Winged Victory*.

At the end of the war, my mistress was now in her sixties, and she moved to the spa town of Bath when she was invited by some friends to retire and rest at their newly bought mansion, Crowe Hall. It was a perfect location to look back upon her life in a spirit of tranquillity. Surrounded by nearly forty acres of forests, she took walks on the terrace and looked down over the lime trees and oaks into the deep valley below. Then she would turn back towards the French windows and enter through a door in the south-facing façade into the study and library, whose shelves were filled with books. There she would sit and read.

This lasted until 1922 when, at the age of sixty-eight, Miss Sarah was appointed first lady of the city of Bath and became Mayoress. The role was established at the instigation of a widower called Cedric Chivers, the Mayor of Bath. He had made his fortune as a bookbinder and had set up companies not only in Bath, but in London and New York, crossing the Atlantic over 100 times. Miss Sarah and he therefore not only shared civic duties but a deep appreciation of books.

I remember the day she showed me to him.

He admired my every page.

He was a booklover, just like her.

My guardian set about attending civic functions, opening buildings, gracing flower shows, making speeches, and handing out certificates, all of which she did with charm, causing her to become admired. But the duties, which increased when Mister Chivers' health began to fail, took their toll and, after two years, my mistress needed a holiday. She decided to go back to Paris, reflecting that it would be good if she spent three weeks in the Spring of 1924 cycling through the streets. She had always taken the view that women in midlife should cycle for up to four or five miles a day, which she regarded as enough for healthy exercise, but not enough for fatigue. "Women incline towards indolence," she once said to a friend. "Regular exercise in the outdoors is unfavourable to flabbiness." In the 1890s, especially in the aftermath of *The Heavenly Twins*, she had become one of the world's most famous 'lady cyclists.'

This plan was confirmed when a friend of hers from London visited Crowe Hall in February. Her name was

Anne-Marie, like the gardener's daughter at Hougoumont, although she preferred to be called Mary. She was wealthy, being the daughter of a prominent lawyer, and beautiful. She had brown skin and short, curly black hair, parted in the middle. Her father had arranged for her to be married to an Englishman but she, being well-read as well as well-off, had fallen for an impoverished poet, whose writings she had come across in *The Crisis.* She visited Miss Sarah at Crowe Hall and heard that her friend was planning a trip to Paris. She knew that this was where her poet friend was living at the time. Having shared the story of her love with my mistress, she suggested they go together. My mistress had nodded. "Your suggestion is timely," she said.

Our visitor looked confused, so Miss Sarah continued. "I should show you this," she said. She presented me to Mary who studied my pages for a moment and then smiled, saying that she thought the book was fearfully and wonderfully made.

Just then a young woman entered.

"My granddaughter Beth," my guardian said. "She is a most interesting person, by the far the most interesting in my somewhat dull family. She is of a mystical disposition."

Beth blushed.

"On one occasion, I saw her in a trance, writing automatically on a score of white pages. It turned out to be a most intriguing and original short story. It really should be published."

"That's astonishing," Mary said.

"Tell Mary about your dream, Beth."

Beth blushed again.

"Don't be shy," my guardian said.

"It was about a week ago," Beth said, her voice low.

"Speak up, child."

"It was about a week ago," Beth said, louder this time. "The dream was about Miss Swanson's book. I saw my grandmother giving it away to a man in Paris. He looked as if he'd fallen on hard times."

Mary gasped.

"There's more," my guardian said, gesturing to her granddaughter to continue her tale.

"The poet was dark skinned, like you, Mary."

Mary gasped again.

"The poet I love is the same," she said. "His great grandparents and grandparents were slaves in the south. There was mixed blood in the family. One of his ancestors was raped by a white plantation owner, hence the lighter skin."

Beth frowned.

"I hope the dream encourages you," she said.

"It does."

"So, you see," my guardian said, "Our sojourn to Paris seems to be written in the stars."

Mary nodded.

"When do we leave?" she asked.

The two ladies agreed the date.

It would be in eight weeks.

When the time came, my guardian took me to London where she met Mary. We took the train to Dover, crossed the Channel to France, and then travelled to the Gard Du Nord in Paris.

On the train to Paris, my guardian asked, "Have I ever told you the story about what happened to a copy of my novel *The Heavenly Twins* owned by a woman who loved the book?"

Mary shook her head.

"She was travelling on a train to a remote village on the coast of Sussex when she fell asleep reading the novel. To be frank with you, I was not surprised to learn that. The book is interminably long and, truth be told, there are probably three novels in the one volume."

Mary smiled.

"When she arrived in Sussex, she woke with a start, left the carriage in a great hurry, not realising that her precious volume was still on the train. When she arrived at her lodging, she was appalled to discover her loss and rushed back to the station."

I shuddered at the thought.

"When she got there, the train had departed, along with the book, so she had the station master send a telegraph to the terminus. It simply read, 'Heavenly Twins left in first class carriage.'"

"Whatever happened?"

"She received her reply."

"What did it say?"

"No trace of the twins."

Mary uttered a long and delightful laugh, more of a series of squeaks and gasps than a bellow or guffaw.

An hour later, we arrived at the busy station in Paris, full of steam and whistles. We were now in the same city where my guardian had purchased me from the kindly Monsieur Alfred at the auction house. A wave of memories broke upon the shores of my mind.

As my guardian carried me out of the railway station, I could not help thinking of Beth. The night before we left, she had come into the sitting room and sat down, a strange look in her eyes.

"You will give the book to the poet," she said.

"I will," my guardian had replied.

"There's something you need to know."

"What is it, child?"

"I had another dream."

"And?"

"And the poet will only keep it for a short while. Although he will esteem it, he will open its covers only once. Do not be troubled by this. He is a go-between, not a guardian."

After saying these words, Beth had a fainting fit and fell back onto the sedan chair. My guardian revived her with some brandy.

I looked on from a mahogany table, concerned about the prophecy. Suddenly, I wanted to remain in the care of Sarah Grand. She had confessed to her friend Maud that she did not possess the natural instincts of a mother.

That may have been true for Archie, but it was not true for me. She had loved, honoured, and held me.

Was I to be condemned to a season of neglect?

What troubles and cares lay ahead of me?

Part 7
1924

In Topeka, as a small child, my mother took me
with her to the little vine-covered library on the
grounds of the Capitol. There I first fell in love with
librarians . . . The silence inside the library, the
big chairs, and long tables, and the fact that the
library was always there and didn't seem to have
a mortgage on it, or any sort of insecurity about
it – all of that made me love it. And right there,
even before I was six, books began to happen to
me, so that after a while, there came a time when
I believed in books more than in people.

Langston Hughes (1901-1967)

Spring arrived late that year in Paris, but when it did, green leaves filled the trees, and the aroma of coffee scented the streets. Arriving late afternoon, Miss Sarah and her friend Mary put on fashionable dresses and headed out to a nightclub in Montmartre called the *Grand Duc*. Mary's poet friend worked there in the kitchen.

"Mister Hughes, it's a pleasure to meet you," Miss Sarah said as the poet walked into the bar at 7pm. A dark-skinned woman was playing a doleful melody on the piano.

"Please, call me Lang," he said.

Lang was a short man. He had black hair – thin at the front, thick at the back – light brown skin and a kind smile. As well as some shiny spats, he sported a grey suit with white squares, and a white shirt with a patterned blue tie, drawn right up to the neck of his white collar.

"Tell me, Lang," Miss Sarah said. "What is that music?"

"It's the Blues – a genre of music that has its roots in the songs our grandparents and great grandparents sang while their white masters were oppressing them on the plantations."

Miss Sarah frowned.

Just then, a pretty waitress appeared, her skin darker than the poet's. She had sparkling eyes and painted lips.

"Hey there, Lang. You want something?"

He turned to Miss Sarah and Miss Mary.

"You hungry?"

They nodded.

"This is on me," Mary said.

The poet smiled and kissed Mary's hand. Her eyes and soft brown skin seemed to shine a little.

"Let's have champagne," Miss Sarah said.

"Champagne it is, Bessy," the poet said, speaking to the waitress. "And bring some Chicken Maryland."

He turned back to Miss Sarah. "The chef – my boss – is famous for his southern treat."

He then spoke to the waitress. "Please tell Florence to play my favourite song."

Bessy strutted on high heels to the piano player and whispered in her ear. When Florence finished her song, she gestured to five men sitting nearby. They strolled to the small stage and took up their instruments. Trumpet, saxophone, double bass, trombone, and clarinet. Florence yielded her stool to a large man in a loose suit. She stood centre stage, took a microphone, and began to sing.

Frankie and Johnnie were lovers
O Lordy, how they could love

Swore to be true to each other
Truer than the sun above
He was her man
But he was doing her wrong.

I was under Miss Sarah's shawl, lying on her waist. I could feel her toes keeping time to the beat. She could not take her eyes off the singer, who was resplendent in an evening gown the colours of a goldfinch, a crown of orchids upon the slick black waves of her hair.

When the song ended, the room erupted.

"Did you like it?" the poet asked, opening a holder, placing an unfiltered cigarette between his brown lips, and lighting it with a frail match from a tiny *Grand Duc* branded packet.

"I loved it," Miss Sarah.

"Welcome to the weary blues," he said.

"It's a strange sound," she said. The song is sad, but the singing of it seems happy."

"Eureka!" Mary said with a clap and a laugh.

"You've just penetrated the mysterious aesthetic of the blues," Lang said. "We laugh to keep from crying."

"I can relate to that," Miss Sarah said.

The poet looked deep into her soul with his dark, exquisite eyes. He knew that she knew. He did not ask. He did not pry. He exhaled some smoke and uttered a sigh.

When the food arrived, it was carried by an enormous, African American man with only one functioning eye. His name was Bruce and he worked in the kitchens as the principal chef of the *Grand Duc*.

"Thanks, boss," the poet said as oval plates were laid at each setting, with the food in the centre of the table.

"Fried chicken in the middle," Bruce said, pointing to some crispy wings, legs, and thighs. "These are corn fritters around the edge, corn bread, and these are beans, baked the way we like them in New England."

Miss Sarah frowned.

Bruce turned to Miss Sarah, his one eye gazing at her. "You from Old England, ma'am?"

"She's a famous English novelist, boss," the poet said.

As they tucked into the feast, Florence took to the stage and began to sing again. This time she began to circle the tables. She lingered around wealthy white Americans, taunting them with her languid eyes and soft furs, refusing their invitations to sit with them.

"Back home," the poet said after the song had finished, "this could never happen. Here, in Paris, it's different. There is greater equality, which is one of many reasons why there are so many African Americans in Montmartre, especially musicians."

Florence stepped down again from the stage and stood next to the poet. She smiled at him, then reached out her long, thin arm and took him by the hand. Hurling her furs over her shoulder with her other hand, she led the poet to the stage.

"Ladies and gentlemen, our sous-chef poet here at the *Grand Duc*, Mister Langston Hughes, will read some of his weary blues."

Florence sat at the piano and began to play. After a few notes, the poet spoke about rivers, and of how his soul had grown deep like rivers that are ancient, older than the pyramids. He spoke about being neither white nor black in a black-and-white world. He spoke about African dance and the low beating of the tom-toms, and of how the negro is as black as the night is black. He spoke about having the weary blues but of not being satisfied. All of it poured like a silver river from his soul.

Before he returned to the table, he said that he was dedicating the final poem to Miss Mary. He began to speak about roaming the night together with his beloved, of travelling across the rooftops of Harlem under the blue light of the moon, singing together while jazz music played in the cabarets below. He ended with an invitation to roam the night together, with songs on our lips.

His words stirred my soul. They carried traces of my mother's lines about roaming, searching, lovers.

As the sound of the poet's voice drifted away and the last notes from the piano faded, the audience clapped, and the poet returned.

"That last poem," Miss Sarah said, once the room was quieter. "It sounded like the Song of Songs."

The poet smiled. "I heard that part of the Bible read many times when I was growing up in Lawrence."

"Are you a religious man, Lang?"

Lang did not answer. He said, "My old pastor in Lawrence used to say that the woman in that poem was black, like an African. He loved quoting her words, 'I am dark, but comely.'"

"I am dark *and* comely," Mary said with a coy smile, tipping her shoulder towards the poet, who kissed it.

Miss Sarah said, "Who else has influenced you?"

"Whitman. Especially Whitman."

Lang bowed his head and recited a poem in which Whitman heard the whole of America singing. Carpenters. Mechanics. Masons. Boatmen. Deckhands. Shoemakers. Hatmakers. Woodcutters. Plough boys. Mothers, homemakers, and seamstresses. All joining in a chorus of song.

"What I love," the poet said, "is Whitman's democracy. He embraces everyone and he does so by using free verse and plain language, language that ordinary people can understand."

"Like Mark Twain," Miss Sarah said.

"Yes," the poet said. "He also is one of my heroes."

"I met him in the early 90s," Miss Sarah said.

"Say what?"

"When I was on a lecture tour in America."

The poet smiled, lit a cigarette, and inhaled.

"Did you notice something about all the people Whitman talks about?" Lang asked.

"They are, I suppose, working class," my mistress replied.

"Precisely. I want to write poems that appeal to the poorest black people in America. Which is why I've written my own homage to Whitman, a poem called 'I, Too', about African Americans being included in that great chorus of voices that make up the American soul."

"Singing the blues," Miss Sarah added.

"Not just the Blues. Poetry. Paintings. Plays. Sculptures. Movies. All emanating from men and women of colour in Harlem."

I thought of my mother's verses as he spoke.

"Sounds like a renaissance," Miss Sarah said.

The poet smiled.

After Florence had sung another snatch of songs, the poet beckoned Bessy back to the table and asked for a box of dominoes. He then set about placing a deck of 28 rectangular tiles on the table. Each tile was made of bone and had black pips painted on their pale facades. The pips numbered between one and six. There was a dividing line in the centre of each piece, and these pips were located both sides of it in two square ends. The pieces made a clicking sound as bone connected with wood.

For the next hour, the three of them divided into pairs and played each other. They manoeuvred their tiles this way and that until Mary had won. After the poet had proposed a toast to the champion, Mary put all the pieces back into their container.

"You see," the poet said. "In the end, all the pieces, black and white, they go back in the box together."

"No segregation," Mary said, showing the contents.

There was a pause as the poet lit another cigarette.

"Do you think there will ever be unity and equality between black and white," Miss Sarah asked.

"Do you think there will ever be unity and equality between men and women?" the poet asked.

"There are some women," Miss Sarah said, "who would almost do away with men, but I am for fairness between the sexes, not for replacing one form of oppression with another."

"How do you see this happening?" the poet asked.

"The New Woman."

"And what is the New Woman?"

"I would say that she is someone who decides of her own free will to be the best version of femininity, as opposed to some distorted and ugly version of masculinity."

The poet smiled. "We have a similar term," he said. "The New Negro. So, you see, we are not far apart in our longings."

"It's time for the walls to come down and for bridges to be built," Miss Sarah said. "The dead stone wall erected by men is crumbling."

The poet took another drag. His eyes seemed almost luminous now. "Yes indeed. She can swim, row, ride, wrestle, shoot, run, strike, retreat, advance, resist, defend herself."

Miss Sarah looked curious.

"Not my words," he said.

"Whose then?"

"They belong to Walt Whitman in his poem 'A Woman Waits For Me'. He gleaned his revolutionary view of women, he said, from his experience of the Quakers ..."

"I am a Quaker," Miss Sarah interjected. "In my faith, women are regarded as the equals of men. We have the right to lead and speak, as the Spirit wills, in accordance with the revelation of the inner light."

"Then you are truly loosed of all limits," the poet said.

"We still have such a long way to go," she muttered.

Lang nodded.

"Do you know what men say of the female brain?" she asked.

The poet shook his head.

"They say it is smaller and lighter than that of a man."

The poet looked startled.

"And that we are therefore created by God and condemned by science to be inferior."

"People of colour face a similar humiliation," he said. "White people claim the relationship between a human's forehead and their jaw reveals their intelligence. White people have a near vertical relation. Ignorant folks say that black people have a more horizontal relationship, like apes. We are therefore primitive and underdeveloped."

"Your poetry is the proof of their stupidity," Miss Sarah said.

With that, Mary closed the box of dominos and the band began to play again.

As the evening wore on, Lang headed to the kitchens for his night shift, saying that he would be back later.

"You won't always be in the kitchen," Miss Sarah said.

The poet's eyes shone again. Then he began to speak. "Today, they send the dark brother to the kitchen. But there I eat well and get strong. Tomorrow, I will be sitting at the table with everyone else. No one will dismiss me to the kitchens then. They'll see how beautiful I am and realize that I too am America!"

As he walked towards the kitchen, Mary watched his every step, gazing at his disappearing form as if she was his shadow.

"You love him, don't you?"

Mary's eyes watered, and she nodded.

In what seemed like no time, the bottle of champagne was lying empty on a bed of ice in the silver bucket by the table.

"Look there!" Mary said

Outside the lamps were burning brightly and a crowd of people had gathered at the entrance of the *Grand Duc*. A man with darker skin and a rounder face than the poet's appeared from nowhere. The people cheered, made way for him, and let him pass.

"That's Palmer Jones," she said. "Florence's husband. He plays piano at the Ambassadors Club. He then comes and joins his wife for an hour before the musicians from all the other clubs congregate here for a session of spontaneous playing. It's spectacular."

It truly was.

For the next hour, Palmer played, and Florence sang. There was such a unity between them, not just in melody, but in movement.

At the end of a song, Miss Sarah took me from underneath her shawl.

"I'm going to give your friend this book," she said.

"Are you sure?"

"Yes. I don't know how long he will keep it, but while he is its guardian, my prayer is that the same spirit that moved its author will move the man you love to a deeper ecstasy of body and soul."

"Oh, I pray that too!"

Mary looked around the restaurant and bar, looking for her love, but he was still away, serving in the shadows.

A little while later, when the sun came up, the poet reappeared with a rich roast of coffee and steaming croissants.

Mary squealed with delight.

"It's high time for me to retire to my bed," Miss Sarah said.

She was about to leave when she said, "I wanted to ask you something, Lang."

She placed me on the table

"Do you love books?"

He answered, "Books can be both a blessing and a curse."

"A curse?"

"They carry traces, memories of the times in your life when you read them, and those memories can sometimes be traumatic, tarnishing the value of the book in your estimation."

Miss Sarah's face was full of curiosity.

"When I boarded a ship to Africa, I possessed a box of books I'd had in Harlem, books that had, through no fault of their own, associations with the traumas from my childhood and my youth. These books had been happening to me since I was a boy, before I was six years old."

"Happening to you?"

"Yes, they had been a happening in my life, just as you are. Books are like people. They come into our lives just when you need them.

"Do you still have them?"

"I threw them overboard."

Even Mary gasped.

"Why?"

"I wanted to leave the past behind."

As he said this, I found myself overwhelmed with gratitude. Miss Sarah had possessed me throughout her ordeals with her cruel husband. Not once had she shown any inclination of abandoning me to wave or flame. She had always cherished me and kept me safe, and for that I found myself profoundly thankful.

"Do you have any books at all?"

He shook his head.

"Then I would like to give you this as a gift, the first book to happen to you in your new life as a poet of the renaissance that you speak about. It's the very first edition, so do take special care of it."

He studied my cover, my spine, my title, my cover pages, everything.

A look of wonder filled his eyes.

"I don't believe this! This is a book I have loved from a distance for a long time, an author I have longed to get to know, one with whom I have always felt a strong affinity."

"Emily was just like you, Lang, a freedom fighter too," Miss Sarah said. "And now I hand her precious book onto you."

"Thank you. Truly. And to have the first edition, with these drawings of William Blake. They shine as the words do."

Miss Sarah nodded.

"If you should ever pass it on," her face was more serious now. "Make sure its new guardian will parent it properly. In the meantime, for however long or short it is in your hands, let it be your adopted child, your pride and joy, the apple of your eye. Then let it be theirs too."

"I will."

"One more thing," Miss Sarah said as she rose.

The poet looked at her.

"Don't ever throw this book into the sea."

With that, she cast a final glance at me, then left.

I spent just three months with my new master, all at no 15, *Rue Nollet* near the *Place Clichy*. Lang and Mary lived at the top of the house. The only other people I saw there was a couple in their eighties. At eight o'clock at night, they would shuffle in and she, with squinting eyes and wrinkled face, would dust the room, including my covers.

When Lang and Mary returned each day from the *Grand Duc*, it was always around eight o'clock in the morning. They would have breakfast in one of the cafés of Montmartre and then slump into bed. They held each other until the afternoon when they would leave for a café. Sometimes they would catch a matinée and watch a movie, a revue, or a play. At other times they would dance at the Moulin Rouge and stroll hand in hand in the woods at Versailles. He would mimic her very English accent, and she would do the same with his "very American, American voice."

"Let's elope and go to Italy," Mary said one day.

The poet wiped his bleary eyes.

"Do you think that's a good idea?"

"If we go now, before my family realises what I'm really doing here, we'll stand a chance of starting a new life."

Mary had come to Paris under the pretence of studying at Raymond Duncan's school of weaving in Paris. She never attended classes but had sent several ornate cloths woven with her own hand back to her father in London to strengthen the illusion.

"But when your father finds out, he will cut your allowance."

"So what? Isn't it better to live in poverty and love well than to live in abundance but never love at all?"

"I have nothing, Mary. My father warned me. A negro trying to make a living off writing is foolishness.

"Please come away, my darling, my beautiful one," Mary said. "Come away with me."

"It is impossible."

Mary could see that he was intransigent. She burst into tears and fell upon his shoulder. After a while, she pulled away, looked into his dry eyes, and asked, "Do you never cry, Lang?"

"Not since I was twelve years old."

Two days later, Lang decided that Mary should go back to England. Mary protested, but the poet was intransigent.

They had one final day together, eating in a restaurant at the top of Montmartre's hill, in the shadow of Sacré-Coeur's pale basilica.

They walked and walked until they were tired.

Mary bought the poet a red rose and then they headed back to the house, bringing cones of strawberries up the steep stairs to the attic room where they sat in silence, dipping the fruit into a jar of cream and staring out of the gabled window at the sloping roofs of Paris.

When they had finished, they remained on the stone window seat for a long time.

Mary was sobbing.

At last, he said, "My little love from London. You must return to Piccadilly. Our hearts may be broken, but they still beat."

She stopped crying.

Pulling herself together, she rose and took one more look at the city. It seemed as if she was trying to stop time itself.

The poet took her by the arm and led her down the steep stairs to the street below.

There he hailed a carriage.

I could hear her crying again.

"Hurry now, Mary," the poet said. "You will miss your train."

When Lang reappeared, he sat at the dressing table, and he began to compose new lines. He talked of Mary as a song that he could not sing for overlong, as a prayer that he could not utter everywhere, and finally a rose that could not stay when summer goes. He penned another poem, once again comparing his love with a rose, celebrating his belief in the symbol, but forgetting the reality – that flowers, and their perfume, wither in an hour. Then a third poem, about the breath of a rose, being no more. It seemed to me that he needed this *tristesse* to compose these lines and to sing his blues, and I wondered if this had been the whole point of it all. As that thought lingered, I grieved for Mary.

But then, for the poet too.

I felt for him.

Trapped between two worlds.

I knew this state.

For I was neither slave nor free.

Trapped in ambiguity.

Just like him.

After Mary left, Lang decided to take me to his favourite bookstore, Shakespeare & Co, on the *Rue de l'Odéon*. When we arrived, I marvelled at the place. Its shelves and rooms were bursting with books. It reminded me of my mother's house in Holt. There were people exploring every nook and cranny, gazing into the pages, as if passing through paper portals into another world.

"Hey, Lang," a woman said, seeing the poet enter. She had wavy dark hair and eyes that went right through you.

"Sylvia!"

Everyone who knew anything about books in Paris knew Sylvia Beach. James Joyce, a frequenter of her shop, had written a controversial novel called *Ulysees* and Miss Sylvia had taken the brave step of publishing it. This work had become famous, and her shop with it. In the summer of 1924, it was a beehive of eager readers and famous authors.

One of these was now standing next to her, leaning on a cane, a lanky man with a huge uncombed head of red hair, a pointed beard, and a thin moustache. Around his neck there was an enlarged tie with what looked like hand-painted flowers in the Japanese style. His trousers were bright green, fashioned out of billiard cloth. He looked like a parrot.

"May I introduce you to Langston Hughes, Ezra," she said.

"I've heard of you," Ezra said in a nasal drawl. "You're the one who writes for the working-class negroes back home. It's all a little too low-brow for me, to be frank with you."

"Each one to his own," Lang said.

Ezra laughed. "I prefer the poetry of your more refined and enlightened colleague, Countee Cullen," he said. "In fact, don't they call him the poet laureate of Harlem, and you the poet lowrate?"

"And don't they refer to you as John the Baptist to the Crooked Jesus, James Joyce?"

As Ezra turned away with a wince, Lang took me out of a packet and presented me to Miss Sylvia.

"This is absolutely priceless," she said. "Where did you get it?"

"Miss Sarah Grand gave it to me, here in Paris, just a few weeks ago. I have always been a fan."

"Sarah Grand, you say. I have a signed, first edition of *The Heavenly Twins* here in the shop. It is a strange book. Too long, rambling, and loosely structured, but it was extremely significant for the women's righters in the 90s, and I'm proud to have a copy."

Just then, she seemed to have an idea.

"Will you do something for me, Lang? Will you read some of your poems to us while you're here in my shop?"

"In return for a good lunch, yes."

"We have a deal," she said. She clapped her hands and called everyone to attention in her strong American voice. "Ladies and gentlemen, Mister Langston Hughes, one of the leading voices of the Harlem renaissance, will read to us."

Within moments, the ground floor of the shop was crowded with book buyers and writers.

"Mister Langston Hughes, the floor is yours."

"You know," Lang said, looking around the room. "There are writers who delight in making simple things hard. They write for the elites and their audience is small. But then there are those who make hard things simple. They write for everyone, and their audience is huge. Never use language as a means of widening the gap between people. Use words to liberate, not to oppress – to unite, not divide."

He recited a poem he had written in the Spring, entitled, 'To Certain Intellectuals,' in which he made the message clear.

The crowd clapped, and the room emptied.

All except one man, another tall American, more broad-shouldered than the man called Ezra, with more colour in his cheeks and more kindness in his eyes.

"I agree with you," he whispered to Lang. "But don't tell Mister Pound," he added with a smile. "He is my friend, and he means well. He has helped many aspiring writers, including me."

With that, he walked away.

"Who was that?" Lang asked.

"An American journalist who's written some stories and poems. Name's Ernest Hemingway."

"I will look out for his work in the future."

As Miss Sylvia handed him twenty francs for his lunch, he thought for a moment. "You know, my time in Paris is almost done and I have plans to travel around Italy before heading home. I'm desperately short of cash. Would you buy this from me?"

Miss Sylvia smiled. "I could give you Miss Sarah Grand's first edition, and some cash. Then you'd have both an investment and the money to see you through until you get back to the States."

The poet smiled.

"Let's do it."

Miss Sylvia fetched the volume, and the money, and the deal was sealed. I had a new guardian and the poet from Harlem had his money. My home was in Paris now, in a house that was not just a store for books, but a lending library, a home for impoverished writers and booklovers.

For me, it was heaven on earth.

At least, for a while.

Part 8

1924-1962

A bookshop is mostly tiresome details all day long and you have to have a passion for it, to grub and grub in it. I have always loved books and their authors, and for the sake of them, swallowed the rest of it, but you can't expect everyone to do the same.

Sylvia Beach (1887-1962)

Shakespeare and Company was a home to works of literature written in the English language. What Miss Sylvia Beach had built there was a bookshop, museum, and lending library, all in one. Some volumes could be bought. Others, of a more antique and precious value like me, were to be admired. The rest were borrowed, with a label portraying Shakespeare adhered to the first page to remind the reader to bring the book back to its home. Here the greatest writers of the age conducted readings. Ezra Pound, T.S. Eliot, Ernest Hemingway, and others awakened the love of countless bibliophiles in Paris, causing many to regard Shakespeare and Company as more representative of American culture than the embassy itself. To begin with, these were days of calm. The halcyon bird with brilliant wings was hovering over us, bringing joy to our doors.

Miss Sylvia had come up with the idea when she had seen the French bookshop opposite. The woman who ran it was called Miss Adrienne and her store was called *The Friends of Books*. One time, I heard Miss Sylvia tell of how she had first met her. "When I crossed the street and entered her shop, Adrienne welcomed me. When I told her of my dream of establishing a bookshop containing only American and English works, she could not have been more helpful. She went out of her way to advise me how to get started which, thanks to a gift of money from my mother, I was poised to do. She was simply wonderful to me."

At this point, Miss Sylvia paused and her eyes glistened.

"When I left her shop, a strong gust of wind blew down the street, causing me to tumble and my hat to fly off my head. Adrienne saw this, ran out, retrieved my hat, then helped me to my feet. When I looked into her eyes, I saw they were a very striking blue-grey colour, just like William Blake's. From that moment, I was smitten. We became business partners and so much more. Our shops stand face-to-face, as we do, forever smiling upon each other."

It was truly a piece of heaven on earth.

But then, as in many an Arcadia, trouble came. An Irish author exploited Miss Sylvia from the beginning to the end of his association with her. I am referring to James Joyce. JJ, as I called him, was a complicated man, in my eyes at least. He was the exact opposite of my mistress, who entertained no thought to herself and who gave her body and soul to supporting someone whose lack of self-awareness knew no bounds. Miss Sylvia was the only person who was prepared to take the risk of publishing *Ulysses*, a novel of his that was rejected by publishers who were in fear of being prosecuted because of its contents.

One day, Miss Sylvia explained why she took this project on in a conversation with her sister. Miss Cyprian was a famous actress and, like her, was bilingual. She had appeared in many popular films in Paris during the 1920s. As a champion of silent cinema, she represented a new medium, one I wondered from the start if it might signal an end to reading books. Like Miss Sylvia, I was anxious whether one day the screen would replace the page, putting places like Shakespeare and Company at risk. The conversation about JJ began with the two sisters debating the merits of both film and book.

"Look at *Les Trois Mousquetaires*," Cyprian said one evening in my guardian's office. "It has revived an interest in Dumas's books."

"But it leaves nothing to the imagination," Miss Sylvia replied. "When people read the original, they are free to paint their own pictures of the characters. Monsieur Berger's film does it all for you."

While she was talking to her sister, Cyprian was sitting at a desk in the backroom doing some accounting and record keeping for the mounting expenses generated by JJ's lavish lifestyle.

She stopped and turned to her sister. Miss Sylvia was at that very moment writing letters on behalf of JJ to an American man called Mister Samuel Roth. He had recently pirated the Shakespeare and Company imprint of *Ulysses* and was serializing it in one of his publications in America. He was a man without a conscience.

"Why did you take on this man, Sylvia? It is consuming all your time and depleting your funds."

She replied. "Do you remember when we were growing up in Bridgetown, when father was the parson there?"

"You were sick a lot," Cyprian replied. "That's my abiding memory. Headaches, I think it was."

"Yes, I had to spend many hours in the parlour, lying on a divan, missing school and church. But there was a bookcase there with the complete works of Shakespeare."

"I remember."

"Do you recall which volume was missing?"

"I think it was *Hamlet*."

"And do you remember why?"

"Granny burned it."

"That's right. She objected to Hamlet saying, 'Lady, shall I lie in thy lap?' I'm sure you remember it."

Just then, an old fear began to surface once again and I trembled, even as the light in the room seem to flicker, threatening to fail altogether. I could not believe that an entire book could be consigned to the flames just because one line had caused offence.

"I took on *Ulysses*," Miss Sylvia said, "because I do not believe that anyone should be denied access to a work of literary merit. There are too many censorious souls abroad who, like Granny, would kill a book before its birth, or cremate it once it has entered the world."

"But he's taking all the royalties, leaving you with nothing. He's treating this shop like a bank. He thinks that just because his book has made this shop more prominent that this is reward enough. Well, it isn't Sylvia. He's not worth it. He's going to bankrupt you."

Miss Sylvia lit a cigarette.

"The book has made my place famous," she said. "And he's fun to have around. A good mixer too."

"But you have rescued no publisher's benefit from the book because he's taking 66% of the profit from each copy. And I agree with Adrienne, who is not impressed by the book anyway, not at all."

"She likes the second part," Miss Sylvia said.

"That may so, but she said of the whole novel that it baffles and mortifies her. Why would you want to support such a work? Why would you want to promote such an author?"

"His book sells well. As do works by other moderns, T.S. Eliot for example. More than Blake and Whitman combined."

"But the multiple services you offer him are free."

"His is the profit. Mine is the pleasure."

"Yet Shakespeare and Company is in danger of being sucked under, drowning, and disappearing, all because of his greed. This beautiful shop is now little more than the James Joyce bank."

Miss Sylvia stubbed out her cigarette. Her brown eyes darted around the room, nervous and restless.

"And he doesn't fit in," Cyprian said.

"How do you mean?"

"Haven't you noticed the way he addresses people?"

Miss Sylvia allowed herself a tiny smile.

"He is so un-American. He refers to you as Miss Beach when our compatriots call you Sylvia."

"I do admit," Sylvia said, "he believes God created Shakespeare and Company for him and him alone. He now even has Adrienne translating his novel into French."

"There's a dark side to his character," Cyprian said.

"What do you mean?"

"I mean that in this very room he moaned about Picasso receiving 20,000 to 30,000 francs for a few hours work while he labours thousands of hours for a pittance. He didn't seem able to celebrate another artist's fortune and success."

Cyprian leaned forward towards her sister.

"And I am not convinced he likes women."

"He is very polite to me," Miss Sylvia objected.

"Chivalry in men can be a smokescreen for contempt. You mark my words, Sylvia, he will breach the contract you drew up for *Ulysses*. He will take from you, spend extravagantly, then come back and back, asking you for more. He is an orphan at heart. Admit it."

My guardian remained silent.

Cyprian stirred herself for more.

"Listen Sylvia, he escaped from his mother, from his mother church, and from his mother country, and he now uses you, his benefactress, as his mother. And as surely as he abandoned them, he will abandon you."

Silence again.

"Look at these ledgers, Sylvia. He makes $5000 every year from his novel. How much goes into Shakespeare and Company? He feels no financial obligation to you whatsoever."

Miss Sylvia rested her head on her hand, looking at the half-written letter on the table, a letter drumming up support from writers familiar with both Shakespeare and Company and JJ's work, petitioning Mister Roth in America to put a halt to his piracy.

Cyprian, who looked around again at her sister, lowered her voice. "When the character of an orphan and the calling of a writer are combined in the same person, there will always be trouble."

Miss Sylvia lit another cigarette while her dog Teddy snored at her feet, and her cat Lucky stretched out on a copy of *Moby Dick* on the armchair nearby.

"I don't find it funny either," my guardian said after a pause. She flicked some stray ash from her smoking jacket.

"Well, what are you going to do with him?"

Miss Sylvia paused, thought for a moment, then replied, "A baby belongs to its mother, not to the midwife, doesn't it?"

In 1933, after JJ had dropped Miss Sylvia overboard, Shakespeare and Company was feeling the squeeze. The excesses of the previous decade were now a guilty memory. American tourists had stopped coming to Paris and many of America's finest writers, who once made a regular pilgrimage to the sacred site of Shakespeare and Company, had left France to return to the United States. The year was accordingly one filled with anxiety and Miss Sylvia suffered from constant headaches. She was further exasperated to discover that JJ was conducting negotiations with Random House Publishers in the USA over a new edition of *Ulysses*. After that, she remained cordial with him in her correspondence, but things would never be the same. The last time he visited, he entered Miss Sylvia's office and left his wet umbrella on her desk, on top of several books that Miss Sylvia was labelling. They were blotched with water stains.

Chief among my mistress's worries was that the loss of *Ulysses* would ruin Shakespeare and Company.

In the end these were unfounded. Having relinquished responsibility for looking after his affairs, Miss Sylvia began to realise the full extent of the drain on her resources, both financial and emotional. She began to feel like her old self again. The migraines diminished. Her conversations were punctuated, as in the old days, with her sudden and lively bouts of laughter. Her brown eyes recovered their greenish glint and her chestnut hair seemed full of vigour once more. Her accounts were no longer plundered by JJ and were stable, even in times of economic impoverishment. As the year ended, although she came to realise that she had made no profit at all from the novel, she also saw with a new clarity that her sister, who was planning to return to America, had been right in her judgement of JJ all along.

One man who continued to visit us was Ernest Hemingway. He loved Miss Sylvia, saying that no one was ever kinder to him during the years when he was a young journalist working in Paris for the Toronto Star. He was always good to her and, unlike JJ, never felt entitled to take liberties. She described him as a good old friend and was thrilled to see him succeeding as a writer.

Two weeks before Christmas 1933, Mister Hemingway sent a message saying that he was passing through Paris and that he and his latest wife Pauline would love to see her, Miss Adrienne, and Miss Cyprian should they all be in residence. Miss Sylvia answered that everyone he had mentioned would be in Paris and that her beloved Adrienne was delighted to cook Christmas dinner for them, after which everyone would be invited to read a favourite passage from a book of their choice. That is how I happened to be present, on Christmas Eve.

When we arrived, Miss Adrienne's rooms were alive with the sound of bubbling. She had been making pastries and preserving jam and was now preparing Christmas dinner. To please her distinguished American guests, who had not yet arrived, she added some homely comforts – stuffing, cranberries, sweet potatoes, and a festive dessert. She had also bought a gramophone and was playing Christmas melodies.

When Miss Sylvia carried me into the apartment, she embraced her friend. They were so different, these two – Adrienne plump and stout, Miss Sylvia lean and wiry. Adrienne had a placid, serene temperament, while Miss Sylvia was fidgety and prone to nervous fits of energy. Adrienne was a spiritual woman who loved to explore the mystical world, while Miss Sylvia rejected organised religion and was a self-confessed agnostic. But they were one in soul and vision. Their stores complimented each other and had become sacred spaces. Miss Adrienne's was referred to as the Monnier Chapel and Miss Sylvia's a place of worship where English-speaking pilgrims found a spiritual home.

Just then there was a loud knocking at the apartment door and Mister Hemingway and his wife strode into the sitting room.

"Papa! Pauline!" Adrienne exclaimed, ushering them towards the fireplace. Papa was a nickname which, for almost a decade, Hemingway had insisted everyone use of him. No one knew why.

Standing before the glowing fire and illuminated by the ceiling light, Mister Hemingway looked even more tanned than when I last saw him, although not enough to obscure a livid scar on his forehead. Miss Pauline, a beautiful woman with short black hair, cut almost in a boyish style, rubbed her hands in front of the flames. A pair of emerald earrings swung from her earlobes, catching the light of the fire.

Papa reached out towards Adrienne and enveloped her in his tall, muscular frame.

Miss Sylvia was to follow. She, being so short, seemed to disappear altogether.

"You look well," Adrienne said.

"We've just been on a safari in Africa," Pauline said.

"Cost us a fortune," Papa added, removing his floppy hat. "$22,000 to be precise. Here, look at these." He withdrew some photographs from his faded raincoat. They revealed five lions that he and his shooting party had killed. The sorry creatures lay lifeless at their captor's feet.

"Well, the trip has left you looking fine and handsome," Miss Sylvia said, "Unlike those poor cats!"

"I agree," Pauline commented, taking his arm, leaning towards his cheek, and planting a kiss there. She then removed her fur coat just as Adrienne announced that dinner was served.

Towards the end of the dessert course, Cyprian, who had imbibed enough wine to loosen her inhibitions as well as her tongue, began to talk about how miraculous it was that Shakespeare and Company was still in business, given everything that the one she referred to as "the Crooked Jesus" had done.

"It's Christmas," Miss Sylvia said, interjecting. "Time for peace and goodwill to all men, including Mister Joyce."

"What has he done?" Papa asked.

"I know you and he are pals," Cyprian began.

"Drinking buddies," Papa qualified.

"Drinking buddies, then, but his conduct since my sister risked everything to publish his novel has been deplorable."

"You mean duplurable," Miss Pauline said, using one of JJ's distorted words, imitating his Irish voice.

When the mirth had subsided, Cyprian said, "His reputation will surely suffer, if he continues to behave like this."

"Reputations are like handkerchiefs," Pauline quipped, running her hand through her black bob. "They are easy to lose."

Miss Sylvia said, "I can see why Vogue magazine loves you. You have a way with words, just as you have a way with clothes."

It was true. Her Louiseboulanger suit was immaculately fitted, as immaculately fitted as her wit.

"But here's my question to you experts," Cyprian said, her shoulders swaying, her words slurring. "Do you think people with ugly personalities can produce beautiful works? Can a perverted film producer create a movie like *Napoleon*?"

Miss Sylvia responded first. "One of our most loyal supporters during the early days of Shakespeare and Company was Malcolm Cowley. Do you remember him?" There were some nods. "I recall him talking about this very subject on one occasion, and he said that he did not believe it was possible for a complete son-of-a-bitch to write a single, decent sentence. I remember thinking that was interesting."

Hemingway stirred. "But note Mister Cowley's words. He said a *complete* son-of-a-bitch. One can be a *partial* son-of-a-bitch and still write a good sentence or two."

"My experience of writers," Miss Sylvia said, "is that they are a strange and complicated mixture. Look at Ezra Pound. He is a true modernist, and capable of writing beautifully, but now he's off supporting Mussolini in Italy!"

"Writers are like everyone else," Adrienne said, her voice calm. "They contain elements of what E.M. Forster calls the monk and the beast. The way these two sides of their personalities fight for dominance in the soul is simply an exaggerated version of the same battle that takes place in all human beings, including us."

Cyprian drained an entire glass of wine. Then she said, "I think writers are selfish, amoral, acquisitive people. I agree with Faulkner, they wouldn't hesitate to rob their own mothers if it meant they could then produce their work."

Adrienne smiled. "I think it's time we retired to the sitting room and read to one another. Leave everything at the table."

Miss Sylvia was asked to read first. She picked me up and read her favourite passage, about the winter being over and the rains gone, the doves singing in the land and the blossoming vines spreading their fragrance.

When Miss Sylvia finished, she looked at Adrienne and smiled. She raised her glass and said, "To the end of winter and a happier and more prosperous spring!"

Adrienne went next and read a festive poem by Paul Claudel called the Song of the Christmas Procession. It was the song of a family making their pilgrimage to midnight mass. On the way, they invite the souls of the dead not to be afraid but to take their place among those making their way to church, even the half-believing, half-doubting. "He who loves us so much," she read, "who from their side would not give him love?" She raised her glass of champagne and quoted the poem, "Today the heavens have become mellifluous!"

"To mellifluous heavens!" Pauline cried.

Pauline then took hold of her T.S. Eliot. She read from 'The Journey of the Magi', introducing it by saying that as a Catholic she appreciated that this subject matter was more suited to Epiphany than Christmas Eve, but that she hoped everyone would understand. As she read in her rich American accent, I felt transported to the cold winter when the wise men visited the Christ Child. As she read, I could not help remembering my fellow inmate in the safe in Bruges, who sung of the nativity of Christ. As she concluded, she raised her glass and said, "*In solsitio brumali*! To the dead of winter!"

Cyprian followed with some pages from film director Abel Gance in which he eulogises about the silver screen, arguing that it brings back to life the greatest artists, as well as the heroes of myth and the founders of religion. "They all await their exposed resurrection," she read. "The heroes crowd each other at the gate!" She raised her glass. "To the music of light and to the wonders of listening with our eyes!"

When everyone had sat down, a discussion began about how Gance had filmed *Napoléon.* Cyprian told us that the legendary director had invented a kind of breastplate, or *cuirasse*, to support cameras that were too heavy for his cameramen to carry by hand.

I remembered the Cuirassiers at Waterloo, their silver armour glinting in the afternoon sun, as they rode not far from Sergeant Billy Massingham at Hougoumont.

Respecting the flow, Mister Hemingway recited lines from his friend, JJ's latest book, *Work in Progress*. Imitating the author's Irish accent, the brash American launched into a passage about a tour through the Waterloo Museum, or "museyroom", on the site of the battlefield in Belgium, which JJ had visited in 1926.

I was not impressed.

I thought that the author, for all his genius, had failed to do his homework with enough rigour. His details about the battle were, at times, wide of the mark and did not correspond to the reality of what had happened that day. He said that Wellington's horse was white. It was not. Copenhagen was a chestnut colour.

I was there.

The conversation returned to present times.

"Hitler's rise to power in Germany disturbs me deeply," Miss Sylvia said. "It will lead to war, I'm sure of it."

"They are burning books," Pauline said.

I could almost feel the flames.

"Including mine!" Papa interjected, his voice raised, his forehead furrowed, his veins bulging.

Cyprian gasped. "Are you serious?"

"I am. In May this year, the benighted German students burned every copy of *A Farewell to Arms* they could find, throwing them into bonfires on the streets, along with every book by Jewish authors."

"But you're not Jewish," Cyprian said.

"My novel is deemed by Herr Hermann to be anti-war."

Pauline explained, "He's the librarian tasked by Germany's students to identify subversive books. Papa's was one of 2500 consigned to the pyres by Hitler's soldiers."

Papa said, "Nothing to me suggests more clearly that Germany is preparing for war. Why would they incinerate my book? It can only be because they despise all pacifist sentiments."

There was silence in the room.

"To peace in our times," Papa said at last, raising his glass, and proposing the final toast of Christmas Eve.

Nine years later, on a sunny day in June 1941, the street outside the store vibrated as rumbling German tanks appeared, then staff cars with German officers dressed in ceremonial uniform, and, finally, grey-clad soldiers, with rifles at the shoulder, their faces expressionless, their boots thumping the ground in a faultless monotony.

Miss Sylvia had somehow managed to keep Shakespeare and Company open until the Germans entered Paris. It would have folded had it not been for André Gide. He started the Friends of Shakespeare and Company which bibliophiles could join if they paid for a two-year subscription. This meant that the shop survived the 1930s. Then, when war broke out, Miss Sylvia kept things ticking over, opening the shop for half days only, and three evenings a week, until 7pm. In this she was ably supported by young volunteers, to whom Sylvia gave board and lodging in return for their hard work in the shop.

Chief among these was a Jewish girl, a Tunisian, called Habiba. One of the 60,000 Arabic speaking Jews living under the French Protectorate in Tunisia, Habiba had grown up with a love of books. Her father, a Zionist, had set up a Hebrew printing press and published the Talmud and Jewish prayer books. She fell in love with a young Jewish printer, one devoted to the publication of French novellas, novels and poetry written by Jewish authors. She loved these works.

When the young printer moved to Israel, Habiba was compelled by her father to stay behind in Tunisia. She was distraught. She heard of Shakespeare and Company and told her father that she wanted to learn lessons from the printing of *Ulysses* that might benefit his business. In truth, she wanted to visit us on her way to find her lover. Almost as soon as she arrived, Paris was occupied by the Germans. Miss Sylvia told her she could stay until the storm clouds over France had lifted. As time went on, Habiba became more and more agitated, not least when Jewish people started being deported from Paris.

One night in the Spring of 1941, Habiba set up a table in the backroom of our shop. She had asked my mistress whether she could hold a Passover meal there. Miss Sylvia replied that it would be an honour. Habiba then covered the table in the backroom with a white, ornately embroidered tablecloth and placed a seven-branched lamp at the head of the table. She had found seven half-burned candles that fitted the brass branches. She had also managed to bake some unleavened bread and acquire some fresh eggs which she part roasted. Habiba had made dishes of a sweet-tasting, mud-like substance which she called *haroset* and had cooked a chicken provided by Louise, a farmer's wife and avid reader who was a friend of Shakespeare and Company.

Habiba invited Adrienne, along with two other Jewish friends, both of whom were due to escape Paris the following day. When the meal began, she told them that this night was more special than any other because it commemorated the Exodus of the oppressed Hebrew slaves from their torment in Egypt. As she lit the seven candles and the smoke ascended to the ceiling, she started to sing a mournful song, and her two friends joined her. It contained a note of celebration within its haunting lamentation, like Mister Langston's Blues.

The meal continued with readings from *The Book of Exodus*, and prayers of blessing, accompanying the breaking of the unleavened bread and the pouring of four separate cups of wine. Habiba spoke these prayers in Hebrew, and, thanks to my mother's love of this ancient and most beautiful of languages, I understood the meaning. "Blessed art thou, O Lord our God, King of the Universe ..."

After the eating of the salad, the eggs, the horseradish, the lettuce and the *haroset*, the meal was served, and the guests ate the chicken and vegetables. Habiba looked on, a glint in her dark eyes as the candles dripped in their sockets. When they had eaten, she and her friends cleared the plates before the final ceremony. Habiba poured the fourth cup, the cup of redemption and sang the final *berakah*. The sound of the wine decanting from the bottle and filling the old clay chalice seemed deafening to me. All their senses were on high alert that night, especially when Habiba continued to pour the blood-red liquid until it overflowed the lip of the cup and cascaded down every side in crimson rivulets onto the while tablecloth, like a sacred and terrible wounding. When the effusion had stopped and the cup had been drunk, Habiba concluded the meal. "Next year in Jerusalem," she cried, and everyone repeated it.

That night, Habiba's two friends made their own exodus from occupied Paris.

The following day, all that was left of the meal was the fading scent of the candle smoke from the *menorah*, which had been taken in a small brown suitcase by the two fugitives, along with the tablecloth, the prayer book, and the sacred cups and plates.

It was a meal I would never forget.

Habiba was given many tasks during her two-and-a-half years at Shakespeare and Company and one of these was to take me out of my display case and clean me. This she did with such a tenderness that I looked forward to her weekly encounters. Her dark and dove-like eyes would stare at my print and pictures. Often, tears would fall down her olive-skinned cheeks as the words and images reminded her of the man she loved. At other times, she would smile, revealing her teeth, which were white as lilies – the coy smile of one who knew and understood the fuller sense of my mother's songs.

"Mama, these poems are so indebted to the Song of Songs," she exclaimed one day. She had started to refer to Miss Sylvia as "mama" a year before. "Almost every page seems to reverberate with echoes from our Hebrew love songs."

"It is a beautiful and much neglected part of the Bible," Miss Sylvia said, nodding her head.

"Have you heard what Rabbi Aqiba once remarked about the Song of Songs?" Habiba asked.

"Please, tell me."

"He said that all the writings are holy, but the Song of Songs is the Holy of Holies."

"That's beautiful."

What wasn't so beautiful was the invaders.

When the Germans started frequenting Shakespeare and Company and browsing its shelves, Habiba had to remain in the backroom, Miss Sylvia's office. All the while she would keep a watchful eye on the display case where I rested, marvelling at my copper-coloured covers, determined that no one should take me from the shop, especially one of the officers in ink-black uniforms, the ones with lightning bolts on their collars and swastikas on their red and white armbands. These were the men that made us all feel nervous.

One afternoon in August, an SS officer arrived and marched straight through the shop into the backroom. He looked at Miss Sylvia and then at her assistant who was preparing some accounts.

The officer pointed to Habiba.

"Who is this?" he asked.

"My assistant."

He told Habiba to stand.

"What is your name?"

"Habiba."

"Papers."

Habiba thrust her hands in her pocket. A look of alarm spread across her face. "I left them at home."

"You are Jewish?"

"I am not. Tell them, Mama."

"She is not Jewish!"

"She should have a yellow star," he said.

"She is a Muslim," Miss Sylvia said.

The man was not convinced. "She will be taken immediately to the sports stadium."

These words caused us all to shudder. The Jews in the city were now being arrested in vast numbers. It was known as *La Grande Rufle*, the Big Roundup. Thousands had been interred in the stadium in subhuman conditions. At least a quarter of them were children.

"Come!" the officer said.

"Mama!" Habiba cried.

"Take your hands off her!" Miss Sylvia shouted.

The officer pushed her away. "Get out of my way or I will have your books confiscated and your shop closed."

Miss Sylvia relented.

Habiba was led away.

I thought she was surely lost, but Habiba had met a young man, dark-skinned like her, with thick, black curly hair. He was called Younes. Whenever he came into the shop, his eyes seemed drawn to me. "You can look at it, just for a few minutes," she would say to him. He would take me in his hands and turn my pages. He would always remain speechless until he made to leave, whereupon he would speak in an unfamiliar language, uttering what sounded like a benediction.

Younes was an Arab Muslim and a devout worshipper at the Mosque in Paris. We learned later that his Director and Imam had been concealing and helping Jews from North Africa who looked identical to Arabs. To German eyes, Jews like Habiba were easily confused with Muslims. They had the same skin, eyes, and hair. They spoke Arabic. Even Habiba's name was the same in both Hebrew and Arabic. "It means Beloved," she said, "in both our tongues."

The saintly Director and his kindly Imam had drawn up fake certificates of Muslim identity for North African Jews and these papers had enabled them to move freely in Paris or return to their homelands. Those who were not Arabic-looking – Jews from Eastern Europe, for example – were hidden in the tunnels below the Mosque. The walled grounds above, adorned by gardens and fountains, were enormous so there was a lot of room below ground. In the courtyards and gardens of the Mosque, senior-ranking German officers were permitted to walk within the tiled walls. These officers were determined not to anger the Muslim population of Paris and allowed them courtesies denied to the Jews.

Until, that is, they began to suspect that the Director of the Mosque was issuing fake certificates of Muslim identity to Jews.

Then the courtesies ended.

As did the issuing of the certificates.

Habiba was the last to be given one. Younes took it to the sports stadium, rescued her, and then escaped with her from Paris. They fled to America. During the journey, she fell in love with him, as he had with her.

I later heard that when they arrived in Manhattan, they opened a store for rare books, modelled on Miss Sylvia's bookshop and lending library in Paris.

As for the young Tunisian printer she had known and loved before Younes, the one waiting for his girl in the Holy Land, Habiba forgot him altogether.

Not every German soldier who entered Shakespeare and Company was like the officer who arrested Habiba. Major Klaus Becker was a case in point. A man of medium height and sturdy build, he was of a far kinder disposition. He was a jovial man with a twinkle in his eye who smoked a pipe whenever he relaxed. His most distinguishing mark, apart from his deep devotion to books, was the fact that one side of his face, the right side, was disfigured while the other was unblemished.

From the first day he walked into Shakespeare and Company, my mistress was courteous to him. There was something trustworthy about his manner. Maybe it was the insignia on his uniform, which indicated that he was a *sanitätsoffizier* in the German Army Medical Corps, or perhaps it was his blue-grey eyes which reminded her of Mister William Blake, whom she admired, and whose hand-drawn illustrations were lodged within my sturdy copper covers.

In the months before the Japanese bombed Pearl Harbour, the Major would often look for American novels and poetry. He bought Nathaniel Hawthorne's works whenever Miss Sylvia could lay her hands on some copies. But it was his love for Walt Whitman that drove him time and again to us. Whitman was his favourite poet and when Miss Sylvia realised this, she invited him one day into her backroom.

After she had invited him to take a seat, she took a key to the lock of a chest that lay behind a curtain. When she returned, she had some old papers in her hands, covered in hand-written scrawls.

"I thought you, of all people, would appreciate seeing these, Major." She then exhorted him to put on a pair of white gloves. "Please take care. You'll see why in a moment."

The Major took his oval spectacles out of a case. He had to balance them with care on his nose. On one side, the bridge was uneven and pitted, as if part of his face had suffered a landslide.

"I apologise for my appearance," he said, adjusting his glasses.

"What happened to you?"

"It was at the battle for Warsaw. I was trying to radio for stretcher bearers when a shell exploded in my trench. All six of my comrades were killed. I survived, but the handset was blown into this side of my face. It's a miracle that I can still see at all, never mind breathe."

"I am sorry," Miss Sylvia said.

"It is war," the Major replied, his eyes sad.

But then, as he studied the first sheet of paper, they lit up and a beaming smile illuminated his pale, scarred face.

"Are these originals?"

"They are."

"This is Mister Whitman's very own handwriting?"

"It is."

"They are wonderful. Simply wonderful."

"They are among my most prized possessions."

"I must return them," the Major said. His hands were trembling now. "I do not want to damage them in any way."

Miss Sylvia smiled and carried the leaves back to their drawer.

"Would you like a glass of wine?"

"That would be most kind."

As Miss Sylvia poured, he reached into his pocket. "Would you mind if I smoked my pipe?"

"I love the smell," she said. "Reminds me of home."

From then on, Miss Sylvia and the Major met frequently. After the shop closed, Klaus would bring paté and biscuits, as well as fine wine and cheese, and the two would talk about books. They would often laugh, and never more heartily than when the Major told her that he thought that the writings of James Joyce were pretentious and artificially difficult, as he felt sure the man was himself. When Miss Sylvia heard this, she could not stop laughing, and nor could he, when he learned what a trial the celebrated author had been, and the nicknames that Miss Sylvia and Miss Cyprian had given both to him and the shop.

Even after the Japanese had bombed Pearl Harbour in early December, and the Americans in Paris were now no longer treated as neutrals by the Germans as they had been in the months before, the Major's affection for the shop and for Miss Sylvia never wavered or waned. He was still friendly, generous, and above all kind, the greatest of all virtues, even though he had to take great care to appear aloof.

One day, he looked like a shelf burdened with heavy tomes.

"What's wrong, Klaus?" Miss Sylvia asked.

"Can I trust you, Sylvia?"

"You can."

"You promise not to tell a soul?"

"I promise, Klaus. On my Whitman papers, I swear."

"Have you heard of Reichsleiter Rosenberg?"

"Of course. Everybody in Paris knows that name."

"Then you will almost certainly know of his intentions."

"I do. We have had several visits from his henchmen here at the shop. They claim to be literary specialists . . ."

"They *are* literary specialists," the Major interjected. "They have been in Paris over a year stealing rare books and transporting them to a library in Frankfurt. It is all part of the Fuhrer's plan to relocate Europe's finest artistic expressions to his own galleries and libraries."

"They did not find anything here," Sylvia said.

"That's because you keep it all under lock and key, away from the prying eyes of the . . . the specialists."

"My treasures are safe," Miss Sylvia said.

"You mean treasures like the Whitman papers, and the first edition, signed, of *Finnegan's Wake*. Now that America is in the war, these men will stop at nothing to have them."

I shuddered.

"There is a man working for the Reichsleiter's no 2," the Major said. "I must warn you about him. He is called Captain Bruno Lohse. He has been tasked with the responsibility of looting the libraries in Paris, both private and public. You must watch out for him."

"But we are just a bookshop."

"And a lending library, Sylvia. That one word 'library' could cause this place to be ransacked. It is like blood sensed by a hungry hound. Every book, picture, publication in this place could be seized, valuable or not."

"How will I recognise him?"

"That's the problem. He has been granted special agent status by Herr Goering, and he travels around Paris in a jacket and tie, not military uniform. It will be hard for anyone to spot him."

"Have you met him?"

"He is tall, handsome, with a full head of dark hair, smartly dressed, and knowledgeable. But he is not to be trusted. He works for an SS Colonel who is trying to use his expertise in art to strip the city of its masterpieces, especially its Jewish artefacts."

"But we have nothing like that here."

"It will not matter. The Colonel is like a magpie. Anything that sparkles, he steals, whether it bears the Star of David or not."

"Why are you warning me?"

The man looked at Miss Sylvia with kind eyes that began to fill. "Because you have made an ugly time more beautiful for me and given me a gift that can never be stolen or sold."

Miss Sylvia tilted her head.

"Friendship," he said. "And in the spirit of that, I say to you, hide your treasures well. Mark my words."

The next day, Miss Sylvia put me in a waterproof jacket, tucked me into a shoebox, and hid me in a cavernous space beneath a floorboard underneath her desk. She tapped the boards around it to make sure they all made the same hollow noise, then she left the room.

I was in the dark again, as I had been in Bruges.

Only this time, I was alone.

In the end, Miss Sylvia need not have concerned herself with recognizing the captain because, on entering, he introduced himself. When the other German customers heard his name, they left. The rest of the browsers, seeing the exodus, followed hot foot behind them. Now the shop was empty, save for the Captain and Miss Sylvia.

"Lock the doors, please," the man said, pointing to the exit with his cane. His voice was calm.

Miss Sylvia secured the entrance.

He then bade her follow him to the backroom where he removed his coat and scarf, just inches above my covers.

"Miss Beach, my name is Captain Lohse. I work for the Reichsleiter. If you cooperate, then this will be over quickly, and you can proceed with selling and lending the appropriate books."

He watched my mistress as he spoke, his keen eyes observing any indications of anxiety or fear.

"You are American, no?"

"I am."

"And so, we are now enemies. Which means I have the right to search this place and, if I find you disagreeable or uncommunicative, have you sent to one of our prison camps."

I shuddered.

"Please show me your ledgers and inventories."

Miss Sylvia produced several big, heavy books from a shelf and placed them on her desk.

The officer flipped through a score of pages in both. Then he walked around the room, inspecting the portraits and pictures, before finally standing in front of my guardian, his face close to hers.

"And what have you not recorded? First editions, for example? Old manuscripts? Pictures? What is there that rises above these commonplace books here on your shelves?"

"Nothing."

"Nothing?"

"Nothing."

"Nothing will come of nothing," the Captain said, smiling at the allusion he had made.

"In this case, it will," she said.

The grim-faced officer scrutinised every inch of the ceiling, walls, and floorboards. Then he took his cane and started to tap on each of the surfaces, listening for hollow sounds.

I heard the thud above me.

"Unlock these cabinets and chests," he said.

One by one, Miss Sylvia opened drawers and doors.

"I told you, there is nothing."

"Consider this a warning," he said as he left the room.

"Why? What have I done?"

"If you are harbouring valuable books, know that these are now the property of the Third Reich. I know, for example, that you have had in your possession a first edition, signed, of *Finnegan's Wake*. I give you two weeks from today to hand over the volume, and any others of material value, or there will be trouble."

"I do not have any valuable books."

"Miss Beach, you do realise that you already have a black mark against your name at the Kommandatur because of your Jewish affiliations. If I find that you have been hiding books as well as befriending Jews, your store will be finished, and you will be . . . relocated."

With that he stomped out to a large, grey military car.

Later that day, when recounting the episode to Adrienne, she said, "The sound of boots is the sound of the Germans. Those boots always make them seem more enraged than they really are."

Two days later, when I had been retrieved from my hiding place, Klaus arrived looking flustered. He hurried into the back of the shop, removed his cap, sat on a chair, and took his pipe. His hands were shaking so much that Miss Sylvia had to light it for him.

"Whatever is the matter?"

"They are coming."

"Who is coming?"

"Captain Lohse and his men."

"Here?"

"Yes, Sylvia. Here!"

He took a puff from his pipe.

"They're going to confiscate everything."

"Confiscate?"

"I mean loot."

Another billow of smoke.

"And they're going to shut this place down for good."

"When?"

"Tomorrow."

"You're not serious!"

"Would I jest about something like this?"

"What time will they be here?"

"Early afternoon. I'm sorry. I would have given you more warning. But there was no time."

He put out his pipe, replaced his officer's cap, and stood. He leaned forward and kissed Sylvia on both cheeks.

"I do not know if we shall meet again. If not, thank you, Sylvia. This place has been a port in a storm."

"Klaus, you have restored my trust and hope in humanity."

"You mean Germany," he said.

He glanced at the books and prints, then he left.

Sylvia hurried into the front room and sold her last book, a copy of Emily Bronte's *Wuthering Heights*. Then she shut the shop and told Adrienne what had happened. She, in turn, passed the information on to the Friends of Shakespeare and Company, putting out an urgent call for immediate assistance.

Within an hour, Miss Sylvia was given free use of the top floor of the building by the owner.

"You can store all the books there too," he said.

Then it hit me.

Shakespeare and Company was about to close.

5000 books and numerous framed photographs were about to be transferred to the fourth floor.

And that included me.

There was no time to mope, however.

Out of nowhere, the helpers were starting to appear.

It was like Whitman's vision of democracy.

Carpenters sawing.

Painters decorating.

People carrying boxes of books and clothes baskets full of pictures from the ground to the top floor.

Adrienne going through the registers, talking about which books needed recalling, which bills paying.

By lunchtime the next day, the place was empty. Even the façade of the shop had been redesigned and the Shakespeare and Company signage covered by several fresh coats of paint.

On the fourth floor, I was tucked into a shelf next to the first edition of JJ's *Finnegan's Wake*.

As everyone left the fourth floor, I could hear a hubbub from the stacked and shelved volumes. It was like the sound of bees in a hive. The books were making honey and the honey was the joy of being saved from almost certain destruction. Every book seemed to resonate and vibrate with the ebullience of it.

This murmuring continued throughout the night and into the next morning.

It enveloped me, like a new cover.

In that space I stayed for many years.

Untouched.

Unopened.

Unread.

And that wasn't all.

One by one, Miss Sylvia's friends started to leave this earthly realm.

JJ had already died in hospital early in 1941 when an ulcer was neglected. Left untreated, it perforated and killed him.

She lost Cyprian in 1951. The bereavement hit her hard. She never lost the feeling that she had been too preoccupied with JJ's needs to properly appreciate her sister.

Adrienne was next, struck down with Ménière's disease. She had started hearing voices. This was so tormenting that for months on end she could not bear the sound and would scream night and day.

A year later, in 1954, she dismissed her friends, including Miss Sylvia, locked her bedroom door, and took an overdose. When they later found her, she was dead. There was a handwritten note by her side. It read, "I am going to death without fear, knowing that I found a mother on being born here and that I shall likewise find a mother in the other life."

Miss Sylvia never recovered from what she called "the swooping down of death on someone you love." She wore the gaze of one who had loved and lost and never found love again.

Hemingway died in 1961. He took a shotgun to his head. In the end, Papa went the same way as his own papa.

Finally, it was Miss Sylvia's turn.

On her last holiday at *Les Déserts* in October 1962, Miss Sylvia over-exerted herself chopping wood. She had planned to make a fire, pour some wine, and read to some local friends from my leaves. She collapsed and was ordered to take a complete rest.

The next day, Miss Sylvia and I were driven back to her fourth-floor apartment on the *Rue De l'Odéon* and told to summon another doctor. She did not. She took herself to bed where she lay for two days and nights. She received no visitors.

At dawn on the third day, her breathing became arduous and her face as pale as an untimely frost. Her eyes opened into a wide stare, away from the end of her bed, into the salon beyond, where so many of her precious books were stacked.

I followed the line of her gaze.

There, standing at the threshold to the room, was a spectre.

It was a figure composed of light, human in outline, and glowing. As I continued to look, the form became more defined.

A man.

He was bald.

He wore an Elizabethan rough.

In each copy of Miss Sylvia's library books, there was a label, saying *Shakespeare and Company*. These had a picture of Shakespeare holding a quill pen above a blank sheet of paper.

It was him.

The bard was at the door.

Miss Sylvia smiled.

He moved forwards and stood at the end of her bed.

He reached out his arms, as if gesturing.

From behind his back, other figures began to appear through the doorway.

On and on they came, surrounding the bed, looking at Miss Sylvia, light pouring from their hearts into hers.

Soon the room was full of them – the radiant outlines of the dead authors of her books.

I saw the Bronte sisters.

I wanted them to see me and hold me.

But it was Miss Sylvia's reunion, not mine.

Above all, I wanted my mother to appear.

I searched for her.

And that was when I knew.

I had always been searching for her.

Last to walk into the room was a tall, broad-shouldered man with a kindly smile on his rugged face.

I saw Miss Sylvia tremble and her eyes flicker. We both knew who it was. When she had returned from her internment in Vittel, she lived as a recluse in her fourth-floor apartment at the *Rue De L'Odéon* until the day the Americans liberated Paris. First to arrive was Ernest Hemingway, driving a jeep, in uniform. He jumped out of his vehicle, rushed up the stairs, and called for Miss Sylvia. She hurried from her room, ran down to her liberator, and Mister Hemingway took her in his arms and whirled her about the small landing. She had felt giddy with excitement at the thought of being free at last. I think she felt the same again now, as her late and beloved friend appeared by her side.

It was said by some that Miss Sylvia had a sad end to her life, that she had given so much of herself to others, and yet she died alone. This was not the case. She was returned, like one of her books, surrounded by the authors whose works she had treasured.

As flights of angels sung her to her rest, they released some old familiar words into the room.

Fear no more the heat o' the sun,
Nor the furious winter's rages;
Thou thy worldly task hast done,
Home art gone, and ta'en thy wages.

Part 9

1962-2030

All a computer can give you is a manuscript.
People don't want to read manuscripts. They want
to read books. Books smell good. They look good.
You can press it to your bosom.

Ray Bradbury (1920-2012)

When Miss Sylvia died, I was confused about what would happen to me. In the case of my previous guardians, I had always become aware of an impending moment of transition, a handover from one carer to another. This time, I was left wondering what my next home would look like, a sentiment shared by all the other orphaned books around me.

It was several days before my guardian's body was discovered by a friend. The focus then was on where she was to be buried. There was a longing, shared by many citizens of Paris, for her to stay in France, but in the end her ashes were transported back to America where they were interred in Greenwich, Connecticut.

While this all happened, I remained in Miss Sylvia's apartment, collecting particles on my cover. I thought of her remains in America. She had become ashes. I was becoming dust.

Then, one day, people started arriving in the apartment. Miss Sylvia's lawyer had come to read her will. By this time, she was a wealthy woman. Mister Joyce had handed the manuscript and papers of *Ulysses* to her a decade after its publication. Miss Sylvia tried to sell these documents in the 1930s, when Shakespeare and Company was threatened with extinction, but to no avail. It was not until she was in her early seventies that she was able to locate a buyer. Now, in the final years of her life, she had found herself a rich woman, at a time when she was unable to enjoy the reward for all her selfless industry.

The solicitor conducting proceedings had a monotonous drone, so I drifted off while he was speaking about the details, thinking about all the volumes that filled what had now become an orphanage for books. It was not until he reached the end of his legal deliberations that I re-engaged my attention. Miss Sylvia had left her wishes about her priceless Whitman papers until then. When these had been communicated, the solicitor announced the one remaining item.

"Miss Sylvia Beach stipulates that her first edition of Miss Swanson's poems, illustrated by William Blake, are as follows: the volume is to be left to Miss Wen Ling, a Chinese student of English literature at Newnham College, Cambridge."

No one had heard of Miss Ling. But I remembered her. She had written to my former guardian a year before, requesting to see her. In her letter of introduction, she had described a little about her background, that she was the first student to go to Oxford or Cambridge from her town in China. Normally, Miss Sylvia was reluctant to give students access to her library, but something made her say yes, and a month later, she had appeared at the door of the apartment.

Ling had clothed her tiny, slim frame in a white dress embroidered with lovebirds and flowers. She had a small and pretty nose, straight black hair, sharp dark eyes, and a wide-cheeked smile. Her long journey to Paris and her presence in the apartment were ample testimony to a steely spine, forged on the anvil of her non-conformities. Underneath her short, jet-black hair, her forehead looked to me like a cliff face at Malham Cove, one I had observed on a picnic with the Bronte sisters. Miss Sylvia liked her immediately. And so, did I.

I overheard the conversation as they sat and drank tea in the salon adjoining the bedroom.

"Tell me about your upbringing," Miss Sylvia had asked.

Miss Ling took a sip then placed her teacup on the small mahogany side table next to her armchair.

"I was born in 1943 and brought up in Macao. My father was a teacher of martial arts and ran a training school. At home, he taught me to defend myself. He was rebellious in many ways."

"How so?"

"In feudal China, it was always the custom for girl's feet to be bandaged tightly from a young age. Their growth would then be retarded. My father always said he would never have allowed this for his only child, which is why people used to say my feet were so big that no man would ever want to marry me."

"You have lovely feet," Miss Sylvia said.

"Thank you, madame. My father was also a lover of books. He read what he enjoyed to me at bedtime. He wanted me to read widely. 'People who read a lot of books,' he used to say, 'know a lot of things.' I have come to learn that he was right."

"He sounds free-thinking."

"Yes, and that put him in danger."

"What do you mean?"

"When the Japanese were causing trouble, they sometimes seized books they deemed unlawful, but my father hid ours well. They never discovered them."

As she spoke, I remembered how Habiba had concealed me beneath the floorboards of the backroom to Shakespeare and Company, and how she had protected me from the Nazis.

"His most precious volume was the Bible. That too had caused trouble. My family's ancestors had been Buddhists, but my father and I became Christians because of Miss Tim Oi Li."

"Her name sounds familiar."

"She is the first woman in the Church of England to be ordained a priest. It happened during the war. Bishop Hall ordained her, much to the displeasure of the Archbishop of Canterbury. She was already a deaconess, but she couldn't preside at the Eucharist. Under Japanese invasion, no priests could reach her congregation. The bishop decided that he should ordain her, so he did. For doing that, he was accused back in England of being uncivilised."

"He sounds courageous," Miss Sylvia said. "I was brought up in the Presbyterian Church in the States. My father was a parson. But it wasn't so much a calling as a career for him. My mother hated it and rebelled against it. For my sister and me, it made us at best agnostics."

"I'm sorry, madame."

"Don't be. If I was ever to have a faith, it would have to be genuine, and it would have to be my own."

Miss Ling said. "I owe my faith to Miss Li Tim Oi. She was a priest in the church in our town. I fell in love with the Song of Songs because of her remarkable teachings . . ."

"Ah, the Song of Songs!" Miss Sylvia cried. "And that, I suppose, is why you are here, to talk about Miss Swanson's book."

My mistress walked from the salon into the bedroom, picked me up and took me to Miss Ling. She passed it to her guest, who bowed with such reverence as she took me in her small and delicate hands that it seemed for a moment that she was receiving the blessed sacrament.

As she turned my pages, her dark eyes began to fill. Several tears fell upon my leaves. Until the clock struck four times, there was silence. Then she closed me, stood to her unbound feet, and carried me to my guardian.

"This is so beautiful. I feel so honoured to see it, so honoured to meet you as well, madame. Thank you."

"Why is this book so important to you?"

"Miss Li Tim Oi often preached from the Song of Songs in our church when I was growing up. I was always overwhelmed when she did. It was her favourite book of the Bible. It became mine too. When she quoted a passage from Miss Swanson's book, her poems felt so mysterious and so mystical, so like the Song of Songs. The book you hold, it is my favourite."

"Did you have a Chinese translation?"

"Yes."

"Who translated it?"

"I did, madame."

I could tell Miss Sylvia was impressed.

"And you are studying English at Cambridge?"

"I am in my third year. I have been asked to write a dissertation on the provenance of this first edition. The people who have owned it. The times it has passed through and the trials it has endured, all as part of a larger study on the poems themselves."

"I can tell you what I know." Miss Sylvia said. "More tea?"

Miss Ling nodded and minutes later a fresh pot arrived. Miss Sylvia then narrated everything she had learned about my time with those who had cared for me, from my mother to Mister Langston Hughes nearly 120 years later. Miss Ling scribbled with a fountain pen while I relived the years, feeling the agony once again of the separation from my mother, but realising how much I had grown, understanding so much more about the strange habits of authors and readers, as well as my own place in this world. As she spoke, I was filled with gratitude for my life, and for those who had protected me.

"What do you want to do as a career?" Miss Sylvia asked.

"I feel called to become a nun."

"Wouldn't you prefer to be a teacher English?"

"No, madame. Before I went to England to study, I spent several years helping in the maternity home run by Miss Li Tim Oi in our church. I would like to devote my life to helping young unmarried mothers and their children. I would like to teach them to read to their children and to appreciate the value of books."

Miss Sylvia smiled.

"There is a place in London, connected to an Anglican convent in the borough of Hackney," Miss Ling continued. "I have applied. They want to see me when I return from Paris. I hope to join the sisters when I have finished my degree."

Miss Sylvia stood. She was tired now and Miss Ling, being watchful as well as respectful, gathered her notes. As she prepared to leave, my mistress looked at her.

"What does your name mean in English?"

"Ling means intelligent, or spiritual, and my surname is Wen, which can mean writing."

"Do you think you'll be a spiritual writer?"

"My father wished it."

"You had a great father," Miss Sylvia said.

"I did. He saved for much of his life to send me to England. He sacrificed everything for me. Macao is a poor place."

"Is he still alive?"

Miss Ling looked down at the floor.

"I'm sorry," Miss Sylvia said. "He would be very proud of you, you know."

Miss Ling looked up and smiled.

"Thank you, madame."

Miss Sylvia let her out.

As one door closed, I had no idea what new door of opportunity had just opened to me.

Two years later, after being kept in safe storage, I found myself in Miss Ling's possession in a rural convent in the market town of Wantage. Miss Ling was no longer clothed in her colourful dress but in a nun's simple habit. Her main tunic was unpleated, light blue in colour, while the wimple over her chest and the coif around her neck were white, as was the bandeau just above her forehead. Her veil was a darker blue than her habit, almost black in colour, and around her neck a silver crucifix hung from a dark cord. This cross, along with her eyes, shone when she took me in her small hands and held me. As she inscribed the courier's papers with her fountain pen, it felt to me as if she was signing a certificate of adoption. I was happy that Sister Ling was my new guardian, and the convent, dedicated to St Mary the Virgin, was my new home.

Right from the start I loved the nuns who shuffled over the cold, stone floors through the endless corridors.

They were all kind, although some could be grouchy and cantankerous, others sullen and disgruntled. Most, however, were cheerful and selfless, living by the golden rule, doing unto their sister what they would have their sister do unto them. And, like books, they came in different colours, shapes and sizes. Some looked fresh and new, like Miss Ling, while others looked old and gnarled, like Sister Agatha, who had been going around for many years saying, "I'm 90 you know." All of them had a story to tell about how they had come to take their vows, although I doubt that any were as extraordinary as my Miss Ling's. From the time she joined the community, she was regarded as different, not in a disdainful way, but as one who, as her father had prophesied, was clever, spiritual and a lover of writing.

Sister Ling's tasks in the early years were menial more than theological, both in the convent in the countryside and on her occasional forays to the community house in London. She spent her time cleaning and gardening, as well as helping in the kitchens. As time wore on, however, her gifts of reading, interpreting, and expounding texts became evident to all. As I saw for myself, from the one shelf in her room, she studied her Bible and her books with intensity and illumination.

"I have been observing your progress," the Reverend Mother said one day. It was 1967 and she had walked into the room while my guardian was pouring over me, scrutinising my mother's poetry, penetrating the mystical mysteries hidden like pearls in a field.

Miss Ling rose to her feet and bowed. Her hands were clasped together in front of her cross. "I hope I have not disappointed you, Reverend Mother."

"Far from it, child. You have kept your vows of poverty, chastity, and obedience to God, and you have been living faithfully by the rule of our community. It is because of that I am now ready to recognise your gifts. In fact, I have a most sacred entrustment for you."

Sister Ling gulped.

The Reverend Mother continued. "I'd like you to give the Lenten addresses in the chapel."

Sister Ling gasped.

"I want you to talk about the Song of Songs. I hear it's your favourite book in the Holy Scriptures. Am I correct?"

"Yes, Reverend Mother."

"Each homily must be no longer than ten minutes," she said.

"I understand."

"Do you, Sister? Let me remind you of one of our maxims. If you can't strike oil in ten minutes, stop boring."

"Yes, Reverend Mother."

The following Tuesday evening, and the four Tuesdays afterwards, Sister Ling gave the Lenten addresses at the recently renovated chapel of St Mary Magdalene. On the last of these, she brought me with her. Most of the nuns were present, all but those away on missions abroad. Next to me lay her copy of the Bible in Chinese. Each week, she had read the passage from the Song of Songs in her mother tongue, and then in the King James Version of the Bible. The nuns had loved hearing her use her own, native language. In her final address, her chosen text was Song of Songs 2:8-13, and her talk was entitled, "The Winter is Over."

As she spoke, her voice calm and soothing, she enlisted all the skills she had learned as a scholar of literature as she talked about the qualities in the poetry of the song. She spoke of the two seasons in Israel, winter followed by summer, and of how the beloved had been in hibernation for the rainy months of the year. Then, she described the approach of the lover, like a gazelle, over the hills, drawing near to his beloved's house, until he was just outside the latticed window. She talked about how he would not enter, but instead wooed his beloved to come out of hibernation, alluring her by appealing to her five senses – the scent of the tender grapes of the blossoming vines, the sight of the sun-drenched land, the sound of the turtle doves calling to each other, the taste of the green figs, the touch of the new and blossoming summer flowers in her hand.

And how she spoke about these flowers.

She told everyone that the Hebrew word was *nizzunim* and how in Israel the landscape can be barren one day and covered with an expansive carpet of these red flowers the next, like a sudden and miraculous epiphany of poppies. These, more than any other of the details the poet mentions, she said, speak of the change in the two seasons, from winter to summer. She encouraged all the sisters to close their eyes, to smell, taste, touch, see and hear what the poet was describing, above all the twofold invitation of the bold lover just beyond the latticed window, "Rise up, my love, my fair one, and come away with me."

"Now imagine that the one calling to you is none other than the Bridegroom from Heaven," Miss Ling said as she continued. "For the poem is not only a song about the love between the king and his bride. It is an allegory of the intimate communion that we are all invited to embrace with the King of Love."

Then she opened my pages and began to read some of my mother's words. They filled the small chapel, echoing around the old stone walls and pillars. The words stirred my heart with longings once again for my mother's presence.

That night was the only time I visited the chapel during these years. My guardian would go there without me. Every day, she would head there with all the other sisters, rising early to attend Lauds at 7 o'clock in the morning, then heading off to Terce, the Eucharist, Sext, Vespers and finally, at 8 o'clock at night, to Compline. Each time she left, I would recall my time in the safe in Bruges with my old friend, The Book of Hours, and how the prayers and songs that graced its illuminated leaves would transform the dark chamber, making it feel as if the membrane between heaven and earth no longer existed, and that the wings of angels brushed against our spines, rustling like silk, leaving in their wake the sweet fragrance of heaven's flowers, of otherworldly *nizzunim*.

I sensed something of this again in the chapel when my mistress spoke that night, hidden in the clouds of incense.

Whenever she went to the chapel, I longed to be there with her, but it was not to be.

Not long afterwards, Sister Ling was moved to St Mary's Community House at 153, Stamford Hill, Hackney, where the sisters had set up a home for unmarried mothers and their babies. For Sister Ling it was the fulfilment of a dream from her days with the mothers and babies in the Anglican church in her town in Macao. In 1967 there were twenty-two young mothers at the residential home, all with their recently born infants, being cared for by the nuns of the Community of St Mary the Virgin. They would teach them how to feed their sons and daughters, how to play with them in the recreation room, how to wash them in the bathroom, and how to pray for them at night. During these days, Sister Ling had a room to herself. Besides her Bible, I was the only book on her wobbly, wooden desk. There was a bed against the wall with a crucifix hanging above it, and a novel by Raymond Bradbury hidden underneath the mattress.

One of the unmarried mothers was a twenty-year old woman called Shirley. Shirley was from Coventry and had become pregnant with twins. The father, a car mechanic with a penchant for stealing, and a knack of getting caught, had no inkling that he was responsible. She had ended the relationship as soon as she had discovered that she was to have twins. She did not love him, and she did not tell him that she was pregnant. Instead, she arranged to travel to London on the train and headed to the Community House. Arriving at the entrance, heavily pregnant, the kindly nuns took her into their care.

Two weeks later, Shirley gave birth to a boy and a girl, whom she named Simon and Sandra. She remained with them for seven months, breastfeeding them at first, then weaning them and bottle feeding them instead. All of this happened under the watchful and compassionate supervision of the nuns, especially my guardian, who was given the task of improving her education.

One day stands out in my memory.

Shirley had settled the twins in their juxtaposed cots and, while they were sleeping, came to our room. She knocked on the door and my guardian invited her to enter. Miss Shirley was wearing a shapeless shift of a dress with a dropped waist. Bright orange with white collars and cuffs. Her hair was brown, long, and wild.

"We'll keep it brief, Shirley," Sister Ling said.

"Thank you, sister."

"Today, I want you to look at a picture with me. It is one of my favourite paintings. I'll describe what it depicts and then you can tell me what you think it means, if anything."

Sister Ling took a poster from her bed. It had been lying face down, its bright white back looking up to the ceiling. When she turned it over, she held it up in front of our visitor and began to speak.

"This is by Vincent Van Gogh. You have heard of him?"

Shirley nodded.

"It shows a large Bible at the top. It is an old Bible, dating from the early 18th century. It is thought that it belonged to the Van Gogh family. Van Gogh's father was a pastor in the Dutch Reformed Church. He and Vincent had a stormy relationship. Vincent felt that his father disapproved of him, that nothing he ever did was good enough, and that whenever he returned home his father would rather have opened the door to a wild dog than to his son. It was very sad."

Sister Ling then pointed to the top right corner.

"Here is a used candle. It has clearly gone out."

She then pointed to the bottom right corner.

"Here is a worn, paperback book. It is a yellowy colour, and it has been well used. It is a novel by Emile Zola, an author whom the painter greatly admired, a novel entitled *Joie de Vivre*, the Joy of Life."

She then directed Shirley's attention to the big Bible.

"See the pages? They are blurred, unclear, unreadable, as if you are looking at them through a window that has been drenched with rain. Except that the pages are open at Isaiah chapter 53, a passage in the Old Testament that is considered a prophetic vision of the suffering and death of Jesus Christ, which was to happen six centuries later."

Sister Ling then turned to her table, fetched a sheet of paper and a pen, and handed them to Shirley.

"This is an exercise in perception, in observation and interpretation. I would like you to write down what you think Van Gogh is trying to say in this picture. You may think he is not saying anything at all and that these images are not symbols. You must decide."

Shirley looked at the picture now lying at her feet. She then began to write. She had fine handwriting. The ink flowed from the pen.

After she had finished, Sister Ling asked her to put her sheet of paper face down on the floor. Then she picked up the picture.

"I am going to tell you what most people think about this picture. It will be interesting to see whether your interpretation is similar, or whether you have come up with something different, unique even."

Shirley's eyes widened.

She was awake now.

"Van Gogh is telling us, through the snuffed-out candle, that his father's life is done and that the days of relying on the Bible for truth are over too. It is a melancholy symbol."

Shirley nodded.

"The lines in the Bible have become blurred, as if lost in the mists of time, although Jesus Christ, the suffering servant of Isaiah 53, is still a person to be admired.

Meanwhile, novels like *Joie de Vivre* compete with the Scriptures as a window onto truth. They are yellow, a colour suggestive of youth. They are full of vitality while the Bible is a dull brown colour, suggestive of age."

She then gestured to the floor next to Shirley, who picked up her paper.

It was her turn to read.

"The Bible is big while the novel is small," Miss Shirley said, her voice stronger than before. "The Bible is sturdy and strong while the novel is worn and torn. The painting says to me that even though the light has gone out, the Bible endures, even if its pages are difficult to understand sometimes. The light of the candle may be the light of faith, which many believe has been extinguished in our times. But the person described in Isaiah 53 is still as fascinating as ever, which is why the pages lie open, like an invitation, an open window or door."

Sister Ling said nothing for several seconds.

"Well, sister. Am I right? Or am I wrong?"

"You are extremely clever."

"Why do you say that?"

"No one I've taught has ever seen what you've seen."

"Does that mean it's wrong?"

"Of course not. That's not really what this exercise is about."

"Well, then, what is it about?"

"The point is that it confirms what I have already sensed that you are a unique individual, Shirley, and that you are a free-thinking person. Do not let anyone ever tell you otherwise."

Shirley's eyes seemed to glisten like snowdrops after a shower of rain. Then she restored her veneer of defensiveness.

"Can I sleep now?"

"You may."

Sister Ling picked up the poster. She walked to the wall above the table where I was resting and turned the large picture of the *pieta* around. She attached the Van Gogh to the back, so that it would be undetected by the more censorious sisters.

Shirley laughed. "You're a cunning one," she said.

"Oh, that's nothing." Sister Ling went to the opposite wall and turned the painting round. There, on the back, was a picture of a young Chinese woman in armour, carrying a large silver sword, marching in front of an army of soldiers. There were Chinese characters all over the picture, and in English, *Lady General Hua-Mulan*. The artist had painted the image with splashes of red and black, with traces of sky blue and yellow."

"What's that?"

"It's a poster for a film that came out three years ago, my favourite film. About Mulan. I have always identified with her. I've seen it so many times I'm concerned that I may be guilty of violating my vow of detachment."

Shirley looked at Sister Ling and smiled. "I like you, sister. You're not like the others here. They're a bit old and crusty, stuck in their ways. But you're groovy."

Sister Ling bowed. "I like you too, Miss Shirley. Let's meet again tomorrow, when the twins are asleep, and let's talk next time about poetry. I have a feeling that you are a writer at heart. There is a well inside you that goes very deep. I want you to let me prime the pump before you are sent back to Coventry."

The time came for Miss Shirley to give away her twins. Sister Ling had spent many hours writing letters to a couple who were known to the Reverend Mother. They had applied to adopt twins. They had a son, and they did not want him to grow up as an only child. After a long and painful birth, they had been told not to conceive any more children. When the Reverend Mother heard this, she put them in contact with Sister Ling. My guardian had been praying in her room while corresponding with them, "Oh Father of the fatherless, give me wisdom. Please guide me, so that these orphans may find a safe and good home."

In May 1967, the day arrived for the handing over of the babies. Miss Shirley came to our room to say farewell. She was carrying the two children. There were tears in her eyes as she tucked them into a pram that Sister Ling had wheeled into her room. They were staring at her, cooing and smiling, blinking while they gazed into their mother's eyes, unaware that this would be the last time they would ever see her face.

Miss Shirley turned away and as she did, the boy's curvaceous arms began to flap against the covers.

"Promise me they're going to a good home, Sister."

"I promise."

"I should be looking after them. But mum's living alone, and she needs so much help."

"I know, Shirley. One day, they will understand."

Miss Shirley held out a bag. "Here. These are booties and other woollen items that I've knitted myself for the twins. I've left my name tag on them. Maybe one day, they may want to find me."

My guardian took the bag.

"Please don't tell the Reverend Mother about the labels."

"I won't."

"Here, this is for you," Sister Ling said. She went to the picture on the wall, reversed it, and removed the Van Gogh print. "I want you to have it," she said, rolling it up and placing it in a carboard tube. "It'll be a connection between us, and between you and the twins."

"Thank you, Sister."

"And never forget, Shirley. Books like Zola's are what you might call the literature of truth. But the Bible, as you once said here, is greater still. It is the truth of literature. Vincent Van Gogh said it himself in a letter. I've written out what he said."

My guardian produced a piece of paper from the pocket in her sky-blue tunic. "He wrote that 'this Christ is more of an artist than the artists.' I believe he was right. Never forget it."

Miss Shirley looked down at the pram. The little boy stopped flapping his arms and smiled.

When she stood up straight, there were tears in her eyes. The boy's arms started waving in ungainly motions once again, until he heard her voice, and then he became calm and still.

"On their first birthday," Miss Shirley said. "If I write a letter to their new parents, and I post it to you, will you see to it that they receive it? I want them to know how much I love the babies, and how much I miss them. I don't want them to think I've rejected them."

Sister Ling nodded.

The door opened.

"It's time, Shirley," the Reverend Mother said. Then, seeing the reddened eyes, "Be strong now, my dear."

Miss Shirley began to walk towards the threshold when suddenly she turned, ran towards my guardian, and threw herself into her arms. "I'll never forget you, Sister."

"Come now," the Reverend Mother said. "The taxi is waiting to take you to the railway station."

Miss Shirley left the babies in their pram, shifting restlessly beneath their blanket, nudging one another's shoulders, looking up towards the ceiling, waiting for their mother's face to reappear. It was Sister Ling who soothed them, pulling on the pram, rocking it in careful, gentle motions, singing a quiet song from the days of her youth.

Minutes later, the Reverend Mother and another lady reappeared with a couple in their thirties. He was tall and dark, with a crooked nose and imperfect teeth, and a hint of gold when he smiled. She had dark hair too, and a demeanour full of joy. They stood beside the pram, waiting while their escort told them about the community house.

"We've been doing this since 1865," she said. "This home was set up by Dr F.B. Meyer, a Baptist Minister and Bible scholar, who, to use his own words, was concerned to make some provision for children whose mothers, mostly unmarried, were unable to care for them."

One of the babies uttered a long sigh.

"The first child to stay here was found crying rather lustily in a Gladstone bag left on the doorstep. A note had been placed with him from his unmarried mother saying that she was too ill to look after him. Her wishes for the four-week-old child were carried out."

The same baby sighed again, this time even louder.

"One of the loveliest things we have ever received is a note from a mother who was a resident here. It was very heartfelt. It simply said, 'He was conceived in love, I parted with him in love, and he will be received in an even greater love.'"

She then turned to the adoptive parents. She looked at them for a moment, then said, "I feel sure, having met you, that you will receive these twins in that even greater love."

The two visitors nodded.

"It is our dream to make them happy," the new father said.

"To give them a safe home," his wife added.

"They are beautiful children," Sister Ling said. "And their mother is a very unusual and special woman, most unlike those we normally have here. The workers say that she is the best mother we have ever had for twins. They say she is such a nice girl, and very intelligent."

Then the lady, who had been standing with the Reverend Mother, began to speak. She was the case worker from the Homeless Children's Aid and Adoption Society and was called Mrs Simpson. She was a plump and happy soul with eyes that smiled.

"All the paperwork is signed, including their medical reports, and you have paid the £1 fee to Reading County Court. The boy has been circumcised, in accordance with your wishes. Both children are in good health. May they become increasingly precious and be made a great blessing to you in the years ahead."

"Thank you," the new father said.

Then the Reverend Mother looked at the babies. "What a lovely pram!" she said, noticing it for the first time. It was indeed lovely, a coach-built pram that the couple had sent ahead to the house. A Silver Cross, in Windsor grey, with spoked wheels and a foldable hood. "Similar to the one Prince Charles had when he was a baby," the new mother said. "It's the Rolls Royce of prams."

"Very good," the Reverend Mother said. "I can see that the babies will lack for nothing. They are highly favoured indeed."

With that, the gurgling twins were wheeled out of the room with their adoptive parents, preceded by the Reverend Mother and Mrs Simpson.

When they had left, Sister Ling sat on her wooden chair and cried.

As that same year drew towards its close, I could sense that Sister Ling was becoming more and more concerned about keeping me in her room. She suspected that I was worth a king's ransom. As she continued to help the poor unmarried mothers in Hackney, she also began to feel the inconsistency between her vow of detachment towards material things and the item of enormous value in her possession. While she was not one to be seduced by wealth, she decided to take me to one of the bookshops on Charing Cross Road to have me valued. The man she intended to consult was one she had met before when searching for a book by John Owen, the Prince of the Puritans. The bibliophile had looked after her well and treated her fairly when he sold her an antique edition of Owen's *Communion with God*, one of her favourite spiritual books.

In mid-December, Sister Ling took me on the bus to Charing Cross Road and entered the shop. I was greeted by row upon row of old books in many different colours and covers – Baskerville, classic, leather and cloth. These were packed into shelves, bookcases and display cabinets, both in the main room, and the smaller chambers that led off it on the ground floor, the same on the second floor. Everywhere we looked there were rows of books. For a moment, I was back in Paris, in Shakespeare and Company, and in the library in Bruges.

The gentleman Sister Ling wanted to see was busy with a customer, so she occupied her time by examining an old volume resting on a table on the second floor. It was entitled *A New History of China, Containing a Description of the Most Particular Features of the Vast Empire*, and written by Gabriel Magaillans of the Society of Jesus in the 17th century. The finely bound volume was an English translation of the French original, numbering over 300 pages.

My mistress turned the leaves with great care, smiling at certain portions of the text. One passage she started to read out loud, seeing as she was the only person in the room.

"*China* is a Country so Vast, so Rich, so Fertile, and so Temperate; the Multitude of the People so infinite, their Industry in Manufacture, and their Policy in Government so extraordinary, that it may be truly said, that ever since the undertaking of Long Voyages, there was never any Discovery made, that might stand in Competition with this Kingdom. These are things known to all the World; and so there needs not much more to be said, to make the Learned apprehensive, that the Subject is large enough to fill many more Volumes then yet are extant, and to employ the most able and judicious Writers."

By the time she had finished, I sensed she was homesick. But then the shop owner climbed the stairs and asked her what he could do for her. She produced me from within the folds of her habit and presented me to him. The moment he set his eyes upon me, he removed his oval spectacles and shook his head.

"This is priceless, Sister Ling. Miss Swanson's poems, in the very first edition, designed especially and only for her by Mister Inkley & Company! With all the original illustrations by William Blake, intact, in good condition! This is a fabulous discovery."

"How much do you think it is worth?"

"More than any book I have ever owned or sold."

The man handed me back as others began to enter the shop and filter around us.

"Look," the man whispered, "this volume is beyond my means but, if you like, I can arrange for it to be sold at auction."

"To be honest, I am undecided what to do with it. It was entrusted to my care by Sylvia Beach . . ."

"Miss Beach? Of Shakespeare and Company in Paris? The original Shakespeare and Company, as opposed to the new one?"

"Yes, the same, and she passed it onto me with the same devotion and sacrifice as our unmarried mothers in Hackney hand over their children to new parents for adoption."

The man nodded, his face grave, his eyes full of understanding. "I often liken this bookshop to a children's orphanage. I take enormous pride in placing precious volumes with what I regard as the appropriate people, although I fear I have, on occasions, got it wrong. But this is not a confessional. What do you want me to do, Sister?"

"Nothing for now. I am a little troubled by the worth of this edition. I must pray some more. My mind is unclear."

With that, she bid goodbye.

As she took the bus back to Stamford Hill, my mistress was unaware that she had been watched and overheard in the bookshop by a man with a studded leather jacket and hair like the deckled edges of an old book. While she had not seen him, I had, and I had become nervous. He was not a bibliophile. He was an opportunist and a thief, someone only concerned about money.

When the bus stopped and we alighted, we were walking down a darkened and empty street when he confronted my mistress.

"Give it to me," he said, brandishing a knife with serrated edges.

"Give you what?"

"I was in the bookshop. I saw it. Give it to me."

"No, it does not belong to you."

"If you don't give it to me, I'll cut you."

"I am a nun, a sister of St Mary's community house."

"I don't care if you're the Queen of England, give it to me now or you're gonna bleed like a fish."

Sister Ling stood her ground.

"I will not."

The man lurched forward with the knife. As he moved, it was like an ancient instinct activated, one from her childhood, from the training she had received from her father. She sidestepped his assault with the swiftness of a gazelle. As he passed by, she thrust out her arm and punched the knife out of his hand. It flew onto the pavement and clattered to a halt somewhere in the darkness.

The man swore and came at her again. This time he reached for her throat with his hands, but she swivelled and then reached out with her foot, kicking him smack in the face. It was just once, but it was so quick and so well placed and timed that it broke his nose, causing a stream of blood to pour down over his lips chin.

"Bitch!" he screamed.

Just as he was about to punch her, we all heard a noise. It was like the droning of a thousand bees. As my mistress turned, she saw a bright light. It startled her but it also blinded her attacker.

"Leave her alone!" a voice shouted.

Our assailant looked uncertain, confused. He had no idea who it was who had shouted at him, or how many of them there were.

"This is not your manor," the voice exclaimed. "If you bugger off now, you won't get hurt."

The man stumbled, then regained his balance, before running away from the scene and into the shadows.

When he had gone, the stranger appeared. He was no more than five feet four inches tall and had a huge mop of curly black hair. He was about twenty years of age and dressed in a tailored suit. Next to him, he was wheeling a small scooter with the word 'Vespa' written on it. There was no one else with him.

"You alright, Sister?"

"I wasn't thinking," she said, her voice shaky.

"What do you mean?"

"I just reacted on instinct."

"Well, as far as I'm concerned, he got what he deserved."

"That's no comfort," she said. "I'm a nun."

"If you ask me, what you did was pretty cool."

"Not if you're committed to a non-violent life."

"True, but that looked like self-defence to me, Sister, unless you're about to tell me that you're in the habit . . . well, of course you're in the habit," he chuckled. Then he finished his sentence. "Unless you're in the habit of wandering the streets of Hackney after dark and kicking the sh . . . I mean the living daylights out of muggers!"

"No, I'm not."

"Where are you heading?"

"The Community House of St Mary's on Stamford Hill."

"I know it. Hop on the back. It's not every day I get to ride with a nun. My Vespa will get you back in time for Vespers!"

And it did. As the rescuer drove us back to St Mary's, people cheered. Mods, young people recently arrived from the Caribbean on the Windrush, Hasidic Jews, everybody. Most of them seemed to know the rider. "I'm a Hackney boy!" he shouted to Sister Ling as he drove. "One of the Ace faces! I went to school with loads of these lads and lasses."

When we walked through the doors into the Community House, all was quiet. No one was about. The driver escorted us inside, bringing what looked like a leather satchel with him.

"Here," he said, fetching a record from his case. "This is a new single I've done called Desdemona. You may think it's a bit rude, if you're anything like the BBC. But it isn't meant to be."

"Do you play in a band?"

"Yep, it's called John's Children. One day, I'm gonna be a world-famous Rockstar. Trust me."

"All right, I'll listen to it. Thank you."

"You're welcome, Sister."

Just then, our deliverer seemed distracted by something. He had noticed the framed print of a famous painting hanging in the foyer. By now, my guardian had persuaded the sisters to embrace art and they had at last yielded. The picture was by the Belgian artist René Magritte. It said '16th September' at the bottom. At first, I thought this referred to when it was painted. But it was the title.

"Love this picture," he said. He was staring at the large tree at the centre of the painting, with a silvery crescent moon seemingly attached to the foliage at the front, stationary and luminous. The evening light above was a blue-grey colour, like Sister Ling's habit.

"You know it?"

"I stared at it the original for three hours in the Louvre not long ago."

"You were in Paris?"

The man nodded.

"What were you doing?"

"You don't wanna know, Sister. Trust me."

"Why do you like it so?"

"I like the randomness of it. Who else would have thought of taking the moon out of orbit and attaching it to the front of a tree?"

"It is good, isn't it?"

"it is, Sister. The artist's playing tricks with our perception. It's chicken oriental."

Sister Ling looked confused.

"Pardon me, Sister. Cockney rhyming slang. It means mental. I like stuff like that. Like in the painting. Making connections that can seem, well, a bit mad really."

But Sister Ling wasn't listening. Something had happened to her. I felt the shock of it when she juddered.

"I need to say something to you," she said. "You may or may not believe in God, but I believe he's just given me a message for you."

"That's crazy!"

"No, it's not."

"Okay, what did he say?"

"He didn't *say* anything. I'm oriental, but I'm not chicken oriental."

The man laughed.

"It's something to do with that painting. It's making me feel very concerned for you, like I'm supposed to warn you to be careful. It feels like a matter of life and death."

"Oh well," the young man said. "You know what they say, those whom the gods favour, die young."

"This is not something to joke about. You must take me seriously. What is your name? I am going to pray for you?"

"It's Marc. Marc Bolan."

The man shook my guardian's hand and said he had to leave. She returned to her room, clutching me to her chest.

The next day, not owning a record player, Sister Ling went to R and B Records, a shop nearby. Lots of visitors thought it stood for Rhythm and Blues, but it stood for Rita and Benny. Rita was warm and welcoming. Benny was brusque and blunt. They were a good double-act. Sometimes, customers needed the motherly approach that Rita provided. At other times, they needed a stricter, more paternal manner, and Benny was more than happy to dispense it.

When Sister Ling walked in, and they saw from her habit that she was a nun from the Community House of St Mary's, both the owners, on this rare occasion, were warm and respectful.

"I'm sorry to bother you," Sister Ling said, "but I don't have a record player and a young man on a scooter gave me this last night. Could you just play it for me?"

"Of course, Sister."

Rita placed the vinyl '45 on the pad and the song blasted out of the shop's speakers. A voice began to shout about a woman called Desdemona. The song sounded to me like a rising cacophony of clashing symbols and thumping bass notes. But I could hear Marc's voice echoing what the lead singer was singing. And he was good. Really good.

"I think he'll go far," my guardian said.

"As far as possible from Hackney," Benny said.

After the attempted robbery, my guardian became even more determined to protect me. She locked me in the community safe in London and left me there. Five years I spent in confinement. From time to time, the door would open, and faces and hands would appear, but it was not until 1972 that my guardian brought me out of my safe house.

When she did, I could see that the community home in London was now almost deserted, and the paint peeling from the walls. It was September and St. Mary's Mother and Baby Home was closing, partly due to the poor state of repair, partly to the lack of clients. The Reverend Mother attributed this to the Abortion Act, which had been passed at the end of the 1960s. She said that after that, homes for unmarried mothers were no longer required, and that the trustees of St Mary's had observed this trend right across the country. "Abortion has superseded adoption," she said with a deep, long sigh.

After the community house shut its tired doors, Sister Ling returned to the convent in Wantage and locked me in the safe in the office. No one knew I was there apart from the one acting as the Reverend Mother at the time, who gave her permission to use the safe.

I counted the days, the months, the years, and finally the decades – nearly four and a half decades in total without a single soul opening my covers and reading my mother's verses. Then, one day in the year 2025, I heard the lock being turned and the door to my solitary confinement was opened. I emerged to find it was around midday. The warmth in the room, which came from the weather rather than the heating system, told me it was summertime.

Sister Ling, my adoptive mother looked almost the same, except there were grey flecks in her hair, her skin was wrinkled in places, and her eyes looked wearier than when I last saw her. Age had withered her somewhat, but not to a degree that I would have associated with her advancing years. She was now well into her eighties but still sprightly.

She was delighted to see, touch, smell, and hold me again.

"Here it is," she said, passing me to a woman standing next to her. "Tell me, Detective Inspector, what do you think?"

"Please call me Anastasia," the lady replied.

The stranger, who was in her mid to late fifties, had fair hair with a tinge of red, skinny blonde eyebrows, a round face, and thin lips. Her eyes were the colour of ice water, and her nose thin and straight. She seemed to me to exude strength as well as beauty, as if she had been forced to fight hard for every inch of ground she had gained in her life.

She donned a pair of white gloves and then held out her hands.

My guardian placed me on the woman's soft cottoned fingers.

Taking care not to put any pressure on my spine, the lady turned me this way and that, then opened my pages and examined both my script and illustrations. All the while, there was a glow in her light blue eyes.

She returned me and removed her gloves.

"Reverend Mother," she said. "All my life, I have lived for love, and I have lived for art, and in this precious volume, there is both."

There was the hint of a Slavic intonation in her voice. The occasional rolled "r", an "s" instead of a "th" sound, a "w" instead of a "v".

My guardian nodded.

The stranger sat. She placed me on her lap and asked, "Am I right to be so careful with it?"

Sister Ling said, "It is an exceptionally rare treasure."

"Do you know how much it is worth?" she asked.

"It could probably fund the building of twelve convents."

The Detective Inspector nodded.

Then the policewoman began to talk, her voice lowered. "It is without doubt one of the most valuable antique volumes in the world. Although, until now, its existence and whereabouts have been concealed, it would arouse great interest if collectors were to learn about it. So, we are right to be careful and to be protective of it."

The Detective Inspector stared at me again. Then she rubbed her chin and turned her eyes from me to the Reverend Mother, as she was now called. "Since I moved from Moscow to work for Scotland Yard," the lady said, "we have been seeing a dramatic increase in black market activity, especially in the stealing and selling of rare books. To me, it is a form of trafficking."

"That is why I phoned your office," the Reverend Mother said. "I have been hearing very alarming stories about the evil done by these book thieves, especially on the news and in the papers."

"I am very glad you called," the stranger said. "Do you know the three top items sold on the black market worldwide today?"

The Reverend Mother shook her head.

"Drugs, weapons, and art. The third includes the theft of rare books. In fact, this is rising all the time."

"Why would people want to steal old books?"

"There are as many answers as there are thieves, but the main reason is greed. Volumes like yours can fetch huge sums of money, giving the criminal a quick route to riches. Pretty well every rare volume has been stolen at least once. My job is to find the book thieves."

"And that, I presume, is why they call you the Book Cop."

"Precisely."

Just then, the Book Cop's phone vibrated. She looked at the screen. "Another theft," she said. "I'm going to have to go."

She tucked away her phone. "Look," she said. "There's another thing to consider. There's been talk of a film about Miss Swanson's life. If they ever get round to doing that, there will be a rush to find first editions. This always happens, I'm afraid. So, you need to be vigilant. If the Swanson film gets made, contact me straight away."

She withdrew a card from her pocket.

"Here's my private email. Don't contact me at the office. Use this address and I will do everything in my power to help you."

"Thank you so much."

"In the meantime, keep the book under lock and key. Say nothing. And tell no one. And remember what Sigmund Freud said . . ."

"What?"

"Collecting antique books is second in intensity only to nicotine addiction."

With that, she exited the room.

My guardian placed me straight back in the safe.

She turned the key.

And the lights went out again.

Five years later, the Reverend Mother's face appeared at the entrance to my hiding place. She had a look of urgency as she gathered me up in her arms and took me underneath her robe into her office. Closing the door, she sat at the desk and cradled me as she typed an email to the Detective Inspector she had met the last time I was brought into the light.

Dear Anastasia,

You told me to write if the film about Miss Swanson was made. As you are probably aware, it is now out and getting a great deal of attention. What you anticipated is also happening. People are going mad trying to find not only early editions, but the very first edition, which you have seen with your own eyes. I am now greatly concerned and would therefore be grateful if you could suggest a solution.

*Also, this is just to let you know that I have retired
from my role as Reverend Mother in the convent as
from last week and am therefore free to come and
go as I please, without having to account for my
whereabouts, or be visible to my sisters.*

I can respond in whatever way you require.
God bless you,
Sister Ling.

My guardian paused at the screen, waiting for a reply. As
one was not forthcoming straightaway, she turned to her
news page and scrolled down the items. Halfway down,
she noticed a headline.

WORLD HERITAGE LIBRARY COMPLETED.

She clicked on the play button in a video newsfeed
beneath the headline. Images started to appear of
a monumental library being built in Iceland with long
corridors and multiple mazes of many-shelved and
capacious chambers. A poet and environmentalist called
Anders appeared and started to speak. My guardian,
realizing that the volume was off, clicked on a megaphone
icon.

"And here we are. This magnificent new building
is destined to be the library where the earth's most
treasured volumes will be recorded, shelved, and
preserved in a repository of excellence. Here the infinite
and infinitesimal details of our world, as seen through
eyes as fresh as the streams from our snow-capped
mountains, will be cherished forever. This World Heritage

Library will be a time capsule for the people of future centuries and millennia, now until the end of time."

Pause.

Now images of ancient books being recovered from thieves.

"In this library, books will be safe not only from decay but from abduction. The world's finest firewalls are in place to keep the book thieves out. This great monument and fortress will mark the beginning of the end for the black market in stolen books. Not even their darkest arts will be able to penetrate the defences and systems operating here."

I could feel my guardian's excitement.

"That's good," she murmured.

As I looked at the screen, I thought this edifice, white and bright under gloomy skies, looked more celestial than earthly. It was a beacon in the darkness. How I longed to dwell in that heavenly-looking house with its many, many rooms.

Just then, my guardian's computer registered a new email in her inbox.

She clicked on the message.

It was Anastasia.

Dear Reverend Mother, it is so good to hear from you again. We are indeed interested in helping you. TBH will certainly qualify for the WHL, if that is what you wish. It will be of special interest to the

Icelandic people for reasons I can explain when we meet you.

Be prepared to leave your convent at 0100 tomorrow morning.

"W" will pick you up.

Bring TBH, some fresh clothes and toiletries.

I make no apology for the urgency. The film, as you say, has increased the need to act quickly, as has the building of the WHL.

"W" will be with you shortly.

Take very good care.

A.

The Reverend Mother turned off the screen and checked her watch.

20:00.

Five hours later, having gone to the kitchen and eaten a small meal, she left her office and walked down silent corridors until she reached her bedroom. She picked up a small case, already packed, and made her way to the Chapel of St Mary Magdalene.

She lit a candle on the altar, then lowered herself to the floor, wincing as her knees touched the cold stone.

Kneeling before the sacred table, she closed her eyes while she held me beneath her blue habit.

In whispered words, she began to pray for the Great Father's safekeeping of her sisters.

Then she prayed a prayer that I had heard from her lips many times in the Community House in Hackney.

"O Lord, support us all-the-day long of this troublous life, until the shadows lengthen, and the evening comes, and the busy world is hushed, and the fever of life is over, and our work is done. Then, Lord, in thy mercy, grant us a safe lodging, a holy rest, and peace at the last. Amen."

My own Amen reverberated within my pages.

She struggled to her feet.

I became aware of a noise outside, a rumbling that caused the ground to shake. The vibrations decreased and the sound diminished. Several moments later, the door to the chapel opened.

In the entrance stood a broad-shouldered man with a round helmet on his head. He was wearing a one-piece, olive-green flight suit with a zip that ran from his groin to his neck. It was covered in pockets and had a badge sewn into the chest, with a bald eagle in the centre.

He reminded me of someone.

Then I remembered.

I had seen an illustration over 150 years before in Monsieur Bonnardot's shop of Captain Nemo in his underwater suit and a weapon in his hand. Drawn by George Roux, it had been in a first edition of Jules Verne's *20,000 Leagues Under the Sea*.

I trembled.

My guardian, however, seemed unperturbed by his presence. She turned back towards the altar and crossed herself before looking at the man.

"Have you come from the Book Cop?" she asked.

The man nodded.

"And you are 'W'?"

The man nodded again.

She took several steps towards the visitor, then removed me from beneath her robe. I was now in the shadow of his headgear, which seemed to me as round and large as a planet.

"It is showing some wear and tear," my guardian said. "The cover is a little more rubbed than it once was, the joints are not as firm as when it was new. The binding is tender. The tooling is faded, as is some of the gilt on the edges. But it's beautiful. More so for ageing."

The man beckoned to the exit.

My guardian turned one last time towards the altar.

She stared at the candle flame.

She bowed her head.

Then we were gone.

Part 10

2030

Round and round
And round I go
I try to stop
I cannot slow
Ground is coming
Oh so fast
Not sure how long
This flight can last

Karl Tearney

The snow began to fall more heavily as the stranger led us towards a field behind a row of terraced cottages, on whose roofs the snow had already settled. When we passed through a jaded gate, the sight of a strange dark green vehicle greeted us. It was about sixty feet long and had some blades above the body of the craft, and a smaller set above the tail. It looked to me as strange and wondrous as Captain Nemo's submarine.

Drawing nearer, I estimated that the snow-flecked body of the vessel was about nine feet wide. On entering through the sliding aft door, I could see there were two seats in the front of the machine, then two benches in the main section, with enough room for about twelve adults to sit on them. One of the benches was behind the front section, the other was facing it. Both had frames made of aluminium tubes and were covered in a faded and frayed canvas material.

"What's this?" my guardian whispered.

W said, "It's an old Huey. A UH-1 to be precise. Built in 1966. Restored on a farm in Northern Ireland."

He spoke with a mixture of affection and pride. "Don't worry. It may be old, but it's in perfect working order."

"Bit like me," my guardian said.

"Strap yourself in," he said, pointing to a bench.

"I'm not sitting back here!"

"You sure?"

The man led us through into the cockpit. He sat my guardian down in the left-hand seat, adjusted the seatbelt and placed a helmet on her head. In front of me, there was a constellation of clock-like dials and silver switches on and around the black dashboard. There was a control column to the left of W's seat and another one, wobblier looking, between his knees.

After an instrument check, there was a roar and the twin blades above our heads and behind us began to rotate.

The next minute, W was pulling on the lever on his left and we were hovering above the ground, then rising as the volume and speed of the disc above intensified. W manoeuvred both columns now. He pressed down with his feet on the spongy pedals below and we started to fly above the ground away from the field and off into the night. It was exhilarating and frightening at the same time. As his limbs moved, he reminded me of a church organist, his hands and feet flowing together in perfect order, even though performing different functions. I marvelled at his skill. Years and years of flying seemed to have made him unconsciously dextrous. His arms and legs moved as if they were part of the vehicle. The pilot and his flying machine were one.

"How fast are we going?" my guardian asked after the convent had been left way behind us in the darkness.

"Cruise speed is about 100 knots. Top speed, a little faster. Ceiling 20,000 feet. Range about 315 miles."

"Where are we heading?"

"A hill in a remote part of the East Kent Downs. It used to be MOD territory. The local farmer's a veteran of the Gulf War. We keep the Huey in one of his ruined barns, off the beaten track."

"Do you have a house there?"

"Not exactly," he replied. "If you don't mind roughing it, then you'll be fine with us."

"I'm a nun. I'm used to roughing it."

The whirring of the rotating blades continued until the pilot called out that we were drawing near to the farm. We started to descend. As we landed, the engines decreased in volume and the blades came to a standstill. The silence was as deep as the night was dark.

As W escorted us out of the Huey, I heard some sheep bleating somewhere in the chilly night.

Three men emerged and pulled the Huey towards the barn.

"They're friends," W whispered.

"Glad to hear it," my guardian whispered.

He led the group of five, including my guardian, away from the Huey's makeshift hanger into an adjacent field, protected by barbed-wire fences, some of which had traces of wool hanging from them where the sheep had strayed too close. We walked over long stretches of grass mottled with cow and sheep dung. W blazed a trail around the black patches as if marking a path through a minefield.

After what seemed like many steps, we reached a hill, whose summit was lined with a long, thick coppice. W paused and looked back down the valley, checking we had not been followed, then entered the woodland. Within a minute we were poised above a hidden doorway in the ground, covered in camouflaged hessian.

The men removed the material and lifted a slab of metal. Underneath, there was a compartment with a locking mechanism in the shape of an old ship's wheel. W rotated it until the portal below shifted. He lifted the large metal lid and we all started to climb down the steps into a corridor beneath, illuminated by soft lighting in the whitewashed walls.

"What is this place?" my guardian asked.

"It's a Cold War bunker," W answered. "One member of our group is a Gurkha rifleman who used to be stationed in Folkestone. He brought us here. It was decommissioned in '87."

W opened another door and we now found ourselves in a spacious and brightly lit chamber, with bookshelves lining every wall. Many were filled with books of all sizes and every kind of binding. I felt the welcome from them, like a gust of warm air on a cold night.

"There's fifteen of us," he said. "But most are asleep. You'll be briefed in the morning. For now, you must be hungry and tired."

"Just tired," my guardian said.

He took her bag and led her out of the chamber down a corridor with doors to the left and the right. At the end, he opened a righthand door and showed us into a small room, no larger than the one my guardian had occupied for many years at the Convent, and before that, in the Community House in Hackney.

"It's not much," he said. "But it is safe."

"It's perfect."

"Do you need anything?"

"Just some water."

He returned moments later with a glass.

"The toilets are communal, I'm afraid."

"I'll thank God for them anyway."

"The boss will meet you in the morning."

"Anastasia?"

"We call her the boss."

The Reverend Mother nodded.

"One more thing," she said.

"Yes?"

"What does W stand for?"

The man smiled.

"Willow."

The next morning, after breakfast, my guardian carried me into the library and sat in a soft armchair. A man and a woman appeared. They asked to look at me. My guardian agreed. They donned some gloves and turned my leaves, admiring the old print, reciting some of my mother's words, marvelling at Mister Blake's ethereal illustrations. As they handed me back into my guardian's care, Willow entered the room and sat on the end of a sofa, a few feet from us both.

"Why do they call you Willow?" my guardian asked.

"I was a British Army helicopter pilot for thirty years."

"You must have seen some awful things."

"I'm afraid I did. Some of the things I saw were very traumatic, especially in Bosnia. For years I had PTSD without realizing it. It was diagnosed late, almost too late."

"I'm sorry," my guardian said.

"I was sent on a therapeutic course run by the army, and after two days, I just couldn't stand it any longer, so

I legged it, did a runner to a river where I climbed under the branches of a low-hanging willow tree and sat inside with my back against the trunk."

Five others had entered the toom now and everyone was quiet. Those drinking coffee put their cups down.

"I was at the end of my rope. But as I felt the bark against my back, I thought to myself, 'you're like this willow tree, all sad on the outside, but inside you're as strong and resilient as this trunk'."

"Hence your name?" my guardian asked.

Willow nodded.

"What was even more interesting, I thought to myself, that would make a great idea for a poem. I wrote one called Willow Tree, and I've written a poem a day ever since. Thousands now."

Just then, a man with brown eyes and dark skin came and sat on the sofa next to Willow. He was carrying an old book.

"Go on," the brown-eyed man said.

"Go on," the others cried.

"Yes, go on," my guardian added.

The soldier looked down at his feet. As his words filled the room, everyone kept still. Every ear was listening, every heart beating faster, as the pilot who was a poet began to speak.

Willow, Willow, Willow Tree
We're very similar
You and me

We weep, we weep, we weep all day
We try so hard
To run away

On and on the poet spoke, one poem turning into another at the request of the listeners. Many of the poems were about war and mental health. Several were about love. All of them were heartfelt, beautiful, almost childlike. They reminded me of the unpretentious simplicity of Mister Langston's poetry.

"What's your real name?" my guardian asked.

"Karl."

"He's a war poet," someone said.

"But I'm not sophisticated," Willow said. "I don't have any formal training, and I'm often criticised for not being refined enough. I call myself a gutter poet. I don't claim to be anything else."

Then he turned to the man sitting next to him on the sofa. "Let me introduce you two. Sister Ling, this is Stafi. Stafi, this is Sister Ling, the Reverend Mother of the Community of St Mary."

"As-salaam 'alaykum, Sister."

"And also, with you."

The man with the deep brown eyes reached out his right hand and, as he did, his left hand appeared. It was holding a weather-beaten book with a cover that seemed to be younger than its yellow parchment pages. The volume was about seven inches by five inches, bigger than me on both sides. There was a thin black chain made of iron attached to a ringlet on the book cover. The other end of the chain was locked onto a handcuff around Stafi's left wrist.

"What's that?" my guardian asked.

"Have you heard of the Hereford Gospels?"

"From the cathedral library?"

Stafi nodded.

While I was under the restorer's care in Paris, I had heard about the practice of chaining books to library shelves. The fore edges of the book would face outwards and the spines inwards. They would be kept secured to the shelves, so no one could steal them. While I understood the idea, the measures taken seemed to me to be severely injurious to books, and I winced at the thought of being bound in that way.

"How come you have it?" my guardian asked.

"Willow flew me to Hereford last week. The canon librarian asked the boss to transfer it to the World Heritage Library."

"But forgive me for asking, are you not a Muslim?"

The man nodded.

"Why are you protecting these Gospels?"

"That is simple, Sister. According to the Qur'an, the Gospel was revealed to Jesus and fragments of this revelation are still to be found in the four gospels in this book. That is good reason to honour it."

"But do you not believe that the Qur'an is the last revelation in time and the final word from God? Do you not claim that your book is superior to the supposedly defiled texts of the Bible?"

"I do, but I say again, Sister, my faith still honours these older Scriptures, even if they have been subject to *tahrif*, to corruption. And in the Qur'an, the Son of Mary is mentioned many times in fifteen surahs. We honour him too, as a prophet. Indeed, the Qur'an, says that the word of Jesus should be believed."

I could feel my guardian warming to him, as I was. Stafi reminded me of Habiba's husband.

"Have you managed to read any of it?"

Stafi shook his head.

"It is in Latin, so I rely on Dr Alexander."

Stafi motioned to a blonde woman, about forty years old, sitting in a wheelchair a few feet away from him.

"Hello sister," she said, her voice strong.

"Are you an English teacher?" my guardian asked.

The woman shook her head.

"Classics."

"You are able to understand this?"

"I translate when Stafi asks me, yes. It is at times quite an unusual Latin. It was clearly from a small community, Welsh most likely, isolated from the larger centres. It is something of a miracle that it survived."

"Why?"

"There were 229 ancient books in the original collection at Hereford cathedral. This is the oldest, dating to around 800. The rest were all burned by a local king in the year

1065. This precious volume was rescued by a good and godly person then. And the same again today."

"Someone's been watching over it," my guardian muttered.

"We believe that there is a book mother in heaven," Stafi said, "and that the books of Moses, the Psalms of David, the Gospel of Jesus and the writings of the Prophet of Islam, blessed is he, are from this one source."

"You believe the book to which you are chained is the offspring of this heavenly mother?" my guardian asked.

"That's right, Sister."

"Speaking of mothers," the Professor interjected. "The end of this volume is interesting. It has a record of a local dispute between a son and his mother about the inheritance of land."

"Isn't that a little strange, having a court record in the back of a rare edition of the Gospels?" my guardian asked.

"Not at all," the Professor answered. "In those days, there was no filing system, no bureaucratic method for keeping records. Wealthy people would store legal documents in the back of treasured books, like they did with this one."

"What happened to the mother, I wonder?"

"We know the answer. The son took his mother to court, arguing that the land was rightfully his. He lost the case and, according to the Domesday Book, it remained in her possession, although it is named there as belonging to her new husband."

"There's a moral in all of this," Stafi said. "You should always honour your mother. Do you not agree Sister?"

"I do."

Stafi continued. "Abu Hurayrah said: 'She is the one who made her womb a vessel for you and nourished you from her breast. You have no option but to love her'. May Allah be pleased with him for saying this."

My guardian said, "Amen."

After coffee, Willow escorted my guardian down several corridors of the bunker to a private room. He knocked and then entered.

"Reverend Mother!"

Anastasia stood, holding out her hand.

"I'm so relieved you've made it."

"I'm just Sister Ling now."

Anastasia pulled out a chair for her.

Willow left the room.

"May I?" she asked, reaching for me.

She examined me in the same way as she had before, cradled half open, so as not to split my spine.

"It's still in great condition, no signs of deterioration since we last met. Does anyone else know about it? The other sisters . . .?

"No, we are the only ones."

My guardian looked around the room and then back at her. Anastasia could see her confusion.

"You're wondering what's going on here."

"I am."

"It's a long story and there isn't much time, so I'll keep it brief. You remember last time we met, that I was working for Scotland Yard, heading up a specialist unit combatting the black market?"

My guardian nodded.

"The unit was infiltrated. It became obvious that our work had been compromised. There were moles everywhere. Even at the highest level. I was . . ." she paused and raised her eyebrows. "Retired."

"You mean you were removed."

"I bowed out gracefully, pretending to be ready for a rest. But, as you can see, I had no intention of withdrawing from the battle. I met Willow and liked him immediately, trusted him too. He told me about his Gurkha friend, and they introduced me to this place. Over the last three years we have been operating out of here in secret."

"Taking books to Iceland?"

"Yes, that's part of our remit. But we are not just focused on the relocation of old books, especially stolen ones. We also investigate book thefts and stop people trafficking books."

Anastasia pointed to an old-fashioned globe on her desk. "There are twenty black-market bosses over the globe who are coordinating book thefts in their countries. See here."

She pointed to twenty, tiny yellow circular stickers as she swivelled the globe with her strong fingers.

"These men have gangs working for them. They are not the usual kinds of villains either. Most of them are self-taught and know a huge amount about books. Some are even sophisticated people, with excellent academic records and refined tastes in books."

She turned the globe and pointed.

"See here? Milan. One gang member spent ten years as a librarian. Worked his way up to the top, until he became the director. Then, in a single week, he managed to strip the library of its most treasured works, both books and prints. He got away with it. Sold everything on the black market, gave half to his regional boss, who then gave half to the man who masterminds it all."

Anastasia sat back in her chair.

"The mastermind is called Mister Antony Forbes-Smyth. He has trained each of these twenty bosses, who in turn have trained the cohorts of thieves that infiltrate libraries, either as customers or employees, and who steal from private collections."

Anastasia withdrew a photograph from her desk. Taken by a street camera, it showed a shadowy figure. He was tall, wearing a trilby and a long dark coat, and was striding across a cobbled street at night.

"This is a picture of him in Bruges, just before a huge heist at the library there. The gang raided the vaults and stole over a million pounds worth of rare books from an enormous safe."

I shuddered.

"But as you can see, it is unclear. You cannot make out the man's face, which is frustrating for Scotland Yard."

"Do you know where he is hiding?"

"He is very evasive. He moves between countries, monitoring the work of the twenty regional and national bosses. He flies in a private jet, using multiple identities and passports. He is extremely furtive and clever, and . . ." she paused.

"And what?"

"And . . . he is charming."

My guardian said, "Evil men since time began have masqueraded as angels of light."

"True."

"Why do you say he's charming?"

"I have met him."

"And you let him go?"

"I'm afraid so. It was when I was working for Scotland Yard. He took me out to dinner on his cruiser on the Thames. Candlelight. Champagne. The works. He tried to turn me to the dark side. He was extremely charismatic, and quite convincing. Told me to call him Tony. If I hadn't had my wits about me, I might have ended up in bed with him, in more senses than one."

"He is your Moriarty then."

"In a way, yes. He is an expert in what we call cultural property crimes. With the help of my very able team here at the Book Theft Programme, we will catch him eventually. We are currently tracking one of his generals, a Professor of American Literature at Ohio State University. We fully intend to persuade him to work for us."

"Persuade?"

Anastasia smiled. "Stafi has a very special skillset."

"I have met him. He is a most interesting man."

"Indeed. You two should get on."

My guardian smiled. She was feeling my covers and running her fingers down the edges of my leaves. She was staring at my markings, which she knew as surely as a mother knows the freckles on her child's skin. "And what of this beloved volume?" she asked, lifting me to her nose, taking a long sniff of my papery smells.

Anastasia turned the globe.

"Willow and two other members of my team would like to take your precious charge to our contact in Iceland tomorrow night, along with two other extremely rare and valuable books. They are to be donated to the World Heritage Library. That's if you approve of Miss Swanson's book being relocated there."

I longed for my guardian to say yes.

"It is the safest place for it," my guardian said. Then she bowed her head a little. "I am in my nineties. There's no point me holding onto it. Where I am going, it cannot come."

There was the sound of a phone vibrating.

"Hello," Anastasia said. "Okay. We'll be right there."

She stood.

"There's a transmission from our contact in Iceland."

We entered a chamber full of computers. Opposite the entrance was a set of clocks in a straight horizontal line with the names of different cities around the world. These hung above a large screen that covered almost the entire wall. There was a map on the screen, and a small red light was flashing from one of the countries.

"This is our communications hub," Anastasia said to my guardian. "And the light on the screen is an incoming transmission."

The map disappeared. The upper body of a bespectacled man appeared. I recognised him. He was the poet from the documentary I had seen on the computer at the convent. He was wearing a black jumper made of wool, with intricate red-and-blue patterns from his shoulders down to his heart. He was also smoking a curved brown pipe.

The poet on the screen began to speak. "No time for greetings, Anastasia. I need to be brief."

"Go ahead."

"We are all set for your delivery Saturday night. Get yourselves by chopper to the Faroes. There's a ferry that stops there. It still comes to Iceland once a week from Northern Denmark."

"Have you any indication of the conditions we'll face on the way?" The voice was Willow's.

"Hi Willow. Yes. But only for one part of your journey. Be very careful when you're travelling from Shetland to the Faroes. Our Met Office is warning of severe weather."

The man took a puff of his pipe. As the smoke curled upwards to the ceiling, he asked, "Do you have the book?"

Anastasia turned to my guardian.

"May I?" she asked.

Sister Ling nodded.

Anastasia lifted me.

"This is the original edition of Miss Swanson's book *The Burning Ones*, with ten illustrations by William Blake. It is every bit as beautiful as you'd imagine, and then some. It will be the pinnacle of the collection in your new library."

"Wonderful!" the man cried. "This will make Christmas very memorable. Miss Swanson's book will have pride of place on Christmas Eve throughout the country. I look forward to having a closer look, and at the other rare books. What else is coming?"

Anastasia said, "We have the Hereford Gospels and a very rare copy of the Slave's Bible."

"Excellent. Well, I look forward to welcoming your envoys on Saturday night. We will have a small reception for you in Reykjavik so you can enjoy some of our Icelandic hospitality."

"Our couriers will see you then," Anastasia said.

"I bid you a safe journey and Godspeed," the man replied. With that, he faded, and the map reappeared.

Anastasia led us out of the room.

"How long does the journey take?" my guardian asked.

"You'll have to check with Willow, but a couple of days at least. He will need to fly low to avoid any possibility of being detected by our enemies. They have spies everywhere."

"Sounds very risky to me."

"Willow has flown scores of missions, and he hasn't lost anyone yet, or any*thing* for that matter."

My guardian frowned.

Anastasia said, "There'll be no flying until tomorrow. That gives us a chance to relax this evening. We have a special meal cooked by our Nepalese chef. Bring *The Burning Ones*."

"I hope it's not a last supper," my guardian muttered, before returning to her room.

That evening, everyone headed to the library. Sanjay, the Gurkha rifleman, had prepared a feast. Anastasia asked my guardian to say grace and then everyone sat. There were sixteen people at the table.

Anastasia placed a white napkin over her arm, poured the finest Bordeaux into every glass and then offered a toast to the ever-smiling Sanjay. After some fine local lamb, slow cooked with Nepalese pakku spices and flavours, the diners tucked into milk cakes and carrot pudding. The dinner was completed with some port.

After the table had been cleared and cleaned, three of the diners brought their cherished books to the table. Each one had been asked to narrate the reason why they loved the volume and why they desired for it to find a home in a country where rare books were treasured. My guardian was the first to speak.

She told the story of my life, beginning with my birth in Holt and my beloved mother's love for me, right up to her own guardianship as the Reverend Mother of the convent of St Mary's. As she spoke of my provenance, you could have heard a page turn, so wrapped were the listeners in my history, spanning over two centuries.

When she had finished, she opened my pages and, at their request, read some lines of my mother's, beginning with one of my favourite quatrains. Her recitation reminded me of Billy Massingham, the night before the Battle of Waterloo, reading the same passage to the soldiers in the farmstead. They were about to begin an uncertain and precarious adventure, just as we were now.

My soul is yearning like a waiting grate
For you to shape, caress, incinerate
The tinder and the coals of my desire
Until they burn and blaze with sacred fire.

On she read, and as she did, I swear her voice grew stronger, as if its volume and intensity outgrew her physical capacity, filling every hidden nook and cranny of the library, moving up through ceiling, floor, root and tree, into ink-black sky and far beyond the shimmering stars past unseen gates into eternity.

And ah, the love in her voice!

The heavenly love!

The golden flames!

The mystic fire!

The blinding light!

My very spine tingled.

The room seemed brighter, cleaner, larger than before. When she stopped, there was silence.

It was my guardian who broke the spell.

"So, you see my dear Stafi, for me, a book's worth is not related to claims about the integrity of its text, nor to arguments about its date, let alone speculations posed by those who want to outdo one another with their holy scripts."

"What then, Sister?" Stafi asked, the swivel of his chain touching the iron circlet on his book.

"The worth of a book should be judged by the love we encounter in and through its sacred pages. The greater the experience of the divine love and the kindness of heaven, the greater the book. If it causes the heart to be filled with compassion and to lean towards mercy, it is a holy book indeed, whenever it was written and whoever wrote it."

As she spoke, I recalled my mother's wish, that I would be used throughout my days to promote in others the ability to give and receive the sacred love that she had known.

"And it is because of that same love," she said, "that I have come . . . I have come to my decision."

She paused.

Every eye was on her now.

"I am not coming with you."

There was a murmur.

"I am too old. I would hold you up. And that's not what you're going to need in the days to come."

"But Sister . . ." Stafi protested, his eyes filling.

"No, Stafi. I am nearing the very end of the final chapter of my life. I am much too frail for such a quest."

"I will carry you," he said, his voice trembling. "Along with the Gospels. I will bear the burden gladly"

"I know you would, but I cannot and will not accept."

"But you will be separated from your precious book!"

"But not from the lover of my soul, the one Miss Swanson eulogises in this blessed volume."

"Who would you like to be its guardian?" Anastasia asked.

"I choose Willow."

She drew a page from inside my back cover. She had spent all afternoon writing it with an old ink pen.

"You see, Stafi, I too have a precious document in the back of my book, just as you do."

She spread the sheet in front of everyone. It had the words CERTIFICATE OF ADOPTION at the top. Then the name of the one releasing me from her care, and the name of the one to whom she was handing me over for adoption. There was space for the signatures of two witnesses, as well as a record of the date, the place and time. When Willow saw it, I could tell before he said or signed anything that he was moved to be asked and that his heart was willing.

She passed the document to Willow, who signed his name, then to Stafi, who added his signature as a witness.

My guardian turned to the man sitting next to her. "I could ask any one of the people here to be a witness," she said. "But I am especially eager to hear your story and to learn about your book."

She was looking at the African American gentleman on her left. He was enormous, built like a great bear. His name was Moses and his ancestors, he said, had been slaves.

"My great grandparents joined in the Great Migration to the East Coast, eventually settling in Harlem. This book was their Bible. A long time before, it had been mutilated by their slaveowner, who had torn out every page from *The Book of Exodus*, in case the readers should be swayed to rebellion by the story of the deliverance of God's people. That is why my parents called me Moses, as a reminder that our destiny is in freedom, and in setting captives free."

"Then you must sign," my guardian said.

Moses bowed his head.

"Are you sure you want me to?"

"Certain."

"Then it will be an honour."

When he was done, my guardian kissed my covers and handed me to Willow, with the adoption certificate folded and inserted inside my back cover. She struggled to her feet and walked out of the room while everyone watched her depart.

Even before she left, I missed her.

Once the door was closed behind her, Anastasia issued instructions for our own exodus.

"Tomorrow night, Willow will fly you to the first of your fuelling stations and then on to Scotland where you will refuel, fly to Shetland, refuel again, and then head to Torshavn on the Faroe Islands, where you will join the ferry to Iceland."

She drained the last of her port before continuing.

"You will have barely enough fuel for several legs of the journey so travel light. Bring your book and a small bag with you. Everything you need, including clothes, will be provided in Iceland."

Willow, Moses, and Stafi nodded.

"Where will we leave the Huey?" Willow asked.

"With our contact on the Faroe Isles."

Anastasia folded her napkin. "One more thing," she said before rising. "Anders warned that there may be extreme weather from Shetland to the Faroes, so take great care. You carry a priceless cargo. Make sure it arrives safe and sound."

The next morning, the three couriers went to the library to wrap their books in protective covers and pack wet weather apparel into backpacks and bags. They only paused for the shipping forecast on the radio. Mysterious words such as "Dogger, Fisher, Sole" filled the air like a litany from ancient shores and distant isles. Willow and Moses made careful notes whenever the Fair Isles, South-East Iceland, and the Faroes were mentioned.

When the time came to leave, Anastasia fetched my guardian and asked her to say a few words. She spoke about how once she had been to the new Shakespeare and Company in Paris. It had been built on the site of an ancient monastery known for its compassion.

"There are beds throughout," she said, "for those who are lonely, nomadic, or homeless. In the entrance, I remember reading these words. 'Do not neglect to show hospitality to strangers, for thereby some have entertained angels unawares.'"

She paused.

Looked up towards the ceiling.

Stared for a moment at the light.

Squinted.

Closed her eyes.

Shook her head.

Then spoke again.

"I believe in angels," she said. A strange peace descended. "And I'm praying that the Great Father will command them to protect you all, including the books."

She recited some words from the Book of Zechariah about an angel that carries books, saying that she had dreamed we would not travel alone, but that this strange celestial being would watch over us. My pages trembled as I imagined such an otherworldly booklover. Finally, she prayed the benediction, spreading her arms, closing her eyes.

The three men tried to urge her to come with us, but she refused, stating again that she would be a burden to them, and that such a quest was for younger folks than her.

Rebutting every effort to bid her a personal farewell, she grasped the sides of her habit with her crooked, speckled fingers and shuffled down the corridor towards her room.

Moses and Stafi each donned an old grey army greatcoat while Sanjay strapped on an army-issue rucksack. Willow checked I was in his large trouser pocket, tapping me twice to make sure.

The three couriers bade farewell to Anastasia and the rest of the group, then left the bunker the way we had entered and proceeded down the hill towards the barn.

Half an hour later, the bunker was behind us, and I was with Willow in the cockpit of the Huey. Moses was in the co-pilot's seat. Stafi sat in the back next to the closed doorway.

Willow checked the fuselage and rotors of the Huey and then hopped into his right-hand cockpit seat and started the engines. The blades above and behind began to turn and, before we knew it, we were on our way north, hugging the coastline of the east coast of England, up to the first of our refuelling points. When we landed, the passengers stretched their legs while Willow talked to our contact, an old man in a cloth cap. On we flew to the next refuelling point where we witnessed a similar routine. A third much shorter leg saw us descend onto a pre-arranged LZ. We exited our vehicle to the sound of seagulls and the distant boom and crash of wind and sea. That night, we rested in a dilapidated stable.

The next day, Friday, we flew to a high and blustery hill about ten miles outside Lerwick. The field where we landed was owned by a farmer and his wife from Oxford who owned a second home. After feasting for half an hour from a table set with a palette of colourful cheeses and meats, everyone had a new spring in their steps. Before we left, Willow urged the group to change clothes.

It was Friday night.

We had less than 24 hours to reach the Faroes.

Willow raised me to his face and inhaled as he smelt my covers. The breath that he took was a long one. It was the breath of a man who was remembering the mission and binding himself to its gravity. When he was done, he wedged me into a cramped space at the bottom of the front windshield, so that I was looking back into the belly of the Huey. He slipped into the nylon mesh of the front right seat, adjusted his shoulder straps, hauled a hood over his head, put on his helmet and attached the radio cord from behind his high-backed seat.

He conducted his customary cockpit check, sweeping his hands over the instruments, from the bottom to the top of the console, adjusting switches, tapping dials and inspecting circuit breakers until he was happy everything was ready. Then he pulled on his leather flying gloves. He flipped the master switch to activate the phones and squeezed the radio trigger. "Flying helmets on, everybody."

Willow glanced into the cargo deck behind his left shoulder to see if Stafi had heard his voice on the intercom. Stafi gave a thumbs up. Willow then looked through the front and side windows, checking if he could see anything outside. Content that all was clear, he rolled the throttle to the starting position and then squeezed the trigger. A hiss emanated from the turbine, indicating that the fire had caught, and we were ready to ascend. The electric motor started straightaway with a shrill sound. The rotors began to move and slowly accelerate as engine, transmission, and blades worked in unison.

Willow looked at the gauges on his side of the panel to check they were all in the green.

They were.

By now, we knew this meant we had passed the danger point for a hot start. The threat of fire had passed.

I was relieved.

"Everything secure back there?" Willow asked.

Moses looked behind him into the fuselage and then turned to Willow and nodded. "All set, boss."

Willow opened the throttle and pulled the collective stick upwards. The nose of the Huey rose first. I could see the ground, illuminated by the wash of light from the landing and position lights. Willow checked to see if there was any drift, then adjusted the Huey, stabilising it as it hovered six feet above the sodden soil. He raised the stick and we started to fly upwards into the moonless sky. When he was satisfied that we were at the optimum height, he pushed the cyclic stick forward and we began to fly over the treeless hills and valleys of Shetland, out towards the coast, then past many islets until we were over the ocean.

Willow doused the external beams. Now, the only source of light was the red glow from the instruments. Sound became the primary sense, with the onrush of the wind and the dull thudding of the main rotors and their distinctive whop-whop-whopping as the Huey sped across the water towards the Faroe Isles.

All seemed to be going well until Moses saw something out of the side cockpit window on his right.

"Lightning!" he said, making sure he was communicating only with Willow on his comms.

Willow looked beyond his co-pilot's shoulder.

There it was again.

A flash of light.

A thin, jagged silver line piercing the darkness, flowing down from the heavens.

"That's not good," Willow said.

Stafi was already standing between the pilots, tapping Willow on the shoulder.

"What is it?"

Before Willow could answer, the Huey was lashed by a bombardment of hail, each stone the size of a musket ball. I thought the windows would shatter but they held.

When the hail turned to heavy rain, Willow turned to Stafi.

"Lightning is my kryptonite."

"Can you navigate through it?"

"Not if we get struck by it."

"Can the Huey handle it?"

"This is not a plane," Willow replied.

Stafi looked confused.

Moses explained. "A plane has a specially designed support structure that runs from wingtip to wingtip. When a bolt of lightning hits the aircraft, it travels along this special brace or spar and then continues its way down to earth, leaving the plane largely undamaged because of its greater metallic strength. I'm afraid the Huey has no such defence."

Another flash.

Nearer this time.

Accompanied by three deafening cracks of thunder.

"What happens if we get hit?" Stafi asked.

"You don't want to know," Moses answered. "Let's just say the Huey's blades need to flex in flight, so they don't have the same metallic strength. If we get hit, it's game over."

Stafi frowned. They were powerless, and he knew it. "Should we turn back?" he asked.

"Too late," Moses said. "Come too far."

Willow was about to add a comment when there was a bang louder than any noise I had ever heard, even at Waterloo. It seemed to explode just above us and, as it did, a bolt of blinding light descended at terrifying speed, striking the Huey's rotor blades.

Stafi was holding onto a strip of metal to steady himself as the Huey started to drop from the sky. The bar he had grabbed was now alive with electricity, sending bolts into his body, causing him to jolt. His mouth was paralysed by pain. Still, he held onto his book, clutching it for dear life, refusing to be separated.

The rotor blades stopped.

The instruments died.

Moses's head was leaning against the window. Blood was seeping down his face from his right eye.

Only Willow seemed to be alive, fighting a forlorn battle to stabilise the Huey and resurrect the rotor blades.

But the engines were shot.

The airframe was now on fire.

The helicopter was out of control, spiralling out of the dark sky, hurtling towards the ocean below.

I sensed the end even before it came.

I foresaw the instant incineration of soft flesh and fragile leaves, leaving the detritus of bone and page, spine and joint upon the cold, black surface of the sea.

I looked into Willow's eyes.

They were desperate, strained, dilated.

He was doing everything he could, but even he was helpless in the seconds before the catastrophic conflagration.

I remembered another loyal soldier, Billy Massingham, and his courage at the Battle of Waterloo.

Then at last, that which I had feared from the beginning of my existence came upon me in a rush.

Death came by fire.

In the twinkling of an eye, my boards and pages were illuminated and destroyed, in a white flash that seemed brighter than the sun and hotter than a thousand pyres.

Nothing could ever restore me now.

I was torn apart.

My particles and pieces were tiny, brilliant cinders, falling like fireflies from the sky, merging with the sea.

I was fragmented and cremated.

A book lost in time.

Part 11

2030

Every book, every volume you see here, has a soul. The soul of the person who wrote it and of those who read it and lived and dreamed with it.

Carlos Ruiz Zafón (1964-2020)

The first intimation of my immortality was a smell, followed by a taste. I could smell the kerosene upon the water and taste the saltiness of the sea. Up until then, I had only ever experienced three senses. I had seen, though not with human eyes. I had heard, though not through any organs known to mortal men and women. And I had felt the touch of my mother, and subsequently others who looked after me. Now I could smell and taste, though how, I knew not.

As I marvelled at the expansion of my senses, a sixth sense was added to the five – a holy intuition of an approaching light upon the dark waters of the ocean. Whatever this shiny entity was, it was tall and slim, with what looked like arms, its hands folded behind its back. When it was only a few feet away, it paused, looked at the signs of death and destruction on the surface of the ocean, and bowed.

The figure approached me. I could see now that it was a woman with dark brown hair, olive skin, and hazel eyes.

As she hovered just above where I seemed to be resting, moving in response to the undulations of the water, the light began to diminish to a glow.

The strange woman above me wore a high-collared shirt whose white arms and sleeves were decorated with drawings of quills and pens. Her trousers were burgundy in colour and leathery in texture. Above them, she sported an unusual waistcoat. It was made of tawny, Moroccan leather, like my covers before they were destroyed, and her buttons, as well as the geometric patterns festooned upon her garment, resembled the gilding on my spine, although far more precious and luminous than any gold that I had ever seen upon a book.

She reached for a timepiece from a pocket on the left side of her waistcoat. It was attached by a chain, like Stafi's Gospels, only this one was golden and encrusted with tiny diamonds.

She smiled and returned the watch to her breast pocket. She opened her arms wide and cried, "To the four winds, I call!" Her voice possessed a strong Latino accent.

She looked down at where my ashes floated. "There is a time to scatter and a time to gather." She glanced at my remains and repeated her cry. "To the four winds, I call!"

A gale picked up and the waves began to rise. A million fragments of board and paper emerged from the darkness, flying at speed towards the glimmering figure. From every direction these pieces flew. Some were as large as a person's hand, others were microscopic in size, although I seemed to be able to see them all.

"And to the sea," the woman said.

Every particle of what remained of me began to ascend from the water towards the woman's open arms.

"Arise!" she said. "Arise!"

No sooner were these words out of her mouth, than the countless scattered pieces unified, fused together within the woman's hands, which she had now lowered and stretched out, palms open, before her body. I heard what sounded like an orchestra playing a sustained and harmonious note, increasing in volume and vibration, until it came to a stop in a sonorous resolution.

Everything that had been separated was integrated.

Everything that had been marred, beautified.

Everything that was impaired, restored.

I caught my reflection in the woman's eyes. Even Monsieur Bonnardot could not have engineered such a reconstruction as perfectly as this being. I was my mother's book again. Pristine, perfect, as I had been at my genesis. But I was more. I contained a multitude of copies and editions, from many times and places, in countless different languages and intonations, from every continent and country. I was the archetype and mother of every edition of *The Burning Ones*, and yet I was unique. I was many – oh, so many – and yet I was one.

"Come with me!" the woman said.

"What of the other books?" I asked, looking down on the mutilated objects on the water.

"They will have their resurrection."

"And Willow? The others?" I asked.

"The sea will give up its dead, as will the land."

"Will I meet my mother again? I have longed to see her face, and now I ache to smell her skin."

The woman looked down at me. "I have a different mission," she said, her voice soothing.

"What mission?"

"You will see."

As this being turned her face away from the debris, I realised that I now possessed another, novel gift.

I had the ability to speak!

Throughout my two-hundred-year life, I had been restricted to the written word. If I had ever wanted to communicate with my mother or my guardians, I could only ever do so through the printed letters upon my leaves. Now that I had been destroyed and then restored, my life was not only revivified but improved. My wounds and injuries were healed, yes, but my restrictions had been removed.

I was enhanced.

I could speak.

I could taste.

I could smell.

I could move without resort to a human carrier.

Positioning myself behind my guide, I watched as from the back of her waistcoat, two sheets emerged, as if they had grown out of her very skin and through the fabric. They were yellowy in colour and resembled papyrus. They spread as soon as they had sprouted. I could see there was writing all over them, although some of the words looked more like hieroglyphics. There were also drawings of strange vessels and objects that I had never seen before, ones that filled me with the same wonder that had gripped me when I first observed the helicopter.

She reached for me and placed me in the opening at the front of her waistcoat, just in front of a tiepin made of brilliant gold panned from the riverbeds of another world. Away from the salt and kerosene, I now smelt the fragrance that she carried – the freshness of Spring and the flowers of Summer, the fruitfulness of Autumn and the purity of Winter, all fused together one moment, then separated into individual odours that lingered for less time it took for me to notice them. Only her voice could have jolted me from my olfactory trance.

"You were being taken to Iceland by Willow and the others, and it is to Iceland we must now go."

The wings at her back extended so that I could see the yellow tips both sides of her arms. They hummed, throbbed with light, then began to flap in steady motions, propelling us forwards, slow at first, but then faster and faster until we were advancing at ten times the speed of Willow's helicopter, accelerating across the moonless sky like a shooting star, iridescent in the darkness, our fiery trail reflecting on the oily surface of the sea like landing lights.

"Behold, the land of fire and ice!" she said.

Her wings ceased their noisy droning and we slowed to a speed no faster than a seabird in flight. Ahead of us, the landmass of a great island emerged in the fading darkness. A faint light was breaking over the hills, far away, like the dim red lights on the helicopter's dashboard, before it was obliterated.

We passed over black-backed orcas surfacing from the ocean depths and blowing like geysers, then over an archipelago of rock stacks and islands, their clefts crammed with nests.

We followed the coast until we reached a concrete lighthouse, over one hundred feet high, surrounded by fields covered in snow-flecked moss, its beams rotating out from the peninsular towards rocks that rose from the grey waves like the heads of ancient, Viking axes.

We passed through a window at the top of the lighthouse and moved towards a radio room filled with mist from a curved pipe resting in an ashtray. Next to it sat the man I had seen on the screen in Anastasia's bunker. His half-eaten lunch was lying on a plate next to a steaming mug. He was speaking in Icelandic, reporting the crash of the Huey and the loss of every soul on board, and the destruction of the priceless books, including *The Burning Ones*.

When he mentioned me, the conversation ceased for a moment.

"Are you there, Prime Minister?"

"This is terrible news," the woman on the other end said. "Not to have the first edition. It is so sad"

"They were unlucky," the lighthouse keeper said.

"Very," the Prime Minister said.

For ten seconds there were no words, just a sound like a distant gale blowing through the speakers.

And then the Prime Minister spoke again.

"Þetta reddast."

There was a pause.

"Þetta reddast," the radioman repeated.

I sensed in my innermost being what those words meant.

"In the end, all will be well."

As I dwelt on the goodness in that sentiment, I remembered what my mother loved to say in her little house, that all shall be well, and all manner of thing shall be well."

Hope began to rise.

Mingled with excitement.

Before the brief daylight ended, we ranged over waterfalls and plateaus, over steaming springs and strange fissures that belched hot air, over beaches with pitch-black sand and stretches of land with stumps for trees, over snowy mountain peaks and sleepy volcanoes, glaciers and unfathomable fjords, over barren lowlands where only bedraggled sheep and thick-skinned horses roamed, right up to the freezing highlands where arctic foxes left their pawprints on the snow.

I had never seen a country so wild and yet so beautiful, so constant and yet so unpredictable. As on the Shetlands, the weather shifted without warning wherever we ventured. Dark clouds would change the canvas of the sky from blue to grey in the flap of an angel's wings. Where one minute the rays of sunlight had warmed the wintered earth, in the next, bullets of hail would pummel the hard soil.

As a thick darkness fell again, we flew towards a city. We hovered above the houses and streets, their lights and lamps piercing the darkness, and my companion spoke to me. "There is something you need to know before we continue. This is a land of booklovers. Its people love to read. More than any other people on the earth. Books that can be touched and turned, held and honoured in the grasp of a human hand."

"You mean physical books, like me."

"I do," she said. "A gift that cannot be handed to another is no gift at all. No one loves to give a book away like the people here. And no one longs to write and publish a physical book like these souls either."

"It sounds like heaven," I said.

"Not quite," she said. "It is very dark for so much of the year and so much of the day that reading books has become a means of survival, a defence against the harsh long winters where the wise stay indoors." With that, we began to descend towards the illuminated city.

My guide alighted just outside a house adorned with Christmas lights. We looked through a bedroom window at a girl, no older than fifteen, sitting at her desk, her head in her hands in front of a journal.

"She is writing a futuristic, dystopian version of the sagas for readers of her own age," my guide said. "Only she has a block."

The guide paused, bowed, and closed her eyes.

"Now watch," she said.

From behind the girl, a man appeared, or one with the countenance of a man. He had huge wings composed of swan's feathers. He drew his wings around the girl's shoulders and stayed there, holding the writer in his pinions, while she remained inert.

"I love this next part," my guide said.

The visitor stepped back and breathed upon the inkwell. The liquid in the pot turned from black to gold. He took a single quill from one of his wings and placed it between the girl's fingers, then manoeuvred the quill tip into the golden ink. As the pen touched the shiny liquid, she seemed to snap out of her inertia. Her face brightened and her eyes quickened. She took the quill to the open page of her large moleskin journal and began to write. Slowly at first. Then increasing in speed until her scribbles were racing across the leaves, filling each with line upon line of golden thoughts until her visitor, seeing that she was overflowing once again, withdrew from the chamber and disappeared.

"This happens often," my guide said. "There are many writers on this great island. Sometimes their hearts become like ice when they need to be like fire. When that happens, they are hugged into life."

"How many people write books here?" I asked.

"Some people say that everyone in Iceland gives birth to a book."

"Everyone?"

"Come. There is more to see!"

We flew to a house with a white wooden façade.

"They are ringing in Christmas Eve," my guide said, as the city's church bells began to chime.

"Look here, now, through the window."

Beyond the pane, a sitting room was decked in festive reds and greens. A father was sitting in a rocking chair. His wife was serving hot chocolate and two children were on the floor, sharing an illustrated book, pointing at the pictures. Four older people were sitting on two sofas nibbling the edges of what looked like ginger Christmas cookies. Grandparents, I surmised.

The man began to read from a book with lacquered antique boards and golden letters. I recognised it from the first sentence. The first words inside my covers. My mother's timeless poetry.

As he read, the eyes of the listeners glistened and tears of his own formed and fell like icicles.

"What is this?" I asked.

"Come," my guide said.

On we flew, from house to house, where the same drama played out. One would be reading my mother's poems while others would be listening, their hearts warmed by the words.

When we returned to the clouds, I asked again what I had just witnessed in these homes.

"There is a tradition in this country," the being replied. "Every Christmas, people give books to each other on Christmas Eve and then read them until the end of Christmas Day, when families and friends discuss them with each other."

"What a wonderful idea," I cried.

"There's something even more wonderful."

I tried to imagine what could be more marvellous.

"This year, the country's Prime Minister has urged that you should be the main book for Christmas. A special hardback edition of *The Burning Ones* has been published and everyone is reading it, including a picture book version for children."

"No!"

I could not believe what I was hearing.

Everyone was reading *me*.

Every citizen hearing my mother's words.

My companion continued. "In Icelandic, it is called the Christmas Book Flood. It happens every year. People choose a book to give away as a gift. They share what they love about the book with each other. It is a most delightful custom."

"But they seem to be reading only one book," I protested. "Not many books, as in the tradition you have described."

"It's true," the being said. "Every year until now, since the custom was started, there have been many books and the publishing houses have worked hard to form a list of recommended titles."

"Then why is it different this year?"

"Because our world has been increasing in hatred and decreasing in love. Your mother's words were deemed to be a fitting antidote to this toxin of hostility. They are hoping that *The Burning Ones* will teach people to unlearn hatred and to re-learn love."

I thought again of my mother's longing, the ache within her soul, to have the song of love within my pages transmitted to every heart upon the earth, however rich or poor, old or young.

And I was satisfied.

Deeply, deeply, satisfied.

"It is a most beautiful thing," the being concluded. "This December, it is your mother's words that have been flooding every home. Everywhere, people here in Iceland are tonight sipping hot drinks and eating chocolates, relishing the song of love within your pages."

In a transition as seamless as her garments, the being took me to a house just outside the city. The light, such as it was, had reappeared and it was lunch, far more simple fare than the meals the night before.

"Christmas Day," my guide said.

At the head of the table, a father sat with a wrapped present in his hands. He had round spectacles with thin golden frames. From the top of his lenses, two bushy, silver-grey eyebrows were growing like uncultivated hedges. The table was long and dressed in a white cloth. Several candles burned in their decorated wooden holders while the mother, four grandparents, four uncles and aunts, and six children waited. One of the children was a boy, no more than fifteen, playing with a game on a small device with a screen. He was disengaged from the proceedings, lost in a world of shifting colours and strange creatures.

"Before we eat the dish that mother has prepared," the father said, "I am going to tell you a story."

"The director of the new world library," my guide whispered.

All but the boy looked at him.

"In the age of the Vikings," he began, "books were very scarce because they took so much time and money to make. Do you want to know how they created a book a thousand years ago?"

There were nods.

"I'll tell you. To make a book of 200 pages, a scribe would have to butcher over 100 calves."

The boy looked up from his screen.

"Those tasked with the job would wear a leather outfit covered in black pitch. As the day wore on, it would be covered in the calves' blood. By the end of the slaughter, they would be exhausted. But their work had only just begun. The next day they would have to skin every one of those carcasses. When they finished, they would remove the hair from every piece of vellum and then stretch it until it was flat and white. When each one was dry, they would be folded in half to form two pages – four pages, if you include both sides. But this was only the beginning. There was some more killing required."

The boy was all ears.

"They would butcher a swan and pluck it. Removing the best quill feathers, they would trim the point and then let it toughen in hot sand. Meanwhile, the scribe would prepare the ink, made from local berries. A book of 200 pages would take two scribes two years to illuminate and write on those calves' skins."

There was a murmur around the room.

"Creating a book was expensive. If a family owned a single milk cow, that was the difference between surviving and dying, especially during the winter months. Slaughtering over 100 calves was an incredibly costly thing to do, and it was for just one book."

"That took far too long if you ask me," the boy said.

The man chuckled. "I don't think you'd have been able to concentrate that long, my son. Do you know what one of the scribes wrote in the margins of one of his manuscripts?"

The boy shook his head.

"He wrote, 'writing bores me'. If devices like yours were around then, I doubt any books would ever have been written. And I haven't even told you about how these books were covered and preserved."

The man could see that the children were hungry, so he told them to pick up their small forks.

It was the mother's turn to speak now. "There is an almond in one of these pastries. The person who gets the nut, gets the present."

"I have it!" one of the girls cried.

"Bravo!" the father said. "Here's the gift."

The girl unwrapped the present and held a book in her hands. It was old but the gilt edges were still visible, as was the title.

It read, *The Burning Ones*.

"One of the oldest editions of Miss Swanson's book," he said.

The girl gasped.

"Why don't you read to us? It will be a precious thing for you to read from such an old and valuable edition."

"How much is it worth?" the boy asked.

"More than ten times your device."

The boy glanced at the pages as his sister read. As she did, I sensed a change in her.

"She will be one of Iceland's greatest poets," the being whispered. "She doesn't yet see it, but she senses something stirring. A yearning. A hankering after your mother's creativity and legacy."

"And what about the boy?"

"He is a fascinating child. His father mistakes his fondness for the screen as an impediment to a love of stories. He is wrong about that. His son loves stories. And one day, he will be in great demand as a storyteller, not in the world of books, but in that same world that he inhabits through his little screen."

"You mean these devices are not the enemies of books?"

"It is, shall we say, complicated."

Before we left the house, the mother applauded her daughter for her reading and thanked her parents for the books they had given her in the book flood. Turning to her mother next to her, she smiled and said, "You once said to me that Christmas cannot be considered perfect unless there is a book for each one of us wrapped up as a present beneath the Christmas tree. It's so true." She reached out and held the old woman's hand as she said these words.

"She is obviously a wonderful mother," I said after the group around the table began to disperse.

The guide nodded. "As was yours."

As we left the family dinner, I turned to the being while we were in flight and asked, "What is your name?"

"You already know."

"Do I?"

"Yes, you do. You have glimpsed me through the corner of what passed for your eyes. You have heard mention of me during past conversations in your presence."

"I don't remember."

"Yes, you do. On the morning of your departure from the bunker, the Reverend Mother mentioned me, saying she had asked the Great Father to command his angels to watch over you."

"I didn't see any angels," I said.

"Really?"

"Yes, really."

"And you think this why?"

"Because the helicopter crashed, and everyone was destroyed in the twinkling of an eye."

"So?"

"So, if angels were commanded to watch over us, they failed to prevent our destruction."

The being paused in flight.

"You still have a lot to learn."

"What do you mean?"

"I mean that everyone and everything on earth sees death as a hopeless end. But what if it is the portal to an endless hope? What if angels are tasked to guide you through the portal, rather than merely preventing you from entering it?"

I remembered Miss Sylvia in her bed in the apartment in Paris. All those years ago, she had approached that portal. She had not been protected from passing through it. She had been visited, accompanied, and escorted from one realm to the next.

"Are you an angel, then?"

The being continued to look into my soul. Its eyes were fiercer now. Not angry. But burning with a furious love.

"It's not whether I'm an angel that you should be asking, but rather what kind of an angel."

And then I knew.

"You are the Angel of the Books!"

The being smiled.

A smile so full of warmth and radiance it made my leaves shudder with the brilliance of it all.

"Do you remember that painting Sister Ling showed to the young mother in the community house?"

"Of the great Bible and the little yellow novel?"

"Yes."

"What about it?"

"The young mother was right."

"About what?"

"About the permanence of divine words in comparison with the transience of human ones."

The being continued to stare at me.

"The writing that comes from the heavenly realms describes realities only seen in the heavenly realms."

"Like angels, you mean."

"The Reverend Mother knew it," my guide said. "She mentioned a passage of sacred writing in which a prophet of old, one by the name of Zechariah, saw an angel carrying a book. The angel caused that book to fly, just as you are flying now."

As the creature mentioned flying, that sixth sense with which I had been newly endowed was activated again. I intuited something deeper in what I was hearing, as if the words the angel spoke possessed both spiritual as well as physical dimensions.

"You're speaking in metaphors, aren't you?"

"Almost," the angel replied.

"Almost?"

"My words are neither literal nor metaphorical, they are both at the same time. The spiritual and the material are not opposites. They are integrated. My words reflect the original unity of all things. They contain symphonies of meaning."

"I don't understand."

"Then think of the word 'fly.' I said that you are flying. You are. You are physically, literally flying. But you are also being read by every soul in the country we are visiting."

"So?"

"So, who do you think was responsible for Miss Swanson's book being so successful?"

"My mother," I said, my voice stubborn, my heart loyal.

"That's true. But who else?"

"All right," I said. "You were."

"That's it! Your mother wrote the most beautiful book, and its success is due in part to her endeavours. But there was something more required to make the book . . . well . . . fly."

The being laughed.

"To make *you* fly!"

I began to laugh too.

"*You* were required!" I exclaimed.

"Precisely!"

When the laughter stopped, the guide said, "It is a mystery to mortal men and women why some books do so well while others, sometimes of far greater merit, disappear into obscurity."

"I have lived with that mystery," I said.

"Some of it is down to worldly things like marketing and money. But this is not the only reason. Sometimes, over thousands of years, I have been commanded to take a book and make it fly."

"Why?"

"Because it has hummed and resonated with love."

"You mean, as I do."
The creature bowed.
"Your mother's words are a song of love."
Suddenly, my heart was overcome with longing.
"When will I see her again, my mother?"
"Come this way," my guide said.

As we continued our journey, my guide pointed to a house even further away from the city, nestling on the brow of a hill. When we arrived, I saw an old man with his shoulders covered in a cotton shawl. He was sitting with a notepad in his hands, writing thoughts on its pages.

"He is a writer, too," my guide said. "He has just had an idea for a book. It will be the last that he gives birth to."

"How can he give birth to something when he is a man?"

My companion replied, "Whether a writer is a man or a woman, the writing process is like conception and birth."

"Like my mother with me?"

"Precisely."

"But she was a woman. This is a man."

"You are thinking with either-or again."

I sighed.

The angel was right.

"Explain it to me, then."

"First, there is the discovery of an idea. That is like conception. Then there is a process of waiting, of growth, feeling the heaviness and weight of what you carry, before the pain and elation of releasing the burden into the world, just as your mother did with you."

I sighed at the memory of it.

"Then there's the joy of seeing what was born wrapped in colourful coverings. There's the ecstasy of the smell and touch of the newly born, one which you shared with your mother."

"And what of my mother?" I asked. "Will I ever be able to see her? Or is she gone forever?"

The woman looked at me. "The Icelanders say, 'You will reach your destination, even if you travel slowly.'"

"That's not really an answer."

The Angel of the Books looked at me and said, "It's not going to be as slow as you think either."

She pointed up towards the night sky and we started to ascend, up and away from the houses below, until the great island beneath our feet was as black as outer space and the pinpricks of light from the houses as tiny as the flickering stars above.

As I turned to look at the sky, something happened to the colours in the heavens. Something I had never seen before, or even dreamed of seeing. A ghostly display of lights appeared, well beyond the infrequent clouds, hundreds of miles above the level of the sea.

Gleaming and shimmering.

Swirling.

Turning.

Trembling.

Mesmerising me with shades of fluorescent, forest greens, both dark and light.

Rippling ribbons.

Bidding, beckoning, welcoming weary souls passing from this wintery world into another dimension.

Transcendent and incandescent.

Up-and-up we went, into and then through a wash of vernal watercolours until we reached the upper atmosphere of the earth.

We stopped.

My guide began to swivel.

Round and round she turned, faster and faster, light seeping from the pores of her body until she seemed transfigured, and I with her.

Then the rotations decreased.

Stasis.

Silence.

Light.

White light.

Fields.

Woodland.

"We're here," she said.

And then we were through and beyond.

Part 12

2030

I have always imagined that paradise
will be a kind of library.

Jorge Luis Borges (1899-1986)

The angel escorted me to the edge of a thick forest of giant oaks. There she beckoned me to join a path beneath their sturdy boughs. When I turned to ask where next, the angel had disappeared. As I continued along the path, the warm rays of the sun reached me through the branches. I smelt honeysuckle and heard the humming of bees. As I touched the lobed fronds of the trees, I shivered with pleasure.

I arrived at a clearing strewn with pine needles and acorns. A log cabin, expertly carved and ornately adorned, backed into the trees on my right. The door opened. A person in a white robe and cowl emerged. I could not tell whether the person was a man or a woman. The figure motioned to me in gestures, summoning me to follow in their steps, beyond the cabin and deeper into the woods. The only words I heard were communicated from mind to mind, not audibly, but in impressions that resembled intuitions more than messages.

The further we proceeded into the forest, the more the trees began to resemble pillars and their boughs the beams of an enormous mansion. I became aware of people hidden within the recesses of the forest in what looked like sheltered clearings. They were sitting on the soft soil listening to teachers speaking to them from oaken lecterns adorned with sprigs. Those listening looked like children in a classroom and yet they were so much older than that, and the space where they were learning seemed more natural than manmade. Each pupil was holding a leaf the size of a shield. These fell from time to time from the branches above; each side of the frond was inscribed with lines of writing.

"Who are these people?" I asked.

The monk-like figure turned. I could not see the person's face, and yet I knew my companion's thoughts.

"They are the ones who always believed they were right."

"You mean religious people?"

"Some, but not all. They are made up of people from all religions and none. Humanists and preachers, anyone for whom being right was more important than being kind."

I heard a long sigh.

"Fundamentalism comes in many guises."

My guide beckoned me to advance down the path, past the apprentices, who seemed to stretch as far as the eye could see, their number in the thousands. As we walked beyond those who were sitting and learning, I saw that some were standing, bowing, and then floating from the ground. Wings made of what looked white vellum appeared behind each one and they began to fly, their bodies catching the beams of the sun and radiating with a dazzling light.

"They have learned the virtue of hospitality from their teachers and are now ready."

As I gazed at the ones who had just ascended, I thought I saw their mentor smiling at me from his lectern. He was a man with a warm and gentle face. He looked like Patrick Bronte, except many years younger than the man I had known and come to love.

"Is that Mister Bronte?" I asked.

"Everyone who in their earthly life preferred the call to be kind over the need to be right is worthy of becoming a teacher here. The leaves that you see are for the healing of stubborn hearts. The teachers are men and women who excelled in the virtues of grace and wisdom."

As I looked at the man, my heart rejoiced that all these troubled souls were helped and healed by one so generous and good.

The figure said, "Restoring old and tired souls is as important as restoring old and tired books."

I was about to move on, when I saw someone sitting at the back of Mister Bronte's class. He looked familiar. As I gazed again, I recognised him. Even though he was dressed in a long white robe and looked rejuvenated in body and soul, it was unmistakable.

"The librarian from Bruges!"

My companion could sense my surprise.

"Do not judge him."

"But he tore pictures out of books in his library. Nothing was left after he had finished. It was so evil."

"I say again, don't judge him. You do not know, and will never know, what pictures were ripped from his own soul before he started tearing images out of the lives of others."

"And what of the book thieves? Are they all here?"

"That is their choice."

"But what if their choice is to come here? Do they deserve to have a second chance after all their malevolence?"

"There is one final lesson you must learn," the figure said. The voice was firm now, although no less loving. "Those who live here do so because they have learned to focus on the precious not the worthless. Do you resolve to do that too, even if it at first offends you?"

There was really no point in resisting.

"I do."

"So be it."

Advancing down the track, the forest began to morph into something I had not expected. The shapes of the trees were still visible, and yet their wood had grown, extending near and far into stairways and landings. Most striking of all were the shelves. On every floor, there were cases filled with books, some sunk into vast tree trunks, others less concealed. I wondered what master craftsman had sculpted such an unusual forest library. The people that had sprouted vellum wings were flying from one stack to another, taking out volumes, reading them under a blue and open sky, some hovering under the sun, others sitting within the shade of the countless recesses within the trees.

"They are reading from books that were denied to them, either by others or by themselves. See the wonder in their eyes."

That was something strange to my mind. Even the best of earth's books possessed what here, in a greater light, might be regarded as imperfections. Even in my own pages, there were words and pictures whose meanings and contours might be considered questionable.

"Are these volumes edited and censored?" I asked.

"To the pure, all things are pure."

I was confused.

The Angel of the Books had been right.

I still had a lot to learn.

On and on we travelled, until I noticed that the trees were beginning to thin out and the temperature rise. The sun seemed brighter and the sky bluer. What trees we now encountered were mainly columns of towering sugar pines, emitting a fragrance as sweet as incense beneath their palm-like coronets. Their brown and purple barks, about ten feet in diameter, looked thousands of years old. They were tapered, scaly and mottled with yellow lichen. The seedbearing cones and sharp needles from their high and sweeping limbs covered much of the soil below, which was turning from the soft turf of the vast woods to the colour and consistency of sand. Around the trunks of these ancient patriarchs, men and women were sitting and meditating, their backs straight and their hands resting upwards on their knees, as if receiving some invisible blessing from the undivided branches, some of which seemed to stretch fifty feet or more.

As the forest undergrowth receded and we passed through a final belt of pine trees, all we could see ahead of us was white sand and more white sand, rising in a slight incline towards a coppice formed from gigantic cedars of Lebanon. We seemed to have crossed over some unnoticed threshold into yet another zone.

Leaving the woods, the sweet candy from the sugar pines was replaced by the taste of salt, carried on the warm wind from beyond the cedars. Cedars of Lebanon had always been my favourite tree. I loved the way their dense trunks twisted and shifted upwards, forking into thick and tiered branches, reaching up towards wide and tabular crowns. When we arrived at the coppice it was like entering a sacred grove. The sense of stillness and serenity filled my spine and made my golden gilding glow. This was a place where no membrane existed between heaven and earth. I felt the green-leaved freshness of it.

At the centre stood a pool of the clearest water, cleaner than the finest mirror. Around it grew plants bearing olives, figs, and dates, each benefiting from the natural spring. My guide gathered some of the fallen boughs and branches on a makeshift stretcher composed of bullrushes and sticks, then, reaching for a branch, took one of the fruits and parted the cloth at the front of the cowl. In my mind, I heard the words, "the fig tree yields its early fruit," and I tasted the juice of it too, even as the figure did. My guide looked up at the high branches of the trees and I sensed a murmuring among them.

"The beams of our house are cedar."

After a brief rest, we walked over the brow of the great dune and started down the slope on the far side of the grove. As the white sand became flat, there seemed to be a long journey ahead. This, however, was an illusion. No sooner had we begun than I began to detect the rich and royal blue of the ocean in the distance and the shape of a large building standing before the surf. At first, I thought it might have been a mirage; the outline was liquid rather than solid. But the nearer we drew to it, the more lucid and real it became.

Then the full shock of it struck me.

There, with its foundations deep within the pure white sand, stood my mother's cottage! Or at least, a version of it. It was far larger than the one I had inhabited over two centuries before. Everything looked cleaner and brighter, its paintwork unblemished and its edges more defined. It was a similar colour to the sand and composed of the same substance, as if human and natural forces had collaborated and, in the process, beautified and magnified each other.

As the excitement grew, I saw five books come out from in front of the house, one by one, moving through the air. One stopped and seemed to do cartwheels. A second flew up into the sky like a firework. The other three laughed at their companions, sharing in the same joy but without the same extravagance. The sun caught their gilt edges and golden lettering, sending the colours of the rainbow in every direction.

"My mother's house!" I cried.

"Your mother's house."

The five books flew past and over us as we made our way towards my mother's cottage.

"Why are they so happy?" I asked.

This time, there was silence.

"And why is my mother's house so much larger than it was?"

We walked around to the front of the enormous building. A wooden deck had been added to the familiar façade of my mother's house. A rocking chair rested in one corner, within range of the hushing of the surf and the bellowing of the breakers.

As we walked towards the entrance, my heart was fearful of being disappointed and yet daring to hope.

Could my mother be alive?

Could it be that after two centuries, I was about to see the one that I had always loved the most and longed to meet again?

Was I about to find her within these whitewashed, wooden walls, in the chamber of her who conceived me?

The figure opened the door.

My mother's rooms had all gone. They had been replaced by a bright and airy, two-floored space far bigger than what seemed possible looking from the outside. There was a glass roof above and the sides of the chamber had portholes through which you could hear and smell the sea. The ground floor was like a theatre, with seats descending from the back wall to a stage leading to the front door. This was covered in marble tables with small grooves in their centre. On one side of the table there was a conventional chair. On the other, a smaller, elevated seat.

The figure gestured for me to follow, and we climbed a spiral staircase to the second of the two levels. I saw wooden bookcases everywhere, only they were not filled with books but thin blocks of what looked like dappled ice or liquid crystal, about the same size as me.

"Take a couple," the voice said.

I walked towards one of the shelves and imagined myself with human hands pulling out two of the slabs.

"Bring them," the guide said.

I descended the stairs and walked to a table nearest the front of the house. On arriving, the façade disappeared and was replaced by a glass wall that extended upwards and outwards for a long, long way.

"Place the slab in the socket."

When I had done that, my companion invited me to take my place in the elevated seat. As soon as I came to rest, a figure emerged in the seat opposite. A young African woman, no more than twenty. She had a scar on her forehead and her right eye was so swollen that she could not see out of it. She looked violated and inconsolable. But when she saw me, the sparkle returned to her one good eye and her expression changed from misery to ecstasy. She started to weep.

"I have longed for this moment," she said between gasps.

"Who are you?" I asked.

"You saved my life."

"What do you mean?"

"I was a victim of abuse, imprisoned within my own home, and the one thing that kept me alive was you. Your mother's words made me believe that this was not all there was to my life, that one day the horror would end, and I would become one of the burning ones."

"And did you?"

"Yes."

I tingled with delight.

My companion withdrew the slab from its glass dock and placed it on a shelf next to the table.

The girl disappeared.

Then the second slab was placed within the slot.

A young man with big, black curly hair and a friendly face appeared. He had a scar that ran like a zip from his forehead to his chin.

"Mate!" he said.

I saw tears forming in his eyes.

"Do you remember when I took Sister Ling back to the community house in Hackney?"

I did.

"She saw me looking at a painting by an artist called Magritte, titled 16th September. It was very cool, but it also rocked me. It showed a crescent moon. Looked like it was fixed to the front of a tree. Couldn't it get it out of my head."

Tears began to fall onto his soft, sweet cheeks.

"Your mother told me to be careful. She was right to. I died on 16th September when I was 29. The car I was being driven in smashed into a tree. Killed instantly. She tried to warn me. Didn't listen."

"I'm sorry."

Marc pulled himself together and looked up at me. "Don't be mate. Anyway, I wanted to say I bought a copy of *The Burning Ones*. You mum's words spoke to me. Very deeply. I'm here because of them. So, I want to thank you."

"Wait!" I cried as Marc disappeared.

My guide said, "You'll have time to speak to him again. And all the others."

"I don't understand."

"This is no ordinary library," my companion said. "Here, the people do not take books from the shelves. You, the books, take people from the shelves instead."

"What people?"

"People that once read you and were changed by your words. Every time you meet one of your admirers in this reading room, you will be filled with the same joy that you saw from the five books that passed us on the way here. You will shine like them."

It was then that I noticed the sounds of his words were no longer in my mind. They were audible.

"I can hear you!" I cried.

"And see me," he said.

My companion lowered the hood. There, standing next to me, was the most beautiful man I had ever seen. I say man, but there were elements that spoke of the most exquisite femininity. His voice was rich and low, like a man, and yet there was a soothing gentleness about it too. In fact, everything about him, if "him", is the right word, seemed to transcend and yet combine the best of masculinity and femininity. His hands seemed rough and strong on one side, but the palms were soft and tender on the other. He had a beard, black and trimmed, and yet his tanned and olive-skinned face seemed far too smooth to warrant it.

"What is your name?" I asked.

"The Craftsman," he replied.

He smiled and then walked outside onto the deck where the fallen boughs of the cedars lay upon the mattress he had pulled towards this strange library by the sea. He reached under a part of the deck and brought out an axe and a saw. There, in front of the ocean, he worked on the wood he had brought, and he did so with the hands of a cunning workman. Within moments, he had produced a cedar display case. In a final act, he decorated the wood with carvings of the same quill pens I had seen in the wings of the creature in the land of fire and ice. He placed glass over the opening in the top half of the small wooden tower.

"This is for a friend of yours," he said.

No sooner had he said these words than a book appeared in his arms. It needed no introduction. It was the Book of Hours that I had left behind in the library in Bruges.

I was overjoyed beyond all words. It was immaculately restored and exquisitely adorned. I marvelled once again at the craftsmanship in this unknown world beyond the world.

"Every visitor to the library can now see this masterpiece. When it is in this case, they will be able to open its covers and turn its pages by thought alone. Every eye will behold its beauty."

My heart glowed.

"And while it's undisturbed and undistracted," he added, "it can begin to write the story of its long and eventful life on earth, something every rare and antique book here is asked to do, including you."

"What happens when it's finished?" I asked.

"A book becomes a portal," he said.

"What do you mean?"

"I mean that a book like you becomes a gateway to another library, one where your own story is kept."

"You mean the story of those who looked after me."

"Yes, and those who didn't as well."

As he talked of these things, my former guardians began to materialise on the shimmering sand. Billy, Anne-Marie, Charlotte, Alfred, Sarah, Langston, Sylvia, Sister Ling. All of them.

They were young and vigorous.

Even Alfred's Spaniels were there, jumping over the breaking wavelets, prancing and snorting in the surf. And Alfred himself, who had always looked old even when he was not, was young again. He, the skilful restorer, had been most skilfully restored.

"But this is not the end," my companion said. "It's not just those who bore and adopted you that you encounter."

"Who else, then?"

"All those who have read you."

"How many is that?"

He did not answer. Instead, hundreds, then thousands of people began to materialise behind my guardians, with Abigail, the young African woman, and the rock star Marc at the front of them all, their faces now healed, their scars invisible.

Behind them, Miss Shirley was walking, holding five leather-bound books under her arms – books that she herself had written, just as Sister Ling had prophesied.

And then, to my surprise, the librarian from Bruges.

His face radiant.

His heart restored.

"I want to hear their stories!" I cried.

"You will have to wait. You will have time, so much time, to talk and laugh and cry with them."

They disappeared.

"There is a singular joy that awaits you."

He turned towards the sea.

"Look and listen!" he said.

I followed the Craftsman's gaze and saw a figure emerging from the surf, a young woman wearing a white linen dress with lattices upon her chest. She was carrying a cream-coloured conch in her hand.

As she walked towards the front steps of the house, her dark and curly hair quivered in the sea breeze.

"Beloved!" she called to the man.

I recognised her voice as soon as she spoke.

"Emily!" he said. The word seemed more of a sigh than a cry, and its sound merged with the waves.

The name confirmed my intuition.

I cried out from the deck.

"Mother!"

The young woman looked beyond the man's shoulder and squinted in the sunlight.

She looked at the Craftsman.

"You didn't!"

"I did!"

She ran across the tawny sand and picked me up in her hands – hands that were unwrinkled and unaged.

She held me to her heaving chest.

She was crying.

Between sobs, she shouted, "It has borders of gold and studs of silver!"

She was pirouetting in the sand.

"Your child," the man said.

"Our child, you mean!"

The man hurried towards her, joy in his dark brown eyes. He took my mother in his arms and held her. I felt the beating of my father's heart and hers against my resurrected pages.

"We are the burning ones," he whispered. "We burn with a most vehement flame!"

My mother laughed.

Then he stepped away and said, "I must go for a while. I have some work to do beyond the woods."

"Over the hills and far away?" my mother asked.

The Craftsman nodded. "But I'll be back in no time."

"Leaping over the mountains," my mother said.

He laughed.

A deep, strong, and innocent laugh.

That afternoon my mother sat upon her rocking chair outside the front of her cottage, caressing my leaves, reading my pages, sniffing at my binding. As the sun went down and the stars came out, she clutched me as she had at the beginning, humming hymns and songs as the chair moved forward and back, the cool breeze wafting from the calm sea.

"The sun rises and falls," I said when she had finished a song. "And the tides come in and out. Do we live in time here?"

My mother laughed and said, "In and out, up and down, far and near, these ideas, you'll find, are not so useful now."

"So, there is no time."

"I did not say this, child."

"What then?"

"Do you remember the English poet who visited Miss Sylvia at Shakespeare and Company?"

"Mister Eliot?"

"Yes."

"And do you remember what he once wrote? That we shall not cease from exploration, and the end of all our exploring will be to arrive where we started and know the place for the first time."

"I remember it."

"Here we live in the stillness between two waves of the sea, just as Mister Eliot said," my mother murmured.

"Forever?"

"Now and forever," she replied.

As the silvery light of the moon bathed the stage in front of the library, my mother lifted me from the comforting folds of her ultramarine throw and kissed me on my cover.

"You are home at last, my love," she said.

There on the deck of her house, where there was no fear in the night, I nestled upon my mother, the fairest among women. I remained there until the next day broke and the shadows fled, gazing at her curly hair, her dove-like eyes, and her flawless skin.

"I am dark and comely," she whispered.

A smile broke out on her glowing face, and we laughed and laughed until the sun rose high in the cloudless sky.

Later that day, the Craftsman appeared, back in no time, just as he had promised.

When he saw us, his face became as bright as the sun.

He ran towards the deck.

There, where the sun kissed the sea, we heard him, and his words gave endless hope to my soul.

"The winter is over!" he cried.

Author's Note

I have in front of me, on the desk where I write, an old, hardback book of poetry. The cover is adorned with hand-woven patterns and lively colours – purple and green. My eye is drawn to a golden emblem with a tree in its centre, and to the name of its author.

Dorothy Ingmere.

As I open the cover, I see her handwriting. It is the script of someone who is elderly, and whose fingers are not entirely behaving in the way that her mind dictates, nor her heart desires.

It reads as follows:

Mark Stibbe

With love

From

D.I.

As I look more closely, I see that the I is not really an I. It is an exclamation point. A smile breaks out on my face, and I chuckle at the countless moments when we laughed together.

Dorothy, in her eighties, lived in a cottage with her oldest friend Denise. Hidden in the recesses of Norwich Cathedral Close, they lived in a house full of books and loved nothing more than entertaining authors – experienced or emerging. People like P.D. James dropped by for a sherry and a good natter about the goings-on among the clergy in the Close. The Dean, whose focus on attracting young people to the Cathedral ruffled Dorothy's feathers, came in for special disdain. Without doubt, she had a mischievous side to her character. Not malicious. Just playful. Hence the exclamation point, instead of a capital I.

When I was studying English Literature at Cambridge University, I went through a phase of my life when I was lonely. I had started to write poetry a few years before and published my first book, *The Drawing out of Days*. Dorothy saw the potential in it, and me, and started to invite me round to her cottage whenever I was home from university. Maybe she saw my loneliness. She certainly alleviated it.

During those many evenings, I lost all track of time. I became lost in a world of stories about what it was to be a young woman reading English at university in the first decades of the twentieth century. I was borne away on the wings of poetry – Dorothy's poetry – with its quirky observations about cats and its sardonic critiques of the clergy. Most of all, I became entranced by her wise words about love. Yet, I never found out whether she had fallen in love. She had been unmarried all her life and was a closed book on such matters. But she spoke and wrote as one who knew from experience what it was to have loved and lost. So, I imagined that she had, but that like many in her generation, she chose not to talk about it directly to me, or to anyone. And that was fine.

Sometimes people ask me where and when I had the idea for *A Book in Time*. I usually reply that its conception was during a writing workshop I was leading in Manchester. I was speaking about unique premises for a novel and saying that the greatest stories do one of two things: they either tell of unfamiliar things, or they look at familiar subjects from an unfamiliar perspective. I then started talking about novels with unique POVs (points of view) and it was during those sentences that I stopped talking. I stood staring at the backwall of the conference room.

"Are you alright?" one of the students asked.

No response (apparently).

"He's had an idea!" one of the other students – blessed with greater insight – remarked.

"What is it?" they began to ask.

I told them that I had just had an idea about a book – a love story told from the book's POV, in which the book yearns to be reunited with the 87-year-old mother who conceived and bore it.

The response was immediate and enthusiastic.

Those students have been waiting for *A Book in Time* ever since!

That is certainly one answer to the question.

But now, as I turn the pages of Dorothy's book, I see that this is not strictly accurate. There is another origin story, one less mystical and sudden, one more down-to-earth and gradual.

I now believe with all my heart that it was in Dorothy's magical cottage that the seeds of this story were first planted – a cottage with winding stairs whose walls were covered in shelves and books, as was every room that I ever entered. The only exception, as far as I could see, was the old dining room where several times Denise cooked the most elegant and succulent dishes for Dorothy and me. We would sit at the ends of a long, mahogany table and talk about faith, literature, and life. They were indeed halcyon days, just as the book in my story says. Wisely, my two elderly friends had not lined its walls with books.

Now, as I arrive at the end of Dorothy's book, I am about to close it when I find a neatly folded piece of paper tucked inside the rear flyleaf. I open it and find a poem – one that was evidently too late to be included in the text, but not too late to be given as a gift.

I am taken by surprise.

I did not even know it was there until now.

And I have had the book over forty years!

The poem is called Stephen's Prayer.

And Stephen said: Lord, let me see my Love
Shoulder with courage her great weight of pain,
And triumph over sorrow. Let her gain

The knowledge that our Lord, enthroned above,
Cares for her grief. Her heart shakes when alone,
And, like a child, she finds it hard to guess
God's unseen Presence. Ease her loneliness,
And comfort her sad heart. Let her be shown
Her usefulness to those who weep likewise,
For Sorrow makes one quick to understand,
And many could take comfort from her hand,
Her heart compassionate, her opened eyes.
She must not grope, tear-blinded, but on high
Look up. For from the lifted face, each tear
Runs down, and leaves the vision clear
For all the stars that spangle the dark sky.
Lord, let her heart be brave; let it not cease
To sing along the road. And at the end,
Within Thy bosom, Father, loving Friend,
Give her eternal peace.

There are tears in my eyes.

It is as if I am hearing her voice for the first time in four decades, and I am overcome by its beauty.

I fold the paper and place it back in its secret hiding place. I turn to the front again to look at Dorothy's handwriting, recalling the cruel symptoms of her arthritis, which she bore without complaint.

I look at the date at the bottom of the page.

July 1980.

Can it be that long since she handed this book to me, in the candle-lit study where we talked?

How has time passed so quickly, and yet each moment – like the moments with my Dorothy – been lived so fully?

Maybe there really is something eternal in the present, and something present in eternity.

As I close the book, I stroke the cover, then raise it to my face, and kiss it, thanking the one she called "Father" and "Loving Friend" for the gift that Dorothy and Denise were to me, for the fact that Dorothy saw the poison of my loneliness, and administered the antidote.

Thank you, Dorothy.

A Book in Time is as much your gift to me as my gift, now, to you.

May we meet again where the sun kisses the sea.

When the winter is truly over.

Acknowledgements

I want to thank those who have helped me in the long and sometimes arduous journey of getting this story into print. Thank you to Juliette and Darren Coffey, Rachel and Saul Kitchen, Manna Ko, Yasmin Kane, and especially Rachel Wilkinson for their very insightful and invaluable comments and counsel.

I'm extremely grateful to my twin sister Claire – an award-winning fellow novelist – for all her encouragements, and to Paula Sheridan and all the many stellar judges at the Page Turner Awards for giving this novel first place in the inaugural awards.

Thank you to the amazing Karl Tearney for letting me use him as a character!

Thank you to Esther Kotecha for the covers and to Kevin Whomes for the typesetting and formatting of my manuscript.

Thank you above all to my wife Cherith for, well, everything.

Acknowledgements

Made in United States
Troutdale, OR
02/17/2024

17751151R00246